The
SWANSONG
of
WILBUR
McCRUM

The SWANSONG *of* WILBUR McCRUM

Bronia Kita

PICADOR

First published 2009 by Picador
an imprint of Pan Macmillan Ltd
Pan Macmillan, 20 New Wharf Road, London N1 9RR
Basingstoke and Oxford
Associated companies throughout the world
www.panmacmillan.com

ISBN 978-0-330-46508-3

A CIP catalogue record for this book is available
from the British Library.

Typeset by SetSystems Ltd, Saffron Walden, Essex
Printed and bound in the UK by
CPI Mackays, Chatham ME5 8TD

Visit www.picador.com to read more about all our books
and to buy them. You will also find features, author interviews and
news of any author events, and you can sign up for e-newsletters
so that you're always first to hear about our new releases.

To my parents, Eunice and Tony Kita

Part 1

I AM DROWNED IN A WELL

The sky was as black as an undertaker's boot and a wind from the east had blown grit in my eyes the afternoon I was shot and went head first into that well outside the saloon. I remember the icy smack of the water, and how the women's skirts I was wearing put up a fight and floated for a moment before the water got the better of them and they sank, taking me down with them. I remember seeing those bubbles travelling upward, like bullets at first, then slowing, the very last one sliding out my mouth and rising up, up toward the surface. You never think much about breathing when you're alive; from the moment you slither out your mother and holler you just get on with it. But when you get to see that last breath leaving your body, it's a different story.

I'd heard tell that a drowning man sees his whole life pass before his eyes, and all at once it was happening to me: some of it rushing past like a hog on fire, some coming by real slow.

That well seemed to have no bottom, and I sank so sluggish you'd think it was filled with molasses, not water. As I floated down I could see little flashes of colour and scraps of pictures, then all of a sudden it seemed as if the water parted just like the curtains on a stage and I was back in my own past. I stopped struggling and let myself sink, and what I saw was me, taking my very first breath in the back of a covered wagon somewhere on the Dakota Trail.

Ma's time has come early and they've pushed aside the sacks of flour and beans and rice, stacked up the boxes of bacon and pilot bread, and propped her up with straw pillows. She can't lie down flat because the medicine chest is behind her, and there's nowhere else to put it. The family Bible is in there, too, and it's real important, the thing you save if you have to abandon your wagon – after the family, of course.

Ma's elbows are dug hard into the pillows, her legs bent at the knees and wide apart. Her chin is pushed down into her chest and she's hollerin' like to die. I feel kind of bad, knowing it's me that's the cause of this, but there ain't nothing I can do, so I just watch, which is more than Pa's doing. He's walking alongside the wagon, pretending he can't hear the noise coming from inside.

There's someone missing, though: my sister Essie. No one's paying any heed to her right now, on account of I'm coming. They can't see her, but I can.

I've a real hankering to look at her face, but I can only see her from the side, and she won't look up. They've put her out the way in the Jenners' wagon. Mr Jenner is driving, Mrs Jenner is helping Ma, so she's sitting there on the wagon tongue in her blue calico dress, every so often chewing on her braid – even though she knows Ma would mind her for it – all alone save for MaryJane.

MaryJane is the cloth dolly Ma's made for her, and she has buttons for eyes, and they don't match: one's bright blue and big, and the other's small and brown. Essie don't care, though, she loves MaryJane, and she's been trying real hard to keep up a nice civil conversation with her, and pay no heed to the noises from our wagon, noises she knows are coming from Ma.

But she can't pretend no more: she's scared, she wants to see her Ma. She's only three, she don't know how dangerous it is to clamber out a wagon that's on the move.

I see her put down MaryJane; I know what she's going to do, but I can't help it, all I can do is watch, and see Mrs Jenner pull my slimy little body clear of Ma, see Essie falling under the wheel, and hear the two screams getting lost in each other.

A COW TRIES TO KILL ME
AND I GET MY FIRST FIT

Ma was real sick for some time after I was born, so they didn't tell her about Essie. When she asked for her they said they'd bring her when they thought Ma was ready, so by the time she found out, there was miles of prairie between us and Essie's little mound of dirt.

Of course she wanted to go back, but they told her she had to think about the new life now – her boy. She never really got over it, I could see that. Oftentimes when Ma came into a room and no one was there but me I'd mind how she would look over my shoulder like she expected to see someone else, like she was searching for Essie.

Even iffen I'd've turned out better than I did, I believe Ma would still have missed her. The farm could be an awful lonely place for a woman, and a daughter would have been someone to talk to, someone better at helping with the chores than me. I was a terrible disappointment to Ma, and although she never said so, I believe she blamed me for Essie dying like that.

I was a puny little thing, small and skinny even then,

with long wisps of hair in a circle around my head, with nothing on top – like a hat without a brim. I had a squint, too, which didn't improve my appearance none. I was a quiet baby, though. I spent most of my days sleeping, which was just as well, 'cause life was real hard for the settlers in the beginning, and they didn't need me to cause them more trouble.

When the law was passed in '62 saying that folk who wanted to move west could claim land for free, Pa thought it such a great chance that he'd persuaded Ma to go, even though her belly was heavy with carrying me. He had to build a house on our little claim out of nothing, 'cause that was all he found there. He cut strips of sod into sections that he used like bricks; the roof was covered in hay and then more sod was laid on top of that. It gave shelter of a kind, but the dust was always trickling down into everything. It got into the food, turned the water brown, and when it rained, we got torrents of mud streaming through the roof.

Then Pa spent near on two years digging a well so Ma wouldn't have to walk to the creek every day, and when finally he broke through, the water was no good. All he got was a great gush of black sticky stuff, so he had to start up again somewhere else.

The cattle were always climbing on the roof, too, to get at the grass growing there, and of course that sent a whole lot more dirt down. One time a cow, stretching out its neck to reach some tasty-looking morsel, fell through, just missing me in my crib. I know I most likely can't remember it, but it seems to me that I can. I hear the desperate mooing of the beast as it struggles to get up, the scuffling of its hooves on the dusty floor of that small room, Ma running shouting through the falling dust and my poor little squeaky cry, more like a scrawny kitten's than anything you'd expect from a human child.

I guess that was the first time a cow tried to get me.

It was on account of the sod roof that Ma and Pa first found out something wasn't right with me. I was a little bitty thing and I'd wandered out the house to play in the dirt, looked around and saw how, since the night before, the roof had burst into colour from all the flowers that had been growing quietly in the soil. There was blue bonnet and bright red Injun paintbrush, and the sight of it all must've been too much for me. I fell on the ground, all stiff, but with my eyes wide open.

I see myself now, waking up on Pa's lap, with him peering all worried into my face. I'd forgotten how blue his eyes were. He gives me a real big smile.

'There you are, son! Now, it's all right. Everything will be just fine. See, Mother, he's fine now. I told you it would pass.'

Ma's sitting in a chair by the table, the last of my well water dripping from her hair. She's smiling, too, but it's a thin smile, and it stays only until Pa turns his attention back to me. I've seen the look on her face: she knows something ain't right; something that can't be fixed, and she'll have to live with it. It's going to be yet another hardship for her to bear.

Ma had thought I was a real easy baby on account of I slept so much. Essie hadn't been like that – she was awake and curious about everything the whole time – but Ma had reckoned I was different 'cause I was a boy, and although she'd had two boy children before me, they'd both died real soon, so she didn't know what was natural and what wasn't.

They soon figured out, though, that I fell into one of these fits when I got worked up about something, so Ma did her best to see that didn't happen. I wasn't allowed to play much in case I got too excited. Instead I had to help Ma with the chores, as there'd be no danger of getting excited doing those. So I spent plenty of time peeling potatoes and shelling peas.

I watch my five-year-old self sitting up at the table, dirty bare feet at the end of bruised legs not long enough to reach the ground. I'm enjoying squeezing the fat green pods until I can see their fleshy white insides. The peas shoot out and hit the colander with tiny clangs, then bounce around for a moment before coming to rest in the growing mound at the bottom. It's kind of soothing to listen to that noise over and over.

Back in those days you didn't see a doctor unless you truly needed one: iffen you'd come off the worse in a gunfight or taken a bad fall from a horse. Truth to tell, most of them knew more about horses than people, and they were as like to kill you as make you well. There were a few who'd learned from the Injuns, and they might know a thing or two, but mostly people got their remedies from the medicine or liniment shows that travelled from town to town. For two bits a bottle they'd give you something that was more liquor than anything else, but it felt good as it was going down.

One time I heard Mrs Jenner telling Ma how some Injuns believed that fits were caused by the spirit of a dead person trying to take over the body of a living one, and that their medicine men had special ceremonies for driving those spirits out. She said that – well, couldn't it be Essie making the fits, trying to come back through me? Ma was real mad at that, and she showed Mrs Jenner the door. I don't know whether she thought it was foolishness, or whether in her heart she maybe believed it, and secretly didn't want to let Essie go.

Pa wasn't as troubled by my fits as Ma – he was different by nature. No matter how dark the sky might be, Pa always reckoned he could see some brightness on the horizon. Most times when he said that we'd find ourselves huddled around the stove listening to the rain beating on our roof, but at least Pa didn't waste time worrying about things before they happened. Of course that meant he was never prepared, not like Ma, who expected the worst and generally got it.

I spent a lot of time trying to make Ma like me more. I did my chores without complaining and worked hard at my lessons. Ma was real keen on me getting schooling. She said it was the surest way to get a job back east, which was where she really wanted to be. I don't know iffen I liked reading so much because Ma made sure that life at home was so dull, or whether I'd always've liked it, but I sure loved books. When I was reading a story I was someone else for a bit, not Willie McCrum who they all laughed at, who was always falling down in the dirt with his fits. I could go other places, too, places where there was more than just sky, and the wind whispering in the grass. In stories there were cities full of people, cities that never really ended, just became somewhere else. Where you never got to the end of the street and found there was nothing beyond but scrub.

Although I liked the lessons well enough, schooldays weren't much fun for me on account of a boy called Jonny Rose, who did his best to get me worked up so's I'd have a fit and he could charge the other children a nickel each to stick pins in me an' see if I hollered.

Books weren't that easy to come by outside of school, but back then folks would often paper the walls of their houses with the pages of old newspapers, which helped keep the wind from blowing through the cracks and gave you something to read in the long evenings and wet days when you couldn't work the fields.

I can see Ma now, standing with her back to me, reading the walls. We've got a proper log cabin by this time, and the walls are covered with yellowing newspaper pages, the ones nearest the chimneybreast blackened some from the fire. Ma is standing with her hand on her hip, resting for a moment, I guess, back arched, like she's stiff. Even though her skirt is made of dark stuff I can see the mud on the hem, and her right hand, hanging down by her side, has calluses all along the palm . . .

GRANDPA AND THE INJUNS

~~~~•~~~~

As I'm drifting down through the water I have plenty of time to think, and I fall to remembering what Ma and Pa told me about how they came to be here. Pa had always wanted to go west, because that was what his Pa had done before him: he'd left the family to try his hand at panning gold, sure he was going to make his fortune. He might have been right, too: one day, when he'd just about had enough and was dreaming of sleeping in a bed again and having someone to wash his clothes and cook for him – something happened. Now I can see Grandpa coming up out of the water, Grandpa, who I never did get to see when he was alive, although his whiskers have grown so bushy all I can make out are his brown eyes shining as he looks down at his pan and catches sight of something glinting in the sun. He takes it out and washes it, and is holding it up to the light when all of a sudden a band of Injuns swoops down the bank toward him, whooping and hollering fit to make a dead man jump.

Well, Grandpa didn't wait around to see what they wanted – he hightailed it out of there as fast as ever he could. But they caught up with him anyhow and took him back to their camp, where he spent a couple of days watching the faces of the squaws as they brought him food and drink, not knowing if he was going to be killed or not.

Of course he couldn't speak a word of their language, so he never knew for sure why they let him go, but he figured they just didn't like him treating their land like it was his. Anyhow, he didn't argue when they strapped him to his mule and tied a burning rope to its tail so it ran for miles before he could calm it down and make his way back to the mining camp.

Once he got over the fright Grandpa couldn't stop his thoughts straying back to that nugget he held in his hands. He was sure it was gold, and each time he thought about it it grew bigger, till it was the size of his fist and he could see it gleaming as if the rays of the sun were coming out of it, like it was something magical. Iffen the Injuns hadn't arrived when they did – if they'd come a few minutes earlier – then he'd probably be thanking them for driving him back to the bosom of his family, but after what he'd seen, he couldn't forget.

So he kept on going back, trying to find the gulch where he made his discovery. Once or twice he thought he'd found it, but when he drew near he saw that some detail or other was wrong, and he'd have to start all over again.

Meantime he had to feed his family, so he found work as a cattle drover. It was hard labour, and whenever he got into town Grandpa liked to enjoy himself, going into the saloon – sometimes still straddling his horse – whooping and letting his six-guns off into the air. He did it once too often, though, and ended up deaf. Which is how the cattle managed to get him back.

One day Grandpa hears this low rumbling noise and turns to his buddies to remark that it sounds like a storm is brewing. As the water sweeps aside I see his look of puzzlement as he wonders where they've gone. He don't have long to wonder before a thousand head of stampeding cattle come trampling over him, flattening him and his horse like a pancake.

That sure is the biggest, shallowest grave I ever did see.

I guess that would have been the first sign there was a curse on the McCrum family, and that the cattle was out to get us.

WHAT HAPPENED TO PA

It might not happen every day, but people do get killed in stampedes. It was what happened to Pa that made me certain. If Pa had listened to Ma he'd've been all right. She wanted to stay put in Independence where they had a little general store that was doing good trade, but Pa had vision – he was always looking to the Future, and he reckoned that Future lay out west.

There we are, standing in front of our cabin, looking out across the prairie, and he's saying to me, 'You don't know how lucky you are, boy. How many people do you reckon have had the chance to be pioneers, to be at the beginning of something like this? Other countries have been settled for years. In Ireland the landowners threw our family and hundreds like them out of their homes as if they were fleas on a dog's back. No one can do that to you here. This land will be ours, and the most important thing a man can say is that he owns the land beneath his feet.'

You see, that was the difference between me and Pa: he believed he could control his own future; he truly thought he did own the land beneath his feet. Me, I could never stay on my feet long enough to control anything, not even my own body, and it's hard to see those wide horizons when you're face down in the dirt.

I loved Pa – make no mistake – it's just that I couldn't *be* Pa, couldn't believe that everything would turn out for the best and all you had to do to get what you wanted was to work for it. Most of my time was spent around the homestead with Ma, and I guess the frustration she breathed out into the air around her got breathed in again by me.

Still, I loved my times alone with Pa. He'd take me hunting with him, trying over and over to get me to be able to at least set a trap, but I couldn't bear to see him killing the rabbits and prairie chickens he caught. I'd fall down in a fit as soon as he took out his knife, and he gave up on trying to make me hold a gun. It got so's I'd have to hide behind a tree iffen he had an animal in his sights, else the sound of me hitting the ground would frighten it right away.

Oftentimes I'd come home looking worse than the carcasses Pa brought for Ma to gut. I'd see her raise her eyes from my face to his, but she never said nothing – leastways, not when I was around to hear. I guess she figured we'd learn for ourselves that trying to train me up to be a man was a hopeless cause.

If Pa had listened to Ma when she said she'd rather be where folks could hear her if she cried out, she'd rather her children had other children to play with, and water from the pump whenever they needed to wash, Pa would never have died, and neither would Essie. I'd've had a father and a sister – and I'd most likely have turned out different, too. It wasn't that I was bad, it's just that I couldn't see any other way to live that didn't mean working with cattle, and I couldn't do that, not after what happened to Pa.

It's coming up now, and I can feel a tightening in my throat. I don't want to see this, I truly don't. But it ain't up to me, it's coming anyhow – I can't do a thing to stop it.

The water moves away and there's the scene I dread to see. I'm ten years old, copying out some schoolwork at the table. Both me and Ma are wondering why Pa ain't home yet, even though the sun's going down. Ma didn't have no more children – she never said as much, but I think it was on account of being afraid they'd turn out like me – so it's just the two of us in the cabin.

I can tell Ma's getting nervous, and I keep glancing up at her, to see what she's doing. She has her back to me, but I know from her movements that she's opening up the dresser drawer, and I hear the click as she checks that Pa's revolver is loaded.

Just then we hear a horse coming up fast, and Ma slips the gun in her apron pocket and goes to the door. She tells me to stay put, but it's too late. I run out ahead of her, just in time to see our neighbour John Gustafson come galloping up, leading Pa's horse Jess with Pa's body tied over the saddle.

I try to look away, but of course I can't – all this is happening inside my head – so I see that Pa's blue eyes are wide open and his flannel shirt is soaked through with blood, and I think to myself that it will be real hard for Ma to wash that clean.

17

But the worst thing is the way he's just hanging there over the saddle, like a deer that's been slaughtered, waiting to be cut up for meat.

I'm staring at Pa for what seems like an age, but the next thing, I fall into a fit. It sure is strange, looking at myself from the outside, because I never knew before what I looked like. I look like Pa. I'm lying there on the ground by the unsettled horse, my head back and my eyes open, just like his. Ma is being comforted by Neighbour Gustafson, so it's just as well there are no cows around to trample me, 'cause no one's paying me any heed.

On account of being unconscious, I didn't hear what Gustafson had to tell Ma, but it seemed that Pa came upon one of our cows lying on the ground, not able to get back on her feet. He decided he'd no choice but to put her out of her misery, but Pa was a tender-hearted man and he was fond of old Jane, so as he was taking aim he couldn't bear to see her distress and had to go round and comfort her one last time, leaving the gun on top of the rock he was leaning on to steady it. Which is when the other cow walked by. The shot echoed for miles, which is how Gustafson came to hear it where he was sawing logs for his cabin, and came running to find Pa already dead, and Jane, shocked by the noise, up on her feet again and looking mighty bewildered.

Ma was real grateful to Mr Gustafson – if he hadn't found Pa we might never have guessed what had happened – and he gave her plenty of cause to go on being grateful, doing all manner of chores that were hard for Ma, and trying his best to help her through her loss.

I see him now, a tall, thin man with a lot of yellow hair, stretching out to put a log on the fire. He drops it and sparks fly up the chimney, making him pull back his long bony hand before it gets scorched. He sits back and makes himself comfortable in his chair. The firelight throws shadows on his face: his eyes are dark pits, and there are deep hollows under his cheekbones. I don't like having him here, sitting where Pa should be sitting; I don't like seeing him working our fields, but I don't say nothing, on account of him making Ma happy. He's the only thing putting a smile on her face.

I do believe she might have married him, if the fever hadn't gotten him first.

After Mr Gustafson died it was just me and Ma. He'd left her his land, but what was that to her, she said, when she had no means to farm it? Pa would surely have been pleased; but then iffen Pa had still been alive I don't reckon Mr Gustafson would have given us the land. Anyhow, Ma sold most of it to some Norwegians who wanted somewhere already settled, and she was able to hire a couple of men to help her with the harder work, like ploughing.

We weren't doing too bad, Ma and me. She made sure I kept up with my schooling – I wasn't much use on the farm before, but after what happened to Pa I just couldn't stomach cattle no more. First Grandpa, then Pa – and that cow that fell through the roof and nearly killed me when I was a baby.

I'd looked at Pa laid out on the table in his Sunday suit and thought about it: there must be a curse on the family.

Maybe it was those Injuns who'd driven Grandpa away from the gold – he'd come back, so they'd laid a curse on him and all the McCrums, and this was the result. It looked a bit like Pa, that thing on the table, but only because it had the same beard and hair. There was no colour to the skin anymore, and the flesh was like something altogether different. Pa was gone from there, and Ma and me were on our own.

So we managed for a while, thanks to Mr Gustafson, but then something happened that took hold of the last part of Ma's heart and chewed it away.

GRASSHOPPERS
TRY TO KILL ME

The pictures slow down and then stop, showing me, pulling up weeds in the vegetable patch. I shrug my shoulders and the drops of water fly off me, reflecting the colours of the rainbow, leaving me quite dry. I'm about twelve or thirteen, and I guess I'm thinking about whatever kinds of things you do think about at that age, when I hear this sort of humming noise, real quiet at first, so I'm not sure whether I can really hear it, but getting louder by degrees. I can't figure out what this noise might be: it don't sound like any machine I know about, and besides, where would it be coming from? We're too far away from the next homestead to be able to hear our neighbours.

Whatever it is, I know I don't like it – it frightens me somehow, and I start to hum to myself, trying to block it out.

That works, for a while: I can't tell now whether the humming sound is coming from inside my head or outside of me. But it's getting louder. And then I notice something else: it's getting darker. There's a giant shadow moving across the ground, coming up behind me. I turn round and see that the whole sky is filled with a silver cloud that's moving toward me – coming lower – as if it's aiming straight for me, and as it gets closer I see it ain't a cloud at all: it's a swarm of grasshoppers.

As they come nearer to the ground they thin out a little: some land on the tree by the house, most go straight for the vegetable patch, but others settle all over me.

I don't know what to do. I have to own that seen from the outside, I look awful comical, standing still, hands held out to my sides, staring at this heaving mass of insects all over my body. And they just keep on coming – hitting me, hitting the house, with a dull, leathery sound. There's a groaning, and slowly a whole branch of the old tree topples to the ground, broken off under the weight of the creatures. Then I hear a shout and turn back toward the house, my uninvited guests moving with me. Ma is standing in the doorway, hollering something, all the while flapping her apron, trying to keep the insects away. But the noise they're making's too much: I can't hear her. All I know is they're terrible heavy and I don't think I can stay standing for much longer. I sink to my knees and fall face downward on the earth.

From time to time I half wake up and see Ma bending over me, trying to get me to drink water or sip some broth. Then I slip back into the darkness. I remember how Ma said I was like that for three whole days – which was the longest ever.

'And it was just as well I was there to haul you inside, else you might have ended up a pile of bones, fit for nothing but makin' fertilizer. Look what they done to you!' She grabs hold of my wrists and I see they're all bandaged up with grey strips of cloth. Those grasshoppers were so darn hungry they'd chewed me as well as the vegetable patch.

MA LEAVES HOME

We lost our entire wheat crop to those grasshoppers. Things were so bad the Government even offered us hardship money, but I guess by then Ma had had enough of farming, enough of me.

The next thing I see is me, rubbing the sleep from my eyes as I come down the ladder from the loft, to find Ma sitting at the table with two bags in front of her and her best bonnet on. I sit down across from her and begin to pick a hole in the corner of one of the bags. It's made of thick, woven material – like a rug – and I play with the frayed ends, rubbing them between my fingers.

'You going somewhere, Ma?'

I try to sound as though it's the most natural question in the world. I know the answer, though, before she speaks.

'I am, son. Now, I don't want you to start fretting; I've seen to it that you'll be all right. I've got you work at the Reillys' farm to start you off. I'm going back to Independence to see if I can't find me some work there. Maybe you'll be able to join me later, and perhaps some day we'll go back east, but I can't manage this place no more, Willie,

24

and you ain't fit to. We's neither of us cut out for this life, it's too hard.

'Neighbour Gustafson thought he was doing us a favour, but in a way he was just dragging things out, like your poor Pa with Jane. If he'd killed her quick he'd still be here, but he stayed his hand and look what happened. I don't want to see that happen to me, nor to you.

'There's things you could do, Willie, I'm sure of it. You've just gotta find out what they might be. If you was stronger it'd be simple – you could work the land, or be a cowhand, but what with being . . . the way you are, and having your difficulty with cows, it's too hard.'

I just keep on looking at the frayed material between my fingers. I don't know what to say. What *can* I say? When you get down to it, she's right: she never wanted to come out west and I ain't suited to running a farm. I could ask her to take me with her but I know that ain't what she wants. It's me she wants to get away from, not just the farm. She wants to start again, make a new life, and how could she do that with a freak like me along? The best thing I can do for Ma is to let go without a fight.

I make my way slowly back up the stairs and put my clothes into a bag. I don't have much, and most of it has been darned so often by Ma there's more patches and yarn than anything else. I drag my hand along the wall as I leave, feeling the rough wood, getting splinters in my fingertips – something to take with me, I guess. I climb slowly into the cart and Ma drives me off toward the Reillys' homestead. We don't say a word to each other; we just shut up the house and leave it. Ma says that Mr

Reilly will try and sell it for us, if anyone wants it, and he'll take the livestock himself.

There ain't enough time to say goodbye – but there ain't nothing much to say goodbye to, just the sky and the dirt and a little house made of wood that will soon rot down to nothing if no one comes to live in it when we're gone.

I look back as Ma drives us away and try to fix it in my mind, but it's hard to feel much. I've never really thought about living anywhere else; it's the only home I've ever known, it's been my world, and already it looks so small and empty.

It comes back to me, watching my fourteen-year-old self moving away in that cart – that longing to feel something, knowing that something important was happening, but not knowing enough to understand it.

I'm soon distracted, though, as we pass the old Gustafson house and I see a woman sitting at the window. We must be the only people she's seen passing that day, but she makes no sign she knows we're there. She just sits with her long pale hair hanging down over her face, rocking slowly backward and forward. I have no idea what might be going on inside her head, and the sight of her spooks me. I glance at Ma, who surely must have seen her too, but she keeps her eyes looking ahead of her, like she's daring me to say anything, so I stay quiet.

I keep wishing this memory would hurry up and be done, but it seems it's the bad parts of my life, the ones I especially don't want to see, that go by the slowest.

THE REILLYS

$\mathscr{I}$'ve fallen into a fit after seeing the woman in the window, and Ma stops the horse before we get in sight of the Reillys' house, and shakes me till I wake. I ain't sure how much they know about the way I am, and I understand I must make an effort if they're to keep me on, so I try real hard to look like a smart and useful kind of boy. It's awful awkward, though, 'cause I can see how the Reillys are trying to act like I'm some sort of long-lost son they're pleased to have back, when they can't stop their eyes showing what they truly feel.

Ma stays just long enough to drink a little coffee, and when she stands up I don't know what to do. What I want to do is run to her and hug her and bury my face in her skirt and beg her to stay, but the only times I can recall Ma touching me are when she brushed my hair – and she was always quite rough at that – so all I do is stretch out my hand. She takes hold of it, pressing on the splinters in my fingers, and though I can feel her staring at me, I can't look at her – I'm too scared of what might happen. If I have a fit right there on the floor the Reillys would be sure to change their minds about taking me on.

So I keep my eyes downcast and think about all the hours I've spent peeling those potatoes, until Ma lets go and I hear the cart moving off and I know she's gone.

When I dare raise my eyes again I catch the tail end of a look that's passing between Mr and Mrs Reilly, like they're asking each other what they've done. Then Mrs Reilly smiles and says, 'I guess you must be hungry, Wilbur?'

Over the days that followed I found Ma and Pa Reilly kind enough, but their children weren't sure what to make of me. Jimmy – who I guess was about nine or ten – kept giving me sly glances, and I reckoned I'd get a hard time off of him iffen he ever had the chance. The baby paid me no heed, since I never fed her, and Suzie kept hiding behind her mother's skirts like she was real shy with strangers. Nattie, though (the eldest girl, who wore a green ribbon in her red hair), was smiling every time I took a peek at her, until I figured she must be getting a sore jaw from grinning all the time, just in case I might look her way. I guess she thought she'd found a new friend – Jimmy made it mighty plain that he thought girls were stupid. I didn't mind, I'd talk to anyone who took the trouble to spend time talking to me – and at school that had mostly been the girls who felt sorry about me.

After we'd had supper on that first day, Nattie said she'd show me around. Their house was bigger than Ma's, with fresh tar-paper chinking to cover all the gaps between the logs and keep the wind out. You could tell there was a man about to do all the chores Ma and me hadn't found so easy. The upstairs was curtained off with sheets, so everyone had a part that was like their own room. Nattie showed me her things: she had a real pretty hairbrush with a back to it that was all pink and shiny, and a doll with a china face and curly yellow hair. I'd never seen such a thing, only ever having had one sister, and her dead before I was born. Nattie said that her doll was called Eliza, and that when Suzie was old enough to play carefully she'd give it her, as dolls were too babyish for her now she was nearly twelve.

She had three books all of her own: one storybook; one about good manners for young ladies; and one full of poems, that had patterns all in gold on the cover. She said I could borrow them to read if I wanted.

'You can read, can't you?' she asked me with a serious face. 'Because if you can't I could always teach you. I was too little to teach Jimmy, and Suzie's not ready yet, and I'd just love to have someone to practise teaching on, because one day I mean to teach school.'

I see her now, through the silver water, with her hands clasped in front of her and her brown eyes shining as she says, 'Just think of it, Wilbur, all those rows of eager little faces looking up at me, waiting for me to teach them how to read!'

I figure to myself that Nattie must have been to quite a different school from the one I went to but I don't say a thing. I'm almost sorry I *can* read, but I tell Nattie I could probably do with some improving – I nearly let slip that I missed quite a bit of my lessons because of my fits, but I bite my tongue just in time.

Then Nattie says she wants to introduce me to all the animals, so we go to the stable to check on the horses, collect a couple of eggs from the chicken coop, scratch the old sow on her filthy back – and then Nattie shades her eyes and points.

'And over there's the cattle.'

My legs feel like they're buckling under me. Nattie frowns, then takes hold of my arm and tries to lead me over to the cow pasture. I don't want her or any of her family to know I'm afraid of cattle, and I'm real scared of having a fit if I get any closer. Nattie's pulling on my arm, but I feel like I've grown roots, I can't move.

'What's the matter, Wilbur, don't you like cows?'

What can I tell her? I take a deep breath and let Nattie lead me on. I know that breathing deep can help me stay awake, so I keep at it as we edge nearer and nearer to those darn beasts.

As we get closer one raises its head and looks straight at me with those big blank eyes. *What're you afraid of?* I ask myself. *It's a cow, is all. They don't bite.* But a little voice in my skull answers back,

But they trampled your Grandpa to death and shot your Daddy.

I can feel the cold sweat trickling down my neck. I lick the salt from my upper lip.

'This is Freckle,' Nattie's saying, just like she's introducing an old friend at a dance. 'She's a real good milker, aren't you, sweetheart?'

She's patting the cow's brown-and-white flank like it's the most natural thing in the world, and I know she's expecting me to do the same. I shuffle forward like my feet are in shackles, and hold my hand above that damp brown muzzle as though it's the mouth of a 'gator. The cow breathes out a heavy breath – I feel the warm air from its nostrils – and I pull my hand back again.

'Oh, Wilbur, don't be such a *girl*!'

I daren't look at Nattie. I make a real effort and force my hand down until it touches the cow's nose.

'There, girl. There's a good Freckle.'

My voice comes out kind of squeaky, so I lower it a bit and it goes too deep. I try to glance at Nattie without her noticing, but she's looking at me and trying not to laugh.

'Don't you like animals, Wilbur? For if you don't you're not going to be much use on a farm, are you?'

'It's just cows, Nattie, honest. Please don't tell your Pa. If I try hard I might be able to beat it, and he needn't ever know.'

'What did cows ever do to you, Wilbur McCrum, to make you so scared of them?'

It comes out all in a rush: 'They killed my Pa and my Grandpa, and they almost killed me, too, once, when I was a baby in a crib, and you won't tell anyone, will you, Nattie – promise?'

Just then Ma Reilly calls for us to come in.

Nattie's staring at me wide-eyed, not knowing what to make of all this.

'Well ... all right – I promise. But don't you ever let on I knew about it, if things don't work out, will you? And I want to hear the whole story about your Pa and your Grandpa.'

'I promise too.'

We spit on our palms and shake hands real hard, and

as I follow Nattie back to the house, watching her skinny legs skipping through the dirt, I feel lighter in my heart than I can ever remember feeling before. I've touched a cow and it didn't do a thing to me, and I've told someone my secret.

COWS AGAIN

For the next couple of weeks I managed well enough. They gave me all the chores to do that they figured I couldn't mess up: I helped Ma Reilly around the house with cleaning and baking and suchlike – things that would normally be girls' work – and outside I collected the eggs, tended the vegetable patch and swept the stables. As these were jobs I used to do for Ma I knew where I was at. I noticed that Ma and Pa Reilly weren't watching me as close as they were in the beginning, and Pa Reilly even took me hunting with him – though I wasn't allowed to hold his gun, just carry the ducks he killed for dinner.

I was starting to feel quite at home with the Reillys, almost like one of the family. In a way it was better than when I was with Ma, because there were other children to talk to – well, there was Nattie, anyhow.

Of course it was going to have to come to an end sooner or later, and it wasn't long before Pa Reilly announced one morning as he was cleaning his gun that I must take the cows out to pasture. Out the corner of my eye I could see Nattie looking at me. As I went toward the door my feet dragged like my boots were made of lead. A little way from the house I heard someone following me. I turned round. I knew it'd be Nattie.

'Wilbur.'

I hear her watery whisper as she gets level with me.

'Wilbur, you can do this. They're just dumb animals, Wilbur. How can you believe they mean you harm? All they think about is getting fed and watered and finding shelter from the storm. The Lord made mankind in His image to rule over the beasts of the field – not the other way around.'

She puts her hand on my arm.

'Don't be scared, Wilbur.'

Just then her mother calls her name, and she looks back toward the house. She turns to me again and says, 'I have to go, but I'll come back and see you after school.'

I walk as far as the barn door and lean against it, and suddenly I'm inside the wood, looking at myself as a boy, smelling the sap, feeling the despair. I – he – thinks he's going to be sick any minute. The sweat oozes out of my face and hands. In that moment I feel completely hopeless. What kind of man will I make iffen I can't take a few harmless beasts out to pasture? I stand up straight and clench my fists tight over the cattle goad.

I lift the bar and open the door. It's dark in there, but light floods in through the doorway and finds its way through chinks in the roof. The cows stand blinking at me. Their smell hits me like a slap in the face.

'Come on, girls! Come on out!' I try to sound like I mean it, like Pa Reilly sounds when he herds the cattle.

I'm amazed when they walk out the door in an orderly

fashion. Hungry, I suppose, and thirsty for some fresh air after being cooped up in their musty barn. They find their own way, all I have to do is follow them to pasture.

After a while of walking along behind those stupid swaying rumps I begin to relax some – I even begin to whistle. Maybe they're not so bad, after all. Nattie was right, they're just dumb beasts, and I've nothing to fear from them. As long as I don't look in those eyes I figure I'll be all right, I'll manage . . .

When I wake I can tell from the way the sun has moved over that it's well after noon. I sit up quick – there's not a single cow to be seen. I look all around: where in tarnation are they? Then a terrible thought comes to me. I turn to the field behind the barn. There they all are, and there the haystacks are, the haystacks that were meant to last all winter – leastways, that's where they were this morning; now there's a field of loose hay being trampled and eaten by excited cattle. I guess they couldn't believe their luck. Maybe that's why they'd been so biddable earlier – they knew all they had to do was bide their time until they could give me the slip.

Course I go running toward them, waving my cattle goad and hollering, and of course I run straight into a big black-and-white cow coming in the other direction, nostrils flared, eyes wide with excitement.

Next thing I know I'm being dragged backward through the dust, and I can hear Nattie's voice.

'Oh, Pa! He's not dead is he, Pa?' and Pa Reilly saying, 'No, I don't believe he's even hurt; he's having some kind of fit, is all.

'It's not him you should be fretting over, anyway, it's

35

that ruined hay. I don't know how we're going to manage through the winter now.'

When we get near the well he stops hauling me. I hear the sound of a bucket being winched up, and suddenly I'm hit in the face by an icy flood of water. I sit up, spitting.

'So you're awake, are you? And what have you got to say for yourself, boy?'

I look up at him, shaking, water streaming down my face and into my mouth as I open it.

'Sorry, Mr Reilly.'

I RUN AWAY AND A WOLF CAN'T
BE BOTHERED TO KILL ME

‌

We jerk forward again, and there I am, lying wide awake in the little bed I have to share with Jimmy. I can hear his breathing, smell his hair, and I'm listening to Ma and Pa Reilly talking.

'It's not his fault, Jim. He can't help being the way he is.'

'Maybe not, but we took him in because he was supposed to help on the farm. We wouldn't have done it iffen we'd known he weren't right. We can't afford to have an imbecile living here with us, eating our food and not able to do nothing useful in return.'

'But his mother asked us to take him in.'

'I reckon we was the ones taken in. Did you know he was like that? I always thought he was a sorry-looking boy, a weakling, but I never suspicioned he was like that.'

'But, Jim, you took his mother's livestock in exchange for boarding him.'

'Well, I wouldn't have done it iffen I'd've known. That woman deceived us. And what kind of work is she fixing to get that means she can't have her own son living with her, anyway?'

'Jim!'

'Well, what's a man to think? First her husband dies in mighty suspicious circumstances, then Neighbour Gustafson passes too. Now she's abandoned her useless son with the only people she could find stupid enough to take him!'

'Jim! That is not a Christian way to talk!'

'At least I *go* to church – when was the last time you saw the Widow McCrum in there on a Sunday?'

'Well, maybe she has her reasons. Now that we know about Wilbur . . .'

I feel just like a stone is forming inside of me, hard and cold. I know that whatever Ma Reilly says I'll have to go. I won't be able to suffer Pa Reilly's black looks, and my fits would only get worse. It was hard enough feeling like I was a burden to Ma, but at least she's my kin. I can't be a burden to the Reillys, too.

I wait in the darkness until the house is quiet, and then I pack my bag and steal out the door. I'd like to say goodbye to Nattie, or even just take a last look at her while she's sleeping, but I can't risk it. I'd probably have a fit and wake her, and iffen she woke she'd beg me not to go, and the noise would rouse her parents.

As I close the door carefully behind me the cold air snatches my breath. There's a whole bunch of stars up there, but it takes a while for my eyes to grow accustomed to the dark. I ain't sure how far we are from town, and I don't know which direction I should be headed in, but I start walking.

I'm not used to being up so late, and I'm getting wearier and wearier. I know I should really sleep for a while, but I'm scared – I ain't never slept out in the open before, and I don't know what manner of beasts might be around.

Eventually I find myself stumbling through trees. I'm in a wood, and so tired and cold I feel completely wretched. I wish I'd never been born. Then I fall to my knees. I'm not about to crawl, so I curl up under a tree and go to sleep right away.

I look down on the small sleeping figure and feel pity well up inside me like a wave of the sea. Then I sense movement. I don't know whether I hear it or see it, but something's there. The moon is shining down through the trees, and I make out the outline of a creature: it's a wolf, a big one. Stupidly, I want to warn myself, but my eyelids flutter open anyhow.

Now you might think seeing a wolf looking at me when I'm all alone at night without a gun would have woken me up and got me running, but I'm so tuckered out I just feel my eyelids drooping until they close and I'm asleep again and in a fit.

Maybe I don't run because I can't be bothered; perhaps it would be easier all round if I let the wolf have a good meal. Then at least one of us would be happy. And maybe the wolf turns and pads away because he senses that feeling in me. Because he figures that a man with no pride in himself, a man who don't value his own life, wouldn't be worth eating, would be like eating the dust from a grave.

*

Next thing I know I'm sitting upright with a start, wide awake in the bright morning light, and there are no wolves to be seen.

A moment later, as I'm pissing against a tree, I realize I have no idea what I'm going to do next. I hadn't liked to bring a single thing with me to eat or drink, and my belly is already protesting. I set to walking again, and find the wood runs along the side of the road that must lead to town.

I HOLD UP THE STAGE
BY MISTAKE

I've been going for some time and I'm awful thirsty as well as hungry when I hear the sound of hooves and turn around to see the stage is coming. It's a good straight road, and I have a while to watch before it reaches me, which is how I have time to recognize the driver. I know that thick dark hair he was always combing; the loud holler that now controls the horses still makes me feel like running away. It's Jonny Rose – Jonny Rose who used to make my schooldays so miserable.

Before I know it, instead of running I've taken off my bandanna and tied it around my face, picked up a piece of branch and lain down by the roadside, levelling it like it's a gun. I figure that iffen Jonny stops to see what the hell I'm playing at I can whip off the bandanna, and when he recognizes me, see if he won't let me have a ride, for old times' sake. I reckon he owes me that much, at least.

He sees me, all right, and he reins the horses in, stirring up a cloud of dust that makes my eyes sting. For a moment he's staring right at me, and I see a look in those pretty blue eyes that I ain't never seen before: fear. Jonny Rose is afraid of me. Of course, he don't know it's me – he wouldn't be afraid iffen he did, but that don't matter. For the first time in my life, I'm the one in charge here. I could end it all right away by pulling off my disguise, but I don't want to, I'm enjoying this too much.

Looking at myself from the outside I can see the mean look in my own eyes. I'd never thought of myself as mean before, but maybe I'd just never got the opportunity, maybe there was as much meanness in me as there was in old Jonny Rose, it'd never had the chance to come out, is all.

Anyhow, before I have time to think about any of this, Jonny twists round in his seat, and in one movement hauls up the box and throws it to the ground. Then he whips up the leaders again, driving away in a farewell hail of little stones. I get to my feet and stand watching the coach disappear, not able to think what I'm to do. I stare at the box and decide I may as well look inside. I prise it open, push back the lid and – it's like opening a treasure chest. If you add up all the money I've ever seen in my whole life it wouldn't come to as much as is in here.

I fall down in a fit, knocking loose one of my teeth on a corner of the box, and when I come round I realize I'll have to work fast in case they're looking for me. I figure out how much of the money I can carry without attracting attention to myself, drag the rest into the wood and bury it, then head off to town to find me some lodgings.

THE WIDOW HARRIS

The lady at the boarding house I was directed to didn't look too friendly. She stared at me down her long nose as if I'd just crawled in under the door, but when I offered her a month's rent in advance she sniffed and showed me to the room without asking any questions.

It was small enough, but real clean, with a proper brass bedstead with a quilt over it, and a chest of drawers and a mirror on the wall. I pulled off my boots and laid down on the bed, staring at the ceiling and thinking about my time at the Reillys', and how good it felt to be part of the family for a while. I knew Pa Reilly wasn't too happy to have me there, and Jimmy would probably have made life difficult for me iffen I'd stayed, but then I figured real families had their difficulties, too.

It was Nattie I missed the most. For the first time in my life I'd found a true friend, and now I'd probably never see her again. That part was bad, but getting the money was real good. I know it wasn't properly mine, that I stole it – even if it was an accident – but what was a boy like me to do? I'd've liked to work, but I didn't know what at: I didn't have a trade, I wasn't very strong, and the way I got when I was around cows was a big problem. Sure, I could read and write, but there wasn't much call for that sort of thing around those parts, unless you were fixing to teach school, and I couldn't think anyone would want to hire me for that – the children wouldn't mind me at all.

I figured maybe this money had come my way to make up for all the bad things that had happened to me. Pa dying, and Ma leaving, and me being like I was. And because it was Jonny Rose driving the stage, and he'd been so terrible mean to me, it was like revenge, even iffen that hadn't been my intention.

Just as I was running all this through my head I heard a commotion down below, and I jumped up and went over to the window. I saw a small crowd going by, with a pale, dusty-faced Jonny Rose in the middle of the group. Jonny looked grim and wasn't speaking, but all the others seemed to be talking at once, and they were waving their arms about and looking real ornery. I ducked behind the curtain and sat down to think about this.

I knew I'd have to take care, but I was pretty sure Jonny hadn't recognized me or he'd never have thrown down the box. Iffen I kept my wits about me I should be fine – iffen folk wanted to know where my money was coming from I'd just say it was from selling off Ma's livestock, that she gave me enough to keep me going until she was ready to send for me. Should Pa Reilly happen into town and hear that story he'd not be about to gainsay it, on account of he might look bad iffen folk were to learn that he was the one who'd really profited from the livestock.

I wasn't fixing to spend enough to make anyone suspicion me – I wouldn't rightly know what to spend it on, anyhow.

When I go down for my dinner that first night the air is fair buzzing with talk of the hold-up. A man with a heavy beard is saying, 'From what I hear he was a giant of a man – more than six foot tall without his boots on.'

'And real mean-looking, too,' chips in an old lady with a brooch on her chest made from a coil of human hair.

'Two guns,' says a younger man through a mouthful of potato. He jabs his knife at the air for emphasis. 'Two guns – one in each hand. Some people can do that, you know,' and he looks around the table to see if we're convinced. 'Fire two guns at the same time.'

'Not much you can do when you're faced with a des-perado like that,' says Bushy Beard, shaking his head. 'If he should miss with one, like as not he'll hit the target with the other. An ordinary man can't hope to stand up against an enemy like that. T'ain't possible.'

Our landlady, who's sitting with her hands in her lap and only eating a tiny morsel now and again, as if she's being forced to for the benefit of the rest of us, sniffs down her long nose again.

'Well, I'm sure I don't know what this world is coming to. Decent folks can't venture out nowadays without tak-ing the risk of being robbed or murdered.'

'To be honest, Mrs Harris,' says the Beard, 'I remember when I first came west as a young man it was just as bad, maybe worse. There's always been outlaws, and no doubt there always will be.'

'All I can say, Mr Jenkins, is that a decent God-fearing person ought to be free to go about her business without worrying about being accosted by robbers and murderers.' And she sniffs again, in a manner that even I, who'm new to the establishment, can tell is meant to put an end to the conversation.

Although it made me feel jumpy to hear all the folks round the table talking about the robbery I was glad the story had gotten so exaggerated in the telling. Of course, it figured – Jonny Rose was never going to let on that he'd panicked, that the man who'd held up the stage and made away with all that money had really been a puny little thing like me. Maybe I'd even grown so in his imagination that he truly did see me as some great big desperado. Anyhow, for the first time in my life I was glad for being such an insignificant-looking person.

I got to kind of like it at Mrs Harris's too. There was food on the table three times a day – although you had to get there early, 'cause she didn't over-provide, and Mr Jenkins would eat anything left over. She even saw to my laundry. According to Mr Jenkins it was uncommon clean, too. He reckoned no bed bug would dare cross the threshold of Widow Harris's establishment for fear of being captured in a jar and held up to the rest of the bug world as an example.

In all the time I was there I don't remember seeing that woman smile once – although I did grow to understand what her different sniffs meant. The most common and loudest sniff said that she didn't approve of something, but there was a quieter, repeated sniff that meant

46

she agreed with you – you didn't hear that one too often – and an irritable sniff that indicated she was in a hurry or had too much to do, and the rarest one of all: the quiet sniff of sympathy. It took me a while to get to know this way of communicating Mrs Harris had, it being all her own, but as time went by I began to see that she was growing attached to me.

Life to the Widow Harris was a series of trials, the worst being the way her guests – most particularly Mr Jenkins – were always trying to eat her out of house and home. She never could abide to waste anything: iffen a potato was green and sprouting she'd still boil it and serve it up, and if a piece of cheese had grown a fur muff she'd just cut that part off and put the rest on the table. She didn't eat much herself, and she'd spend most of a mealtime watching Mr Jenkins like a hawk, taking note of how many slices of bread he buttered, and how many sausages disappeared behind that beard.

Mr Jenkins was a friendly, easy-going sort, but the Widow Harris didn't like him one bit. It wasn't just his appetite for food, it was everything about him: his size, his hearty laugh, the smell that sometimes came off of him on warm days, and worst of all, that great bush of a beard. I believe she'd have liked to creep into his room at night and cut it off, iffen she could've done it without touching him, and gotten rid of that symbol of abundance for good and all.

Mr Jenkins so obviously enjoyed life, was so full of vim, that you couldn't ignore him. It went completely against the Widow's belief that human existence was a vale of tears and that a body should think only of her reward in Heaven. If you had too good a time in this world, what would there be left for you to look forward to on the other side? That was why she liked me, if you could say she liked anybody – I was so clearly not making a good job of this life. The first time I had a fit in front of her she was asking about Ma and Pa and before I knew it I was on the floor, arms pinned down in the grip of her bony fingers, while she hissed the Lord's Prayer real fast just above my right ear.

Here she is now, her long nose emerging from the water that streams down on either side of it, her voice coming strong through the roaring. 'O Lord, help this weak creature who cannot help himself. Help him to make the best he can of his brief life on earth, until Thou gather him to Thy bosom, O Lord, and make him whole again with Thy perfect love.'

I'm finding it kind of hard to breathe, but if I jerk my arms to let her know this, she only tightens her grip, and if I try to say anything it comes out as a gargle, muffled by her corsets. I'm beginning to think the Lord might be about to get a visit from me earlier than expected.

'O Lord, ease his pain and help him humbly accept his burden. Amen.' Finally she looses her hold and I fall back gasping to the floor.

'Supper'll be ready in half an hour,' she says, as if nothing untoward has happened, smoothing down her skirts as she walks out the door.

Once I'd realized that Widow Harris kind of enjoyed my fits, I almost felt I should fake a few more, just to make her happy. I even began to wonder whether Mr Harris might not have gotten himself killed on purpose, on account of his wife. She told me he'd been taking his evening constitutional and just happened to be passing the joy house, when a man, hearing his angry wife trying to find him downstairs, jumped out the window with his pants in his hand, breaking his nose, and Mr Harris's neck.

Of course the Widow forced the marshal to get the joy house moved out of town, but I can't help thinking it did both her and her husband a service. I couldn't imagine what being married to the Widow Harris could be like, but when I saw how hard she rubbed the glass on her dead husband's picture on the mantelpiece I think I got an idea.

MR JENKINS TAKES ME ON

Now, although I had plenty of money to live on, thanks to Jonny Rose, I knew I'd have to find some work sooner or later, so that people didn't suspicion me, and it was Mr Jenkins who gave me a job. He was the blacksmith and he lived with the Widow because he didn't have a wife to keep house for him – well, he did, but she was busy keeping house for someone else in another town, so Mrs Harris told me.

I believe Mr Jenkins took me on because he felt sorry for me, but he said he needed an apprentice and I'd do, so I started to learn how to fashion horseshoes and mend bridles. He didn't let me fit the shoes to the horses, but I wouldn't have minded too much, as I'd nothing against them, even though I knew it didn't make no sense, being afraid of cows, when a horse, or even a mule, can deliver a kick that can kill a man straight off.

I was beginning to feel quite different: I believe I was happy. For the first time in my life there was no one around who made me think I was a burden to them. Widow Harris's praying was hard to take sometimes, but it seemed like I was being of use to her, which was a real good feeling. Things could've gone on that way for a long time I guess, iffen Jonny Rose hadn't gotten in my way.

It was a few days after I arrived before he took account of me, being still shook up from the robbery, I suppose, but when he'd recovered himself he was soon tormenting me again, just like when we was at school.

The first time he sees me I'm crossing Main Street and he's leaning with his elbows behind him on the hitching rail outside the saloon.

'Why, if it ain't little Willie McCrum. I heard tell your Ma left home without you. That true, Willie? Even your Ma can't stand you no more?'

He's got that old swagger back, that old look in his eye – the one that says he's the boss and I'd better do what he tells me, and I know that if I stay where I am for too long I'll end up having a fit and he might even start taking money off passers-by in exchange for sticking pins in me.

'That's right,' I say, standing as straight and as tall as I can. 'She's gone to Independence to look for work. When she finds something to suit her she'll send for me to join her.'

Jonny pretends to laugh, bending over and clapping himself on the knees, like this is the funniest thing he's heard in a long time.

'Sure she will, Willie, sure she will. And then you'll get some fancy job in a bank or a store and find a sweetheart and get wed and you'll all three live happily together for ever.'

It sounds such an ordinary life he's talking about, such a wonderful, ordinary life, but when he says it all like

51

that I know that life will never be mine. I'm seeing flashes of black in front of my eyes by now, and I know I must get away from him, so I stutter out that I have to get back to work, and just make it to the blacksmith's before falling into a fit.

Mr Jenkins knows about them, but he's never really seen one before this, on account of the Widow Harris always taking charge and shooing people out the room when they happen. For a big man he's awful nervous about such things, so he never argues with her. He's looking kind of uncomfortable when I wake up again.

I pull myself to my feet, brushing the sawdust off of my pants with one hand and pulling bits of straw out my hair with the other.

'Sorry, Mr Jenkins.'

'Oh, that's all right, boy. You can't help yourself.' It's quite some while before he seems his usual self again, though, joking with me, and singing songs that he'd never dare sing at the Widow's house.

JONNY ROSE
LEARNS THE TRUTH

I stayed at the town of Turkey Gizzard nigh on five years, and they were good years. I'm real sorry to see Mr Jenkins dissolve into clear water again, but we're moving on.

Jonny Rose was always hanging around somewhere, like a thorn in my paw that went in deeper the more I tried to pull it out. He'd managed to keep his job driving the stage – he was good with horses, and people liked his handsome face. Handsome people do have a way of getting what they want in the world – but I could tell by the look that was sometimes there in the twist of his eye that he was still sore about the robbery. I don't know if he suspicioned me from the start – I guess not – I figure he just used me as his whipping boy and found out the truth by accident. Anyhow, one day when I'm at my secret place in the wood, digging up some money to supplement my wages, I hear a twig snap.

I start, feeling the fear strip my spine clean out my back. I can't see nothing unusual, so I figure it must have been a deer or a prairie dog – but a moment later I almost jump plum out of my skin when I feel breath on my ear, and wheel round to see Jonny Rose standing right behind me.

I look like a coward, shying away from him while he stands there real casual, with his thumbs hooked in his belt, and that smile on his face.

'Well, well, well. Who'd've thought it? I must say I never figured on little Willie McCrum being our fearless highwayman. Might say I see you in a whole new light now, Willie.'

I'm breathing so hard I can hear it. I guess I'm too darn scared to fall into a fit. Mr Jenkins has given me an idea. I'd told him about how I tried to stop my fits by remembering all those potatoes I'd peeled for Ma, and he said why not keep a potato in my pocket, to give me something to hold, like a lucky charm? I've got a potato in each of my pants pockets – I can see them now, bulging – but back there I'm too plum scared to move, and I've forgotten all Mr Jenkins' advice. I just stare at Jonny Rose, and my eyes feel set to pop.

'Well now, Willie, what you got to say for yourself? What's the matter – lost your tongue, have you?'

I'm just standing there, looking at him, but then I find my voice. 'Well, I guess you got me, Jonny. What're you gonna do now? Gonna tell them, Jonny, tell them who it was held up the stage? Only it won't look too good will it, iffen they find out how it was me robbed you all along?'

I'm pleased by the way I'm handling this. I can feel my heart hammering against my ribs, but I'm awake and I'm talking, I think now it was on account of having sensed that power I had over Jonny when I held up the stage. Things have changed between us, and it feels good.

'Lookit, Jonny, they'll never let you ride a stage again iffen they find out you can't even stand up to a fella like me.'

'Oh yeah, and what would you know about it, Willie?'

'They don't want no yeller bellies working for them, Jonny. Even I know that much. They don't want someone who'll ditch the box every time a jackrabbit flashes its tail at him, who cries uncle whenever the wind blows a bit loud through the treetops.'

Jonny's eyes are narrowed now. He's listening to me, wondering what I'm leading up to.

'How's about I just take what I've got in my pockets, add a little more for luck, and leave the rest to you, Jonny? I figure you can return it to the stage company, or you could maybe think of another use for it – after all, you deserve it, Jonny. It wasn't real neighbourly of them to take money from your pay like they did. They owe you something for that, Jonny. But of course, if you just let me leave I'll never have cause to know what becomes of the rest of the money.'

Now it's Jonny's turn to fall silent. He looks down at the ground, as if he's thinking, and turns a stone over with the toe of his boot. He squints sideways at me. 'How do I know I can trust you, Wilbur?'

'Because I got nothing to gain by staying around to tell tales, Jonny.'

This is too much for him: he throws his hat down on the ground.

'Dammit, Wilbur! You ain't as dumb as you look. All this time I had you figured as some kinda mental defective, and you've been running rings around me – and the lawmen! How'd yer do it, Wilbur?'

I can't help laughing as I watch myself answer him with a smile. I can't hear my words, though, because the water swallows them up and I'm swept on as it goes rushing by.

I MEET SOME OUTLAWS

⟊⟊⟊⟊ૐ⟊⟊⟊⟊

I never found out what Jonny Rose did with that money, as I made sure to put as much distance as possible between us. I hightailed it out of there without ever going back for the things I'd left at the Widow's. I don't know what she thought happened to me – probably figured I'd fallen into a fit and gone down a gully. I hope so, iffen it made her happy. I could picture her keeping my things in a cupboard and bringing them out to show people from time to time just to prove how you can't ever know what the Lord has in store for you, and how it's best to be prepared. I felt kind of sorry, though, to think she maybe missed me some.

Through the rush of water I can hear another sound now, a regular, rattling sound. I begin to feel it in my bones before I can see it: I'm on a train, trying to get as far away as I can from the town of Turkey Gizzard.

There's a strange mix of feelings going on inside me: I'm kind of sad to be leaving so sudden when I hadn't been planning on going anywhere, but I'm mighty pleased with myself, too, for having got the better of Jonny Rose for a second time – and this time he knows it was me.

I'm sore at having to leave some of the money behind, but I've got enough to keep me for a while, and besides, I've been earning a wage working for Mr Jenkins – I figure maybe I can find another blacksmith who needs an apprentice.

I'm so full of thoughts it takes me a while to realize the train's not going anywhere. There's nothing out of the ordinary about trains stopping in the middle of nowhere – cows take a fancy to standing on the line, the rails get broken up – so no one's too surprised. It don't do to be too impatient when you're travelling by train.

As time passes, though, folk begin to look at each other, a little nervous. A man across the way from me says, to no one in particular, 'If this is a hold-up, I wish they'd get on with it.'

A few people laugh, but not like they mean it. A fella two seats in front of me gets up, sticks his head out the window and has just pulled it back in again and said that he can't see anything untoward, when two men shove through the door at the end of the carriage. I guess from the way he's dressed – in overalls – that the first man is the engineer or the stoker, and he looks awful anxious, probably on account of the second man has an arm round his neck and is holding a Colt .45 to his ear.

The fella across the way groans.

The one with the gun speaks: 'Now, folks, as long as you ain't troublesome to me, then I won't be troublesome to you. The quicker we get this over and done with, the quicker I'll be out of here and you all can be on your way.'

58

He don't sound angry, or even rough, just like someone who's come into a store and wants to do business. The next thing he does is puzzling, though: he tells everyone to lay their hands in their laps, palms up, and does a kind of inspection, like we're all in school, and he's looking for inkblots and dirty fingernails, still holding on to the railwayman the while.

The first one he comes to is the fella who put his head out the window, and when the robber looks at his fingers, he tells him to hand over his wallet. The man don't move – it's hard, being first in line at a time like this, and I guess he wants to see what'll happen iffen he decides to act tough.

The fella with the gun says, in a reasonable kind of way, 'Now, in case you hadn't noticed, Samuel here is the driver of this engine. Say hello to the ladies and gents, Sam.'

The poor man has the look in his eye that a hog sometimes has when you've got it by the neck and it seems to knows it's about to die. He don't make a sound. The outlaw jerks him backward.

'I said to say hello, Sam. Didn't your Mama teach you manners when you was a boy?'

Samuel manages to stutter out, 'Hel . . . hello,' and the other man says,

'That's better. A little courtesy never did hurt. Now listen, my friend,' he says to the man whose wallet he's asked for, 'I'm sure you've got important business somewhere along this fine railroad, so I suggest you do as I asked, or I'll be forced to shoot Samuel's brains out,' we can all hear the whimpering noise Sam makes, 'and no one will be going anywhere. Unless there's someone here knows how to drive a train?'

The passenger, realizing he's beat, produces a fine-looking wallet with some initials on it, and the outlaw moves on to his next victim.

It's plain this ain't the first time some of these folk have been held up. They look more antsy than frightened, and somehow I ain't frightened, neither. When Samuel and his dancing partner get to me I look up into his sweating face and see his eyes silently begging me not to put up a fight.

It's the eyes of the outlaw that interest me, though: there's something not right with them, they can't seem to keep still. The lids have strange lumps over them, and they flutter all the time. His eyes don't stay still for long, neither. I wonder for a moment whether he might be going to have a fit, but he seems able to carry on with what he's doing while his eyes flicker away like candle flames in a draughty church. He's managed to take a look at my hands, and he says, so everyone can hear, 'Seems like you're a working man.'

He takes the gun out of Samuel's neck long enough to poke my right hand with it, meaning I'm to turn it over.

'Plenty of dirt under those fingernails. Looks like your pocket's full, though. What you got in there, boy?'

He taps my pants pocket and I slowly slide my hand in and take out . . . a potato.

I look up to see Samuel's face lose its red glow and turn white, like a fire fading to ashes. There's a moment's silence, and my head begins to feel real heavy on my neck as I wait for the explosion that'll put an end to either Samuel or me. But when the explosion comes it's of a different sort – the man with the gun is laughing.

'Well, will you look at that, Samuel – a potato! Looks like our young friend had the good sense to bring along something for the journey, in case he should get hungry!'

I hear the other passengers joining in the laughter, nervous, not sure what might tip the balance of this whole situation into disaster for us all. I don't think anyone doubts this fella's serious.

'Well, son,' the outlaw carries on, 'I don't make it my business to steal from honest working men like yourself. Put that potato back in your pocket and I'll make do with a little something from one of these fine gentlemen I can see around me.'

He studies at everyone in the carriage, his gaze resting longer with the people who are dressed more fancy.

Now my turn is over I'm beginning to enjoy this. Of course I wouldn't tell him that the reason my hands are so dirty and my knuckles all grazed is on account of my fits. I've always been ashamed of finding it so hard to keep myself clean; I never thought to be glad of it, 'specially since I happen to have so much money with me.

The man with the gun continues his shuffling dance with Samuel down the carriage, asking only the folks with soft hands to empty their pockets and open their valises. The fella two seats ahead of me says, to no one in particular, 'Was that who I think it was?'

'Reckon so,' answers the man across the way. 'He only ever takes from the folk that look like they've got enough to spare. And did you notice his eyes – how they couldn't keep still? That's a condition he was born with. That was him all right!'

I look around. I don't like to speak, on account of not having been robbed, and not wanting to draw attention to myself, but someone asks the question for me.

'You're gonna have to help me out here, fellas. Seems you know something I don't – who was that?'

'Why, sir,' says the man in front, 'that was Jesse James, leader of the James Gang. They rob banks as well as trains. But they don't take from people who have to labour to earn their bread – that's why he asked to look at your hands. And why I've just lost fifty dollars,' he adds, in a dry voice.

Well, what d'ya know? I want to laugh, watching the expression on my face as I settle back in my seat and look out the window. I've met with a famous outlaw and he's let me go without taking any money. I'm happy, too, because I didn't have a fit. It'd've been a real embarrassment to me to have fallen on the floor in front of Jesse James and the people in the carriage, who are all taking it as calm as you like. Poor Samuel might've ended up shot, iffen Jesse had decided I was just playing possum. Maybe I was growing out of the fits? Maybe I'd be able to start living a life like anybody else.

I'm feeling kind of warm and contented, which I suppose ain't the usual way to take a train robbery. Another thing is making me feel worked up inside, though: there's something wrong with Jesse James – he's not right, just like me, but that ain't stopped him. I've got some money, I've got life ahead of me, and now I've got an idea shaping up inside my head.

I GET A TOOTH PULLED

Without warning the train suddenly dissolves into water and we're rushing on again. The next thing I see is a town, laid out like a grid, with streets running north to south and east to west. It's bigger than most of the places I'm accustomed to; there are all manner of stores, hotels and boarding houses, restaurants, theatres, crowds of people going about their business. There are plenty of horses – but no cows to speak of. This is Tombstone, Arizona, and I like the look of it.

I've come here because I've heard there's a silver mine, and I figure I might get some regular work. The idea of living in a big town is awful appealing: somewhere a man can hide away, mind himself and no one else. I find some lodgings and go look around.

There's one thing spoiling my day, though: I've a tooth that's paining me. It's been giving me trouble for a while, and it's gotten so bad I need to find someone who can fix it for me. I go into a saloon to buy some liquor, figuring it might ease the pain some, and ask the fat bartender whether there's a dentist in these parts.

'Not official, but there's a doctor comes in here regular

could fix you up, if you buy him a few drinks. Won't be in till later, though – he's not one for early rising.'

So I wander around town until noon and go back to the saloon.

The bartender points out a real skinny yeller-haired fella with a pair of drooping moustaches, and I go over and ask if he can help me.

His face comes up real clear before me, bright blue eyes sunken in their sockets above hollow cheeks. It's hard to tell his age, on account of being so thin is probably making him look old before his time. The thing that really bothers me, though, is the way he's coughing into a handkerchief. He looks awful sick, and I ain't sure I want him near me. When he takes a slug of whisky and then holds the bottle out to me, I shake my head.

We go to his lodgings, and he lays a cloth on the table and arranges all manner of metal instruments on it. I'm shooting real nervous glances at him every time he clears his throat. He turns his back on me to go and fetch something and when I see it I break out in a cold sweat: it looks like the kind of thing they use to geld cattle, only smaller. As the doctor comes toward me the room fades to black, and as I feel the cold metal against my tongue I fall to the floor.

When I come round he's cleaning up in a basin of water, and as he turns to face me I see the cloth in his hands is tinged with pink. I still feel cold as ice, and my mouth tastes of metal, of blood.

'You wouldn't believe me if I told you how often grown men faint in these circumstances,' he says to me.

'They're far worse than the ladies for it. Guess they just don't like to face their fear.'

Then he starts on another coughing fit and I'm up and out of there as fast as I can move.

It's not until later, when I can't sleep, that I realize the pain's still there: he's pulled the wrong darn tooth! There's not much I can do about it till the next day, though, so I watch myself tossing and turning through a restless night. I know from what the bartender told me that the doctor ain't likely to be out and about in the morning, so I somehow manage to make it through till the afternoon, when I go over to the saloon again.

The fat bartender looks uneasy when I ask him where I might find the doctor.

'No, he's not been in, but some friends of his have just left, and I've a feeling he'll be joining them soon. They were heading for Fremont Street, I believe – but if I was you I'd steer clear of them; there's trouble brewing.'

Usually I'd've heeded that kind of warning, but today the pain in my jaw is just too fierce, so I push my way one-handed through the batwing doors (the other hand is holding my sore face) and follow in the direction the doctor's friends took.

I can see four figures a way ahead of me, all dressed in black and striding on steadily. One's smaller than the others, and he's got pale hair, so I guess it must be the doctor and his friends, on account of the way the folks lining the streets are looking at them. I call out, 'Hey there, Doc! Doc Holliday!' But they're too far off to hear me, and too intent on their business.

Then they turn left at the corner, and I lose sight of them. As I'm scurrying after I hear gunfire, and that makes me slow down some. It's all over real quick, so I decide to keep on going.

It's awful quiet as I move down the street, and kind of eerie. As I reach a building with a sign saying 'Fly's Lodging house and Photographic Studio', a movement catches my eye and I crouch down low, looking left to see the sheriff, bending over what looks like a dead man, dressed like a cowhand, lying on a vacant lot. Two more are spread out in the dust, but there's no sign of the doctor and his friends.

I don't need to see any more. I don't know what this fight was all about, but I figure it might have been something to do with the doc's dental work, and at least toothache lets you know you're still alive. I'll pull that tooth myself somehow. I decide then and there that Tombstone's too violent a place for a fella like me, and straightaway the water covers me, the sheriff, the dead men and the stables of the OK Corral behind us.

THE AUSTIN BOYS

⟜⟝⟞⟟

I can feel it in my bones, what we're going to see next. I just make out the pictures of me finding another lodging, this time in a town called Deadwood. My new landlady is much younger than Mrs Harris, though she's a widow, too. There are a lot of widows about these parts. This one's called Eudora Massey, and she's mighty handsome, with a figure like one of the statues they have in big towns, supposed to represent virtue, or chastity or one of those ideas, but are really an excuse for a man to look at a lady without many clothes on.

We're not stopping to look at Mrs Massey, though, and her features blur as we rush on by. When we do slow to a halt the water parts to show me settling down on a bluff overlooking a ravine with a road running through it. I know what I'm doing: I'm waiting for the stage, and this time I've got a real gun, and a flour sack over my head, with holes in it so's I can see. I'm getting all worked up: I can feel my heart hammering against my ribs like it's in prison waiting to escape. I'm seeing black flashes now and again, so I start muttering, 'Potatoes, potatoes,' just like Mr Jenkins said I should. I can't put my hand in my pocket on account of I need them both to keep the gun steady, but I know I've got one in there. It's kind of green by now, and it's sprouting, but it'll do just until I can take another from the kitchen while the landlady's back is turned.

I can hear the horses' hooves now. They're going real fast, but I've chosen this place because the stage'll have to slow down some to come up the hill, and I've blocked the road with a big tree branch to be sure. The driver'll be took by surprise when I stand up.

Well, it ain't just the driver gets took by surprise when the stage appears. I stand up and show him my shotgun, he reins in the horses, then I say, 'Throw down the box,' only I realize too late that I forgot to cut another hole in the sack for my mouth, so it comes out more like 'O down the ox'. The driver, a broad-shouldered fella of thirty or so, looks puzzled. Still he can work out what it is I want from how I'm got up and the way I'm waving a gun at him. But it's what happens next that really confuses the situation: all of a sudden I see something move on the other side of the road, and when I look up there are two men wearing black masks pointing rifles at the stage.

'Hey!' the shorter of the two shouts across to me. 'What do you think you're doing?'

'Whaddya mean, what'm I doing?' I try to answer him, but the sack muffles my words again, and just then some flour that's still sticking to the inside makes me start to sneeze. The two men just stand there staring at me, but they're soon distracted, as with a crack of the whip, the stage driver takes his chance, and before we know it he's

68

disappearing into the distance. The shorter man fires a shot into the air, but it seems more like he's doing it out of frustration than because he really believes it'll have any effect. It does, though: it makes the horses quicken their pace.

The two men turn back from watching the stage disappear and stare at me again. I can't seem to stop myself sneezing, and before I know it everything's going black.

I wake up on the ground with both of them looking down at me. They've taken the sack off my head, but my nose is still itching from the flour. The short one looks real ornery: he has his hands on his hips and he gets up and paces backward and forward, muttering to himself. The other one is crouched by my side, studying me like he's found a rock with a new kind of lizard under it that he's never seen before. I sit up, sneeze a couple more times for luck, and take a good look at them.

The one who's pacing about's no bigger than me, with a broad face and brown hair and eyes. The other fella's much taller – more than six foot, I'd say – and thin as a hitching rail. His long face has a nose that seems to have been broke a few times, and his eyes are a bright pale green. It's not the colour that's unusual, it's the way he stares at you, like he's never going to turn away, like he can somehow see your insides working and the blood running through your veins. He spooks me a bit, so I try not to look at him.

'Oh, so you're awake, are you?' the short fella says. 'D'you realize what you've done?'

He's still pacing about, he's so mad, and when he's got

his back to me it's kind of hard to hear, but I make out, 'We'd been planning that job for months. Months! And you come along and mess the whole thing up in a couple of minutes.'

I just stare at him. There don't seem to be much I can say. I could tell him that I'd been planning the job for a long while, too, but it wouldn't do much good. Nothing's going to bring the stage back, and it ain't no use robbing just any old stage: you have to know there'll be money on it, more than just what's in people's pocket books and on their fingers.

'I've got a little myself – we could stick together, plan another job.'

It just comes out, but then it don't seem such a bad idea after all. The way I am, it makes sense to have partners; managing on my own will always be hard. The short fella widens his eyes and looks at the other one, who's been staring at me all this time.

'You hear that, Cal? This fella wants us to be in his gang. Does that sound like an attractive proposition to you?'

I can tell from the way he says it he thinks the answer is no, but the other one seems to be taking it seriously. He finally takes his eyes off me and looks up.

'Well, Dan, they do say three heads is better than one, don't they?'

The shorter one looks surprised. 'Maybe they do, Cal, but not when one of them belongs to this fella.'

He's stopped his pacing up and down and come to crouch by me, too. Now they're both staring at me, and I slip my hand into my pocket and close my fingers round the potato, feeling its eyes with the ball of my thumb.

'What d'you think, Cal? Shall we give him another chance?'

'Reckon so, Daniel,' is all the other says in reply.

I soon learned that Caleb left most of the talking to Daniel, and that despite their different appearances they were brothers by the name of Austin, and they hadn't been outlaws for much longer than I had myself.

Daniel wound himself up about a lot of things. He was always pacing around, waving his arms about and shouting at me and Cal, though it didn't take me long to realize he didn't mean much by it.

Caleb was altogether different. Whole days would go by without Caleb saying a thing, just making a few noises, some of which I figured were meant to signify 'yes' or 'no'. Then all of a sudden he'd come out with a question like, had I ever wondered what it would be like to walk on the moon?

I can see him now, lying back, staring up at the sky, and behind him, crouched on the other side of the fire, I see Dan, and the look on his face is just like he's about to cry. Then the water closes over them both and we're moving on again.

The thing with Dan was, he was always worrying over Caleb, like Caleb couldn't take care of himself. He told me once that Cal was nearly three years old before he started to talk, and that their Ma and Pa had given up on him saying anything. When he did, what he said was, 'Ma, why does the river always flow the same way?'

I reckon the reason Cal and me were good company for each other was that I can't see nothing wrong with

71

that question. When we talked about such things, though, we did it when Daniel was sleeping, because iffen he'd've heard he'd only have got that look on his face again – the one that said he despaired of both of us, and what was he going to do with us, and how'd a plain man like him ever get saddled with such a fine pair of fools?

Dan and Caleb's family were of a more practical turn of mind. For years they treated poor Cal like some kind of idiot. They were real nervous when he got to school, in case the teacher wouldn't take him. When she called them in one day and said she couldn't teach Cal no more they weren't surprised; it was what they'd been expecting all along.

Cal's Ma said to the teacher, 'He's such a good boy, you know. I'm sure if you let him stay on a bit longer he'd start to get it. I know he's willing to learn, he just can't help being slow.'

The teacher stared at her for a moment and then she said, 'But, Mrs Austin, you don't understand. I can no longer teach Caleb because I'm not equipped to do so. He's by far the cleverest boy, and probably the cleverest person, I have met with in my entire life. I've never known anyone who can figure sums like he can.'

Leaning forward and almost whispering, she added, 'I can't be sure, but I think your boy might be a genius, Mrs Austin.'

Now it was Caleb's parents' turn to stare. Eventually his Pa found his voice and asked, 'We are talking about *Caleb*, ma'am? *Caleb Austin?*'

'Why, of course, Mr Austin. There's only one Caleb. I would strongly advise you to take your son to a big city and enrol him in a school there. Preferably one for gifted children – he should be among his own kind. It would not be fair to keep him here. He has a highly unusual nature, and very little in common with his schoolfellows.'

Daniel only learned about this later, of course, but he knew something had happened as soon as his parents came home. Neither of them said a word. His mother took off her bonnet in total silence; his Pa went out to check on the livestock, and Dan watched them, real worried that something bad had happened, that the teacher had said Caleb would have to be sent away to an institution, like that woman who'd run through town in the Fall, smashing all the glass windows she could find with rocks wrapped in pages from the Book of Revelation.

Cal himself, of course, hadn't noticed anything. He was staring into the fire, lost inside his own head, as usual.

It took the Austins a couple of days to get over their shock, and it was then Daniel heard them talking in whispers at night, trying to figure out what they should do for the best.

'Do you think she was right, John? Should we take him to the city?'

'But what about the farm, Caroline? Who'd mind it while we were gone? And how'd we make us a living in the city? And what about Daniel? Out here we've got land, we're not beholden to any man – this is our little piece of the earth. Once you go to one of those big places you've got to work for someone else, and you can be sure he'll do better out of the deal than you do. And the cities are so full of people, you can't protect yourself or your family from the bad ones. It's like an ocean that'll swallow you up and drown you. We're better off here, Caroline. It's better for the whole family to stay.'

'But what about Caleb? You heard what the teacher said – about how it's not fair to keep him here, away from his own kind.'

'Well, I'm not so sure about that. What use are clever people to the world, Caroline? If he goes to some fancy school what's he going to do with all his learning – become a college professor and wear a starched collar and cuffs? In a few years we wouldn't know him, he wouldn't be our boy any more. He'd be *ashamed* of us, Caroline. We wouldn't be good enough company for him.'

'But, John, aren't we being unfair to him?'

'Well, it's not just him we need to be fair to, is it, Caroline? There's four of us in this family, and we all deserve equal consideration. Besides, to my way of thinking it'd be unfair to turn him into something he's not. He comes from a good, simple family. We're plain folk, Caroline, and it's my opinion we should stay that way. Cal was born to be a workhorse, just like me and my father before me. We weren't ever meant to be fancy Arab stallions.'

So that was the last of the talk of sending Cal to the city. Dan wasn't sure what he thought of it. He was curious about city life, but kind of scared, too, of making the change. And he didn't want to lose Cal. The farm had suffered terribly from the grasshoppers, and the bad winters, too, and he'd taken Cal off to try and earn their living when he saw his Ma and Pa couldn't support them no more. They found work as farm hands from time to time, but Cal's dreaming and his odd ways were always getting him fired, and as Dan couldn't leave him to manage on his own, he'd have to quit, too. That's how come they'd decided to start robbing.

WE ROB STAGES AND BANKS

*Dan figured there was enough money around for the two of them to be able to take some of it without doing much harm. They didn't mean to hurt no one – Cal wouldn't carry a loaded gun, just in case, and it was no good arguing with him. He never said anything about a subject until he'd made his mind up about it.

Daniel did load his gun, but his eyes weren't too good – he needed spectacles – so he tried not to use it in case he killed someone by mistake. And me, I've had this squint since I was born, so I ain't never been much good with a gun, neither.

So we made a real promising gang, the three of us: two who couldn't shoot straight, one who wouldn't; one who was always daydreaming, and another who had fits when he got worked up – although for some reason I didn't have so many of them when I was around Cal. Once I'd got myself accustomed to the way he stared at you I found he used to calm me down somehow. Most likely it was the way he didn't often get wound up about things himself. Because his mind was always somewhere else he mostly didn't realize when a situation was dangerous.

Course, this had its bad side: Daniel used to like Cal to be standing there when we held up a stage, on account of he was much bigger than either of us and might be more frightening, but it was devilish hard to keep Cal's mind from wandering off on its own. We used to pull his hair sometimes, if he stood still too long, or maybe poke him in the back, but then he might come to with a real start, or even turn on us, not realizing who we were at first.

Through the water I catch little glimpses of us holding up more stages. Hauls could be as much as $3,000, and that would last a good while.

Suddenly I come to a halt in front of a picture of the three of us looking down at a box we've just broken into. I remember this one, all right. We thought from the weight of it it must be filled with gold, but now we can see it's nothing but rocks. Wells Fargo have been getting real annoyed at road agents like us relieving them of so much money, and sometimes we've been getting shot at. It ain't an easy way to get a living any more, and besides, express companies are starting to send their treasure by train, in locked cars, as it's much safer.

Which is why we decided to turn from being road agents to becoming train robbers.

Of course, trains were a different matter altogether: for one thing they moved real fast and were harder to stop than stages, and for another, they were often full of people, and some of them would be carrying guns they were ready to use.

When a train's going up a grade, though, it'll slow down, and you've got a chance to climb on. The place to hide once you're aboard is a space at the front of the express car, which they call the 'blind baggage' on account of you can't be seen there: the express car has no windows, and you can't be seen from the engine in front because there's a tender full of coal or wood in the way.

Once you're on, you can crawl over the tender and surprise the engineer and the fireman and make them open the mail car.

The problem we had with this, though, was that Cal really loved trains, and he wouldn't let us use dynamite in a way that would damage any part of the train itself – we could blow up rails or throw it on either side of the track to frighten folk into doing our bidding, but we couldn't harm the darn train.

Now I don't much hold with violence myself, but to my mind Cal took things too far. The way he wouldn't carry a loaded gun or let us blow anything up on the train was unnatural, in my opinion, but Cal being how he was, there was no arguing with him. He'd refuse to come iffen we didn't agree to do things his way, and iffen we tried to trick him, he wouldn't come with us again – maybe he'd even get so mad he'd start rocking backward and forward like he used to do, groaning in a way that Dan and me'd do anything to stop – and we knew we needed more than two men to do those kind of jobs, 'specially with one of them being me.

So there we were, trying to rob trains without guns or explosives, and me having to stick my hand in my pocket every once in a while to touch my lucky potato. Looking back at it, I figure it really was some kind of a miracle we lasted as long as we did.

All of a sudden there's a muffled bang, and the water

shoots up like a fountain. What I see next is Dan's face. It looks like he's staring at me, but of course I'm not really there: he's gawping at something behind me. I look over my own shoulder and see what he's seeing: a safe – or a big lump of metal that used to be a safe. I remember it now – this was the time we tried to use dynamite in a bank in Cheyenne 'cause we couldn't wait for the time-lock to open. Only we didn't know how much to use, and what we ended up with was one great big lump of twisted metal that was no use to anyone.

Dan's staring at it like he can't believe what his eyes are telling him. Then Cal comes forward and I see Dan's hand shoot out and grab his brother's wrist. He was going to touch the metal, see, and it would have burnt him.

'Let's get out of here,' Dan says, in a flat voice.

When it happened I was too busy getting away to think how Dan must be feeling, but facing him like this I can see the beaten look in his eyes. I guess he realized before Cal and me that we didn't have much of a future as outlaws, and although this wasn't our last job, maybe he already knew there was no point to it.

I want to speak to him, to pat him on the shoulder and tell him, *There ain't no use worrying, 'cause you can't change things. Whatever's going to happen, will happen, and if you think there's anything in the world you can do to stop it, you're fooling yourself. Life ain't fair, and that's about the end of it.* But of course I can't speak, and anyhow the water gushes down between us like a wall, and he's gone. Through the water I can see smoke and the glint of light on metal, hear Dan's voice calling out commands.

Some hauls were good, and we wouldn't need to do a

job for months. I liked those times the best. We had us a little cabin in the Black Hills where we'd stay. I was real good at keeping house, seeing I'd spent so much time doing those chores for Ma, and I did most of the cooking. No one ever said I had to do it, but I guess I liked it; I liked skinning and peeling and chopping and putting everything in the pot and getting something out at the end we all could eat. Daniel cooked sometimes, but he used to get real ornery over it, and Cal's only contribution was to arrange all our cans, which he'd sometimes do for ages, making towers and bridges with them. Asking him to try his hand at cooking didn't seem like a good idea, somehow.

So when we weren't planning a job we got along just fine, but when the money was running low and we had to start thinking again I'd get more nervous.

I can see us now, sitting around in the shanty, talking over our next job. Daniel was always the organizer: he loved drawing pictures of how it was going to work. He wasn't too good at drawing, though, so I was always having to ask him what they meant, and then he'd get antsy.

WE HOLD UP A TRAIN

When the water sweeps aside I'm looking down from above, and I can see Dan's picture laid out on the ground. He's pointing with a stick to a mark next to a big boxy thing that's supposed to be a train.

'This is you, Cal. You're keeping an eye out for nosy passengers. Anyone sticks their head out the window, threaten to shoot them iffen they don't mind their business.'

I nod and say, 'Uh huh.' I have to make noises and pretend I'm following what he's saying, so he don't notice Cal's not attending, and start yelling at us.

'Wilbur, I'll be keeping watch on the stoker and the engineer while you deal with the express car.'

Look at me, wriggling – I must be fingering the potato in my pocket.

But I'm moving on again now. The water streams in, and I'm watching the train slow to a halt in front of logs we've dragged across the tracks. The stoker and the engineer put their hands up all right, but while Cal and me are in our positions, guarding the train so Dan can get the money, I see movement out the corner of my eye.

I'm supposed to be watching the train crew, like I've been told, but when I glance to my right I see sunlight glinting off a gun barrel – one of the passengers is taking aim at us. I look back at the stoker and the engineer.

'Cal,' I mutter through clenched teeth, keeping my eyes on the two nervous-looking men. No answer.

'Cal,' I say again, a bit louder and more desperate this time.

I steal a quick look around and catch sight of Cal's legs sticking out from under the train. I know exactly what he's done: he couldn't help himself getting off his horse and taking a look underneath the engine. I realize it's down to me to do something and I turn in the saddle and shout out, 'Drop the gun, mister.' Then I shoot in the air, to scare him. Only it's not the fella with the gun is scared, it's Mabel – my darn horse – who takes fright and hightails it away from there as quick as ever she can.

I hear more shots behind me, but there's nothing I can do: she won't stop.

I wake up in the dirt. The sun's going down, and I don't know where in hell I am. I raise my head and see Mabel cropping grass like nothing's happened. Being a horse, she's forgotten it already. I persuade my legs to get me up onto my feet. I ache all over, like an old man with the rheumatism. And I know I've done it now. Dan will be mad as hell. Then it occurs to me they might not have gotten away – what if it was an ambush, and they've been caught, or even killed? What have I done?

I take hold of Mabel's reins and limp off in what I hope is the direction of our shanty.

When I get there and see there's no smoke coming

from the chimney my heart sinks into my boots, but I whistle anyhow, so if they are there they'll know it's me. When I hear a voice I jump.

'Wilbur, you darn idiot! Get in here quick!'

Dan's voice is hoarse – he don't want anyone to hear us, anyone who might still be hunting us.

I push open the door. It's kind of dark, with only one lamp lit, and that one on the floor. I can just make out Dan, crouched beside Cal, who's lying on a bed of straw in a pool of yellow light. I know at once that he'd've asked Dan to lay down that straw – he so hates a mess, he wouldn't want to get blood on the floor.

He's been hit in the shoulder; he's prodding the hole with the fingers of his left hand, just like he's digging worms out the ground to take fishing. Dan twists around to look at me.

'Will you tell him, Wilbur? Tell him he needs to have a dressing put on this before he bleeds to death, or gets an infection. He might listen to you. He never listens to me – I'm only his brother, after all!'

Cal's still poking the wound as he asks me, 'Do you think you bleed more if you're hit nearer the heart, Wilbur?'

'Oh, for the love of God!' Dan's voice cracks. 'What are we gonna do? We can't carry on the way we are: you two ain't fit to rob trains, and I can't do it on my own.'

'We could try and get some regular kind of work,' I suggest.

'*Work*!' Dan seems like he really is about to cry, now. He's spitting as he speaks. 'And exactly what kind of work are you two about to get? *He* can't keep his head in the real world for more than five minutes at a time, and *you* fall into a fit whenever someone hollers at you! I tell you, Wilbur, I've had enough, I truly have.'

I say I'll go and keep watch outside, but really I just want to be on my own. We've come to the end of our time together, the boys and me, and although I knew it had to happen someday, I still feel bad. I'm real sorry, seeing myself so downcast, recalling what it felt like, knowing I was about to be alone again. But then even iffen I could talk to myself, what would I say? *Come, now, Wilbur, one day you're going to be shot and fall down a well wearing women's clothes, and get a chance to live through all the things you done wrong all over again?*

DEAD INJUNS

Through the rush of water I begin to hear a different sound: an eerie howling, and I can almost feel the bitter cold freezing my ears, my nose, my toes inside of my boots. The water's slowing to a halt, and I see it turn, from top to bottom, to a sheet of ice.

It's the tail end of '90, and I'm on my own after the boys and me went our separate ways. Dan's taken Cal off to look for a doctor they know – he's their Ma's cousin, I believe – and I'm trying to make my way in the world without them.

It's been a good few months now, and I've managed to make a living taking jobs here and there with blacksmiths and the like. I've quit one town on account of everyone knowing about my little problem (I had a fit at the pump because someone walked a cow past when I wasn't expecting it). I'm crossing Sioux country and I'm kind of wary, but all I can think about is the cold. It's so darn cold I reckon all the Injuns will be huddled up round their fires. They ain't going to take a bit of interest in me – iffen they can even see me in this blizzard. I've just crossed a creek and I'm fighting my way toward the

Sioux village. Things are so bad I'm sorry I started at all, and I'm wondering whether I shouldn't go right up to one of their tepees and ask whoever I find there iffen I can't go in and warm myself. I figure even a scalping can't be worse than dying out here – at least I'd die in some comfort.

Each step costs me a huge effort, and the freezing air makes my breath so short I feel like retching. Seems to me the wind wants to take my breath to add to its power – and I begin to fancy that's maybe what a real powerful wind is – the breath of a thousand dead men, trying to steal the life from those that are still living. I know it won't be long before the cold gets me – and then I stumble over something and fall on my hands and knees in the snow.

I pick myself up and beat my hands on my chest to warm them, and as I'm doing it I look down and see that what I tripped over is a man – or leastways it was once. It's clear he's dead – he's lying there in the snow with the top half of his body raised for all the world as if he's trying to get up. One of his legs is bent, and his arms are bent at the elbow, with his hands raised. He's got an old scarf wrapped around his head, but I can see he's an Injun – an old fella – and as I look about me I realize there's more of them. There are bodies everywhere – men, women, children, some lying almost covered in snow, others making strange twisted shapes, like they're still alive and struggling to get to their feet again.

I brush some snow away from a squaw who's lying curled up on the ground, and I see her body's wrapped around a little papoose. She's got one arm around its belly, and a hand cradling its dark head. They look like they're sleeping, but they're both dead. I try to shovel some snow back over them, but the wind ain't having it. I turn to a big brave sitting cross-legged nearby. His eyes are half open, and he seems to be looking up at me from under his lids. His regular shirt is torn and fluttering in the wind, and underneath I can make out brightly coloured material.

I try to lay this brave down, but when his back's on the ground, his crossed legs stick up in the air. If I push down on his legs, his body shoots up in a sitting position again, spraying the fallen snow all about. Being kind of comical makes it even more sad. It's some sort of miracle that I don't have a fit, 'cause iffen I was to lay down in these conditions I know I'd soon be dead. But it sure does make me feel melancholy. I've seen dead people before now, but never this many at one time. I almost start to cry, only I know that iffen I did, my tears would most likely freeze to my eyes. I don't know what's happened here, but these folks sure didn't die of the cold: their clothes, their hair, even the snow around them is stained with their blood. They've been shot to pieces, and I feel like iffen I should stay any longer they'll have my soul for their own. So I leave off trying to bury the bodies and struggle away through the blizzard, knowing the snow will cover my tracks as soon as I'm gone.

A BAD THING HAPPENS

All at once the ice melts like a waterfall. The thing I see next is smoke coming from a chimney. I've been travelling for two days now, and I'm making my way toward a little log cabin. The snow has nearly gone and I'm powerful hungry and thirsty. I'm getting desperate: I've been out of water since the day before, and iffen I don't get a drink soon I figure I'll just have to lay down and die. Desperation's driven out any fear I might be feeling, and I'm about to go up to that cabin and get me something to eat and drink.

I creep to the corner of the house, crouching low and trying to keep from being seen. I stand with my Colt ready and raised in the air and my back pressed to the wall, easing along it till I'm able to peer through the little window.

I can see a stove with a pot boiling on top, and I can hear voices – a woman, and what sounds like two children. Then the woman moves into view, bending over the pot to stir it. She's got red hair and she's thin. Her clothes are shabby, with patches on the skirt and the apron. I can't see her face. She pushes the hair away from it with the back of her hand, and I feel a wave of pity. She's tired, and I'm about to burst in and scare the wits out of her. There I go again: all this feeling badly about other folk is no use to me at all. I need to eat, and she's got food – I ain't fixing to hurt her. There's no sign of a man about the place, and I can't see a horse tethered anywhere nearby, so I should be able to get in and out pretty fast.

I ease my way along to the door, slowly raise the latch and spin into the room with my gun arm stretched out ready. The woman starts, and drops the ladle she's been holding with a clatter. There's a high-pitched little scream from the other side of the room, but the children don't move.

I can see the woman's face now. Her skin's as pale as snow, and she looks like she's been kicked by a mule: her top lip's been split, and one of her eyes is bruised. Her red hair's tied back loosely, and strands of it are escaping every which way. Her brown eyes staring at me look terrified. But then I see a change: her face relaxes, and I see something push out the fear – she knows me!

'*Wilbur?* Is it you, Wilbur?'

I have to stare at her a bit longer before I realize who she is.

'*Nattie?*'

I can't keep the shock I feel from creeping into my voice.

I lower my Colt and carry on just looking at her. I can't believe the change in her: she looks years older than she really is, even without the scars and the bruises. But there's something else, too, something worse – the light's gone out of her eyes. She's not the Nattie I used to know.

Then, both together, we say the same thing:

'What are you doing here?'

We stand staring again, before I say,

'I came looking for food, Nattie. I'm kind of on the run. I've done some things I shouldn't have.'

She don't seem to mind this, and says, 'Why, what am I thinking, Wilbur? May I offer you some coffee?' Just like we're two old friends visiting with each other. And she turns and lifts the coffee pot from the hearth. As she's pouring she asks, 'Are you an outlaw, Wilbur?'

'Well, I guess you might say that – but I never meant for things to turn out this way, Nattie. It just kind of happened. You know how I am – I couldn't keep a job with my fits.'

I don't know why it is, but I feel like I've got to explain to her, like she'll be angry with me. But instead she just looks sad: her eyes are full of tears.

'Oh, Wilbur, it's all our fault! Pa promised to look after you, and he didn't. I should have told him how you were scared of the cows, then maybe you wouldn't have had that fit, and things would have been all right. What would your Ma say if she could see you now?'

I don't want to think about Ma – there's too many memories coming back.

'It wasn't your Pa's fault, neither – I went because I wanted to.'

I can see she still don't believe me. She looks away, so I ask her, 'What are you doing here, Nattie? I thought you were fixing to be a schoolteacher.'

'Oh, I was.' She's tracing something on the table with her fingertip, some pattern she's imagined. 'Things change, Wilbur. You can't ever know what's coming, what's around the next corner. We all got the fever and ague. Jim and the girls and me got better, but Ma and Pa – they died, Wilbur, and we had no one to look after us. It was up to me and Jim, because we were the eldest, so I had to keep house and care for the little ones, while he worked. Then when Mr Lieberman came courting, Jim said I'd have to marry him, so that the girls and I could have a proper home. I didn't really have any choice, and he seemed pleasant enough. He always looked so clean when he came to call, and his hair was all brushed down. He had really nice manners in those days . . .'

Her voice trails off, and she puts her hand up to the cut on her mouth. She's keeping her head down, now the surprise of seeing me has worn off some, and I know she's embarrassed. I feel sorry for doing such a bad job of hiding how shocked I am.

'Did he do that to you? Did he hit you, Nattie?'

She glances up sharply, then looks away again.

'I'm not so good at keeping house, and Mr Lieberman is most particular. However hard I try – and I *do* try – I never seem able to get the place clean enough, and there's always too much salt in the stew – or too little. Seems I can't do anything to please him.'

'He shouldn't do that, Nattie. He didn't ought to hit you, however dirty the house is, never mind how much salt there is in the stew.'

'Maybe he shouldn't, but he does, because he can. What can I do, Wilbur? I've got two little ones of my own now, as well as my sisters. How would we manage without a man to provide for us?'

'Well, what about Jimmy? Where is he?'

'I wish I knew. Once I was married to Mr Lieberman he took off. Figured he'd done his bit, I guess. He wanted to be a cowhand, so maybe that's what he did.'

'So you never did get to be a schoolteacher, Nattie?'

'No, I never did get to be a schoolteacher, Wilbur.'

I sit down at the table and look around. Only now do I take proper notice of the children: there's a girl cowering in the corner behind me, and a small boy with his hands in his pockets looking at me with some curiosity. I hear a noise from the ladder leading to the roof and turn around to see a young woman peering anxiously at me.

'Suzie? There's no need to be scared, I know I ain't had a shave nor a wash for some time, but I'm not as rough as I look. I'm Wilbur, Wilbur McCrum. I lodged with your folks for a while when you were a little bitty thing. I don't suppose you remember me.'

She moves over to Nattie's side, and the girl rushes over and takes hold of her skirts. The boy moves more slowly, still with his hands in his pockets.

'Suzie doesn't talk much,' Nattie says, smoothing back a strand of her sister's hair behind her ear. Suzie just stares at me, round-eyed.

'She's scared of Pa,' the little fella says, in a matter of fact way.

'Are *you* scared of your Pa?' I ask him.

He looks down at his boots.

'Sometimes, but I'll grow up to be a man one day.' And he shoots me a defiant look.

The sight of them all huddled together in this shabby hovel makes me feel bad. It's so different from the Reillys' house: there's no glass in the windows, there's gaps in the walls for the wind and the dirt to come through. Nothing to make it like a real home. I feel so bad about Nattie living like this, but I don't know what to say. There's words humming in the air around us, but I can't find the right ones to describe what's inside me. So I look anywhere but at her.

Nattie sees me looking around.

'He doesn't like me to do anything to make it homely. He wouldn't even let me bring my books with me. He's a Calvinist, you see. He doesn't like to see me reading, because he can't. I don't know what's to become of us, Wilbur, I really don't.'

I don't know how to answer her, but then I don't have time to say anything, because the door suddenly bursts open. I take hold of my gun and jump to my feet to find myself looking at a stocky man of forty-five or so with a wide jaw and mean-looking eyes.

'Who the hell are you?' he growls, and that's all I hear before the room turns black and I hit the ground.

When I wake up the first thing I see is the same man, sitting on the floor with his back to the wall. He's got an expression of real surprise on his face, which I guess is down to the bullet hole right between his eyes.

I scramble to my feet, and my gun drops to the floor. I must have been holding it the whole time. I look round to see Nattie staring at the dead man in a strange way. She still looks tired, but she don't look upset. There's a hardness there I ain't never seen in her before. The girls are huddled together behind her, and the little one is whimpering, but the boy walks over and looks at the body, then up at me.

'I guess he's dead, mister.'

'Nattie, what have I done? Is that him? Is that your husband?'

'Not anymore.'

She's still standing there with that look on her face, like she don't want to move and break some kind of spell.

'I'm sorry, Nattie. I didn't mean it. I had a fit. The gun must have gone off. What are we going to do? Should we get a doctor?'

'I think it's too late for that.'

At last she looks at me, and it's as if she's come out of her trance.

'You'd best get out of here, Wilbur. I'll give you some food and a change of clothes, but then you'd better go.'

'I should turn myself in, Nattie, say it was me, else they might think you did it.'

She looks at me sharply again, and that hard expression spooks me.

'The children will say they saw you kill him, won't you, children?'

Her son goes over to her and slides his hand into hers. Looking up at her he says, 'We'll tell them, Ma.'

Then he looks back at me, holding my eyes with a steady gaze.

'You've got to get out of here, Wilbur. The folks round here believe my husband is a mighty fine God-fearing man. They'd lynch you if they found you.'

It's clear that Nattie's in charge, so I do what she says. She covers her husband's body with a bed sheet and sets about getting me water so I can wash. Watching her while she's shaving me I feel sad inside. She's so careful about what she's doing, and I can imagine her being a real good wife to someone who treated her right. Why'd she have to end up with a man like that?

I FIND DAN AGAIN

The water carries me off in its embrace once more, and I can see myself, a week or so after I went on the run from Nattie's place. I'm leading my horse through a chaparral, keeping low, my gun in my hand, looking awful nervous, when I hear a sound.

At first I think it's breaking twigs, but then I realize it's more regular than that: it's something creaking. It creaks, then it stops, then it creaks again. I walk through the trees, looking all about me, holding on to my lucky potato with my free hand – and then something brushes against my shoulder. In front of my eyes I see a pair of boots – and if that weren't strange enough, I know those boots. They used to be mine, until Dan won them off me in a poker game. All this goes through my head in the time it takes to blink an eye, and I don't want to look up. I don't want to look up because I know what I'm going to see when I do. But I can't help myself. My eyes travel up the legs, and there above me, hanging from the end of a rope, is Dan himself, his head leaning horribly to one side. He's got a sign hanging round his neck which says *'This is wat we do to no good catel theeves.'*

I wake up in the dirt to the sound of that damn creaking, and the first thing I think is that I've got to get him down. I know he's dead, but I've got to get him off that rope. So I climb the tree they've strung him up from, and cut it. The noise his body makes as it hits the ground is so terrible I feel everything going black again, and I have to cling on to my branch like a baby to its mama to stop me from joining him.

I climb down and slump on the ground beside his body. I feel so tired now that all I want to do is fall asleep, and never wake. I almost wish I'd go into a fit so bad I'd dash my brains out on a rock and that'd be the end of me as well as Daniel. But I know what I've got to do: I have to bury him.

I stare at Dan. Apart from being all black and blue, he looks kind of peaceful. Leastways, more than he ever did when he was alive. The thing about Dan was, he thought Cal needed him, that he couldn't manage without him, but it seems to me that really it was Dan who needed Cal. He was the sort of person who has a need to be needed. He might act all despairing about Cal and me, but really Cal didn't much mind where he slept, or what he ate. He found the world such a curious and mystifying place that he'd be fine anywhere, just so long as he wasn't starving or freezing to death.

It looked like Dan and Cal had parted ways, and maybe Dan hadn't known how to live with no one to look out for. Leastways, it was him ended up dead.

I brush away a beetle that's crawling across his face, and look around for somewhere to start digging.

I'm glad when the water closes again. I wouldn't want

to see myself burying Daniel and then riding away, not knowing whether I'd dug deep enough to stop the coyotes clawing him up again. The only thing that could put my mind at rest was writing Caleb, to tell him what had happened. I sent the letter to the place where they'd gone looking for their cousin, so I hope it would have gotten to him, iffen he was still alive himself. I knew it would make him awful sad to know Dan was dead, but I figured he'd rather know what happened, than always be wondering.

It was after putting Daniel in the ground I made the decision that changed everything for me. I wasn't real good at making decisions – usually I just let things happen – but after seeing Dan like that I fell to thinking about life – and death. I thought about all the things I'd never done. I'd never climbed a mountain, nor swam in the sea, nor been to England or France. There weren't much I could do about any of those things, but one thing I could remedy: I'd never been with a woman and, as I'd got a bit of money left, I could find one. It wasn't the best way – like most everyone else, I guess, I'd always dreamed about meeting some girl and falling in love, and getting married, but that was easier to do when I was a boy, and it was something far off in the future. Now I was *in* the future, and I had to admit to myself it would never happen to me like that. I didn't know whether Dan had ever been with a woman. He'd never said anything about it, so I guessed probably not – and now he was dead, and it was too late. So I made up my mind that this was one thing I'd do before I died, and I was going to do it for Dan, too.

IDA MAY

Vacanegra's a small town, not far from Laramie, and I didn't so much choose it, as happen upon it. Once I'd found out from a bartender that it had its own joy house, I got myself a place to stay, freshened myself up as best I could, put on a clean shirt and went to find me a woman.

I see the madam now, a Scots woman from the sound of her, with a broad back and a nose that seems like it's been broken in a brawl, but still handsome in her own way. She gives me a look that makes me think she can tell I've never done this before. I have a hand in my pocket, and she says, 'All guns must be left down here with me, mister.'

'Oh, I ain't got a gun on me.'

'Well, you won't mind if I make sure, then,' and before I can say anything, she's putting her hand in my pocket and pulling out the potato. I stare at her, not knowing how to explain, but she just arches her pencilled-in eyebrows at me and says, 'Now listen, mister, once that bedroom door is closed, what goes on between you and my girl is just between the two of you, but I want you to know that I won't have any violence on these premises.

This is a respectable establishment, and my girls are of the finest quality. Anyone who tries anything funny will feel the sharp end of more than just my tongue.'

I grab hold of the back of a chair for support. I'm beginning to think this is a mistake. I'm sweating already, and I ain't even seen any of the girls yet. I put on some cologne before I came out, and it's so powerful it's making my eyes sting. Then the madam pulls aside a curtain in the doorway, and the curtain and the water become one. I can follow her through it, and see three girls sitting side by side on a fancy upholstered sofa.

'This is Helga,' she says, waving her hand at a big woman with what looks like a lot of false hair. 'She's from Germany, and she's as strong as a man, so you needn't fret that anything you do might hurt her.'

She glances down at my pocket and then back at my face in a meaningful way.

'And this is Sadie – she used to be a bare-back rider with the circus.' She nods toward the golden-haired one who's drawn on a beauty spot to show off her pout.

'And that there's Belle,' she says, like she's run clean out of enthusiasm.

I'm staring at the third girl all the while she's talking. This one is dark, and much skinnier than the other two: her low-cut dress sticks out from her chest where she's nothing to fill it. She seems kind of sulky, too, like she don't want to be there, and don't much like me, neither. That's fair enough – I guess I'd feel the same in her situation. The others are simpering away at me like I'm the best-looking man in the territory, but in spite of that – or maybe on account of it – I like Belle the best, and a few minutes later it's her I'm following up the stairs to her room.

I'd thought my cologne was powerful, but the smell of that room is far stronger. It's women's scent – some kind of French perfume, I guess, and it's like she's soaked every scrap of material in it. And there's a whole lot of material in that room: heavy brocade curtains, and a bedspread in rich colours, shawls hung over the door, the chairs. I can feel my eyes beginning to water, and I start to sneeze. Belle looks up from the bed, where she's taking off her slippers, and asks me whether I'm all right.

'Yes, yes. Something tickled my nose, is all.'

I go over to the window, hoping to find something to say. I stand there for a moment, my hat still in my hands, but all I can see is a cart passing by with some barrels on it. When I turn round, Belle's standing there in nothing but a corset and stockings. I hit the floor straightaway.

I open my eyes to see Belle kneeling over me, slapping me none too gently around the jaw. She looks worried, but just as soon as she sees I'm awake the sulky look slips back on her face.

'What d'you mean by passing out like that? You gave me a real fright there for a minute. Thought you'd upped and died on me before I'd even laid a finger on you – or your money.'

I sit up and shake my head, to clear it. 'Why, I'm sorry, ma'am' – she snorts when I say that, and turns her head away, arms folded tight across her chest – 'it's just something that happens to me whenever I get worked up about something, and I guess I ain't never been so close to a beautiful woman before.'

This time the snort turns into a hooting laugh, which is so loud it takes me by surprise.

'Well, sir, that must make it mighty inconvenient for you, most especially when you're with a lady friend.'

'That's just it, ma'am. I ain't never had a lady friend on account of it. You were about to be the first.'

She begins to laugh again, then stops short and stares at me.

'You mean you ain't *never* been with a woman – not once?'

'Never.'

'Truly?'

'Truly.'

She looks to be thinking about this for a while, then she turns to me again.

'Why me?'

I feel hot, and I can't meet her eye, 'Well, I guess I must have liked the look of you.'

She hoots again, then she shoots me a coy look, and pats the bedspread.

'Well, are you going to come and sit beside me, or are you figuring to stay there on the floor all evening?'

Although I'm scared of having another fit iffen I get too close to her, I feel real foolish sitting down there, so I get up and go over to the bed.

'You know, we don't have to do nothing you don't want to. You've paid for me, so you get to decide what we do. If all you want to do is talk, then we'll talk. It'd make a change for me; most of the men who come here ain't interested in talking to me anymore than they'd talk to their darn horses – less, probably.'

And that's what we did. I'm real sorry to see the curtain of water close over me again. It felt good to remember when we first met. I told her everything there was to tell about me and Ma and Pa – and Essie. I told her about my fits, and how they got in the way of everything, how I had to leave the Reillys' house, and the Widow Harris's lodgings, about Jonny Rose, and Dan and Caleb, and my time as the worst outlaw in the whole of the West.

Thing is, she listened to me like I was the best storyteller she'd ever heard. She felt sad for me when Ma left, and when I had to leave Nattie, and there were tears in her eyes when I told her about finding Daniel hanged. Other times she laughed, like when Jonny Rose found me with the gold, and she even said, 'Oh, Wilbur, you're so clever!' which I couldn't recall anyone ever having said to me before.

She told me about her life, too: how her real name was Ida May Longden, but she was known round these parts as Gap-Toothed Belle; how her Ma had been a beautiful Irishwoman with black hair and blue eyes, and her father had been a rough fella who spent too much time in the saloons; how her mother had died having a baby, and her Pa had married again; how her new Ma had hated Ida May, and had treated her like a slave until she ran away and had been taken in by Lady Muldoon, the madam.

'She's a real lady, you know. She married a Scots lord, only he was awful cruel to her and kept her locked up, wouldn't let her see anyone, nor go to dances or nothing, until one day she ran off with a man that worked on the estate, and they came out here to try their hand at ranching, but it didn't go right and he went crazy and tried to shoot her, so she had to get him put away, and she ended up selling what they had left and starting this place.

'She's not so bad, really. She looks after her girls, which is more than some do, and she's let me stay, even though I don't bring in much money. I just can't seem to make myself friendly like the other girls can, and I ain't all plump and soft. Lady Muldoon even tried giving me extra food to fatten me up, but it didn't work – just gave me bellyache. If you hadn't picked me out tonight I don't know how much longer I'd've lasted here before she decided to give the room to someone else – a girl who could bring in more business.'

I couldn't understand how any man could be so blind as to find either of those simpering girls prettier than Ida May. To me she'd have been well nigh perfect, iffen only she'd had a full set of teeth.

I'd never talked with a woman the way I did with her, and we talked for almost the whole of that night. The madam gave me another of her up-and-down looks on my way out, but this time it seemed to me her face was softer than before.

I saw Ida May regular after that, and I got me a job in a sawmill. It was real noisy work, and I could hear the buzzing in my ears even when I wasn't there, but it suited me, because all that loudness made it hard for me to think about much, apart from what I was doing. And it brought me in a wage. I didn't want to end up like poor Daniel, swinging on the end of a rope with my hands tied behind my back, so I needed to keep away from anything that might get the lawmen – or the vigilantes – on my trail.

Trouble was, the more I saw of Ida May, the more the notion kept rising in my mind that maybe we could get married. I'd take her away from the joy house and we'd set ourselves up somewhere and have some babies, and live like a regular family. I'd never been much of a one for making chests at the girls, but Ida May was different.

A MOST SURPRISING
THING HAPPENS

You don't have to listen to my story for long to realize that as a general rule nothing happens like I expect it to, and it was the same with me and Ida May. Things were real good with us – Lady Muldoon made me pay to see her, just like everyone else, but she let me spend a lot of time there, provided I did chores like chopping wood for the fires, and filling baths for the girls. When she found out I liked cooking she let me do some of that, too, helping out her regular cook, a Chinaman with a long braid down his back, like a woman, who everyone called Jock and who never spoke.

I'd've been real happy to carry on like that, iffen one night I hadn't noticed Ida May weren't saying nothing.

I'm sitting on the edge of the bed pulling my boots off and telling her about a saw breaking, and how it was lucky no one got hurt. Normally she'd come and help me, but when I turn round to look at her I see she's lying on the bed staring up at the ceiling, chewing on her lip like she wants to gnaw right through it.

'What is it, honey?' I ask, putting my arm across her and leaning over to look in her face.

She glances at me, but then she goes back to staring past me again.

'Wilbur, I've got something to tell you.'

She don't sound like herself when she says that. Her voice is quiet and serious, and it strikes a chill in my heart. My first thought is that she's found a new beau – she does sometimes entertain other men when I'm working.

'What is it, Ida May?'

'Wilbur,' she turns her head to look at me properly now, 'Wilbur – you're going to be a father.'

I'd been so sure she was about to tell me something real bad that I don't understand what she's saying at first. She must see that, 'cause she says, 'I'm having a baby, Wilbur.'

'*My* baby?' It ain't so much that I don't believe her, just that I didn't think giving a woman a baby would be that easy.

She pulls her skirts round and kneels up, facing me, colour rising in her cheeks. 'Of course it's your baby! What do you think – that I let other men do what you do with me?'

She looks like an angry cat, and as ready to spit, but I'm so happy all I can do is laugh. I reach out to take hold of her, but Ida May ain't having it – she swings back her arm and hits me round the face, knocking me backward onto the floor. It stings some, but it don't stop me laughing, even when Lady Muldoon, hearing the commotion above her head, comes stumping up the stairs and bursts into the room with a gun at the ready.

'I'm trying to run a joy house here, not a music hall. I'll trouble you to contain yourself, Mr McCrum!' Then lowering the Colt, she turns to Ida May and says, 'So he knows, does he?'

I raise my head from the floor and look at Ida May, who's still spoiling for a fight. 'So you told her first?'

'She told *me*! How was I meant to know? I ain't never been in this condition before, and I wouldn't be now, if it wasn't for you, Wilbur McCrum!' and she marches over to Lady Muldoon, takes the gun off her, and stands over me with it.

'That's enough from you two lovebirds. You can talk this over quietly, or you can go elsewhere. I have gentle-men downstairs, and they aren't in the mood for waiting.'

Ida May sits back down on the bed, looking ready to cry now, and I get to my knees and shuffle over to her.

'Hey, sweetheart, it'll be all right. I'll take care of you, of both of you. It'll be just fine, you'll see.'

She pushes away my hand as I try to stroke her hair. 'How's it gonna be fine, Wilbur? I can't work much longer, and we can't live here forever. We'll need a place of our own. We'll need to be decent, respectable folk, Wilbur, if we're having a baby. What's it gonna say when it's old enough to figure out what this place is, what its mama is?' And she put her hands to her face and begins to sob like her heart's broke.

It near breaks my heart, too, to see her like that, which is why I say what I do.

'I'll take care of you, Ida May, I promise. I'll get us some money, enough to find a home of our own, just the three of us. Trust me, Ida May, trust me, honey.'

I see Lady Muldoon's face, with its nose tilting to one side like it wants to talk to her left cheek. She's trying to look stern, but I know her heart ain't really in it.

'I'll let you stay as long as you work in the kitchen. This isn't a charitable institution, mind, everyone has to earn their keep.'

I look at Ida May, to see what she's thinking, and I can see she's none too happy. Kitchen chores call to mind her Pa's new wife, and she don't want to think too much about those years. I smile and jog her arm with my elbow, trying to make her more cheerful, and she sits up and raises the corners of her lips. When Lady Muldoon turns away, though, she jogs me back, and her expression ain't exactly grateful.

I don't want to be torn away from the memory of that time, even when she's looking at me so angry, but we're moving on again. I see Ida May over and over, a little bigger each time with the baby growing inside her. Sometimes she's shelling peas, sometimes she's at the sink, washing the dishes, oftentimes she's yelling at me, but me, whenever I'm in the picture, I'm grinning all over my face, 'cause for the first time in my life I can see the future, and it's a real future this time, not a make-believe one.

Then we slow down and I see what I've been hoping to see ever since this picture show began – me, walking up and down outside while I wait for Ida May's confinement to be over. She's sure been making a lot of noise, and I don't reckon it'll have done much for Lady Muldoon's finances, but she's a soft-hearted woman, and she couldn't bring herself to turn us out on the street with nowhere to go and a baby on the way.

Ida May makes one final God-awful sound, like a cow being slaughtered, and then there's a silence that frightens me more than the hollering did. Next there's a thin little wail, and I realize that must be the sound of my child filling up its lungs for the first time. I run inside and take the stairs two at a time. As I reach the door of her old room, which she's been allowed to have back while the baby's on the way, I go smack into Helga, who's just coming to fetch me. I pick myself up and go in, but before I get any further, a strong hand grabs me around the arm and I'm forced into a chair, then my head is pushed down between my knees. I guess Lady Muldoon don't want me passing out, but I want to see Ida May and the baby, so I keep struggling to sit up and take a good look at them while she keeps my head down, like she's dunking me in a barrel of rainwater.

After a couple of minutes of struggle, and muffled complaints from between my own legs, she says, 'You sure you aren't about to keel over, Wilbur McCrum?'

'I can't promise nothing, but this sure ain't helping, I tell you.'

She leaves go of my head, but keeps a grip on my shoulder so's I stay in the chair.

The first time I get to see my son I've got them stars in my eyes and I'm dizzy as hell. Ida May's lying back on the pillows with her eyes closed, and looking so bad I'd think she was dead if I couldn't see she was breathing. The baby's in the arms of a girl called Black Sarah, who's looking into its face and cooing to it. She holds it so I can

see it better and says, 'It's a boy, Wilbur. You're a daddy
– you got a son.'

I look at the little screwed-up face and try to see a
person there, but I can't. It's blue and red at the same
time, with sticky white stuff in its hair, and Ida May's
blood still on it. All I can think is that he's to blame, this
little squalling creature, for making his mama so exhausted, for draining her face of colour like that, and now
we've got to look after him, somehow, until he's old
enough to look after himself.

'Don't you wanna hold him, Wilbur?'

I don't, but before I can say anything, Lady Muldoon
answers for me. 'Maybe that's not such a good idea, Sarah
– leastways, not yet. Let him get used to the idea first.'
And the hand on my shoulder loosens its grip and pats
me like I'm a good dog.

I twist round and look up at Lady Muldoon. 'Is she all
right? She's going to be all right, ain't she?' I feel like a
child myself. I need someone to tell me what I'm to do. I
can feel my eyes filling with water, and I'm not used to
that, on account of I usually have a fit in any situation
that'd make other folk cry.

Lady Muldoon smiles down her crooked nose at me.
'She'll be just fine, Wilbur. She's young and strong – but
it's a hard business bringing a baby into this world. I did
it once, and that was enough for me.'

I must look surprised, because she carries on, 'Oh, yes,
I have a son, too. He'll be a grown man by now, and for
all I know, already a great Scottish laird.'

'Don't you ever think about going back to see him?'

'That was another life, Wilbur. I left all that behind a

long time ago. This is where I belong, with my girls, doing something useful. I was bored out of my wits sitting in that great house all day with nothing to occupy me but choosing the dinner menus. I was born in the wrong place, and I married the wrong man, so I had to get out before I made any more mistakes. My husband and son were better off without me, and I'm better off without them.'

I'm trying to imagine leaving behind all that money, that easy life, but then it clearly weren't so easy for her, and money ain't the most important thing, after all. Then Ida May makes a noise and I turn to look at her again, and the picture dissolves.

I ROB A BANK

Money may not be the most important thing in life, but you can't do much without it, 'specially when you've got a wife and child to take care of. I didn't want to, but I decided to do just one more job – a big one this time, so we'd have enough money to go back east and set ourselves up somewhere. We'd lead a quiet life: I'd do regular work and Ida May would keep house; we'd grow old and be respectable. Maybe I'd even track down Ma and show her I wasn't as much of a good-for-nothing as she'd thought I was.

Because money was more and more often shipped by train by this time – and robbing a train on my own was too risky – it seemed to me that the best thing would be to rob a bank. That'd be risky, too, on my own, but I figured if I planned it well enough so's I knew how to get away, and what I'd do if things went wrong, then it was still my best chance.

I spent a few months travelling around looking for a likely place to rob, and in the end I happened upon Fortitude, Kansas. It suited me because although it was a small town, there was more than just one main street – 'cause the last thing you want when you've robbed a bank is to find your way out has been blocked by angry citizens. That's the big risk with a bank job: you're surrounded by people who sure don't want you riding off with their money, so you need to be in and out as quick as you can. It was far enough away, too, for no one there to know me iffen they saw me.

The best thing about this particular bank, though, was the chief clerk: he was a small man – no bigger than me – with narrow shoulders and thinning hair. He wore spectacles, too, and I figured that iffen I got them off him he'd have less chance of recognizing me later.

I camped out in the woods near the town and got to know the place well enough. The good thing about being such a plain-looking person is you can pass around almost as iffen you was invisible. Iffen you're a big, tough-looking fella like those friends of Doc Holliday's all the men are likely to take heed of you, and iffen you're the handsome type, like Jonny Rose, then all the ladies will. As long as I didn't have a fit, nobody was going to pay attention to me – leastways, not until I robbed their bank, and I was figuring to wear a real good disguise for that. Ida May had made me a mask out of black satin, with cord loops to hook over my ears and a beard made of unravelled rope. I'd tested it to make sure it wouldn't make me sneeze, and I'd practised what I was going to say in front of Ida May's mirror – with her listening, to see that the words was clear. I'd walked around the streets of that town until I knew every corner, what was in the window of every store – even the dead flies. Nothing could go wrong . . .

Here it comes: there's the bank, rising out the water, and there's my problem – or there it ain't. The hitching rail's been taken down by workmen who are making a new sidewalk. There's nowhere for me to tether Mabel, so I have to hide her down an alley a block away. This makes me anxious, and I'm breathing deep as I put on my mask and slip in through the doors. There's only one person in there, apart from the two clerks – an old fella who looks like a farmer is leaning on the counter, having a conversation. As he's got his back to me he's the last to notice me standing there, but the others freeze straight away, and it don't take the old man long to guess from their faces that something bad is happening behind him. Then he looks over his shoulder at me and stops talking, too.

'Now, folks,' I say, 'this won't take long if you use your heads. I don't want to hurt no one. All I need is some money, then I'll be on my way.'

I'm trying to think of Jesse James robbing that train, and how civil he was to the folks he was stealing from. I figure that a little courtesy never did no harm, and they're more like to do as I say if I don't panic them. I have to sound as if I mean it, though, so I've practised making my voice go deep.

Although the chief clerk don't look like the kind of man to put up a fight, he must've been told he shouldn't give in too easy, so he tries to reason with me.

'Now, son, much as I'd like to oblige you, there's a time-lock on the vault here, I can't do anything about it.'

I snort, hoping I sound angry, rather than like I'm sneezing. 'Sure there's a time-lock, mister, but it opens at half after nine. Whad'ya take me for, a fool?'

This makes him look mighty uncomfortable, and then the junior clerk chimes in, 'Give him the money, Frank. It's not worth dying for.'

The fella with the moustaches is real nervous now. I can see he'd like to look at the younger man, but he don't want to take his eyes off me. What's left of his hair is sticky with sweat, and his face has turned grey. I wonder what I'd do if his heart failed him.

I'm starting to feel real sorry for him. All he's doing is his job, and then I come in with this darn mask on my face and point a gun at him. I try to think about how mean I felt the last time I saw Jonny Rose, but this just ain't the same. This man's done me no harm – I'm the one doing *him* harm. If he refuses to give me the money he might well end up killed, and if he hands it over, the townsfolk might decide to lynch him. Either way, he loses. I know I can't keep thinking like this or I'll have a fit and be in the jailhouse before I can blink. I daren't put my hand in my pocket, so I do the next best thing: I start muttering under my breath, 'Potatoes, potatoes.'

The look on the senior clerk's face changes to puzzlement, and he cups his ear and leans toward me, trying to catch what I'm saying. 'What's that, son?'

'If you want my opinion, Frank, this fella's crazy.'

That comes from the old farmer, and it's enough to jerk me out of that sympathy I was feeling. I lunge forward, and pull the old fella toward me. I'm a bit shocked at how hard and muscled his arm feels, but I stick my shotgun in his side and say, 'Open the vault, Frank, or I'm gonna repaint this bank with your friend's guts.'

This sounds so mean and nasty that I make myself feel quite sick, but it works. Frank backs into the room behind him and I move over with the old fella so's I can watch him through the door. He unlocks the vault and comes back pretty quick with a bag full of money that I make him open, to be sure it's real.

It's as I'm reaching to take the bag that it all starts to go wrong for me. The old farmer sees his chance and knocks my shotgun upward, letting off a shot that brings a shower of dust down on our heads, blinding me for a moment. As I'm bending over and coughing, the old man grabs my mask and pulls it off. We stare at each other for a moment, before the dust starts to make his eyes stream, too, and I pick the bag up off the floor and hightail it.

I can hear the people inside the bank still coughing and spluttering, so I know I've got a minute or two's advantage. The gunshot will've attracted attention, though.

I'm about to start running toward the alley where I've left Mabel, but I see a fella come out of a building carrying a gun. Lucky for me he's looking the wrong way, and I turn in the other direction and duck down between a saloon and a saddler's store. There's a pinto pony tethered to a wagon outside the saloon, and I put my bag of money down while I take off one of its saddlebags, then stuff the money inside it. Then I start back toward Mabel, being careful not to run, and trying to look like someone who's just going about his business. I can't pass the bank again in case Frank or the others see me, so I tip my hat over my eyes and cross the street to walk behind the buildings on the other side, hoping to go back in a loop and find Mabel. I'm losing hold, though:

with each step the world's turning blacker, and I can't keep going much longer. I fall forward on the sidewalk.

A few moments later there's a thundering of hooves. I'd always wondered what happened while I was in that fit, and now I know. I'm in the shadow of another saloon, and I've fallen on top of the saddlebag. The marshal and four or five other men – one of them the old farmer – ride by, looking for the bank robber. One notices me and looks over, but the marshal keeps on riding, and another man calls out, 'That's just some old drunk, Bull.'

So it was my fit saved me.

As the horsemen grow smaller and smaller on the horizon I see myself raise my head, looking kind of dazed, and I push myself up to my feet and dust myself off, before going to find Mabel and riding away as fast as ever we can in the other direction to the posse.

I ESCAPE, DRESSED
AS A SALOON GIRL

The scene dissolves to bubbles of water, and we're rushing on again. Almost at once it parts, and I'm sitting with Ida May on her bed, counting the money that's piled up between us. It's wonderful to see that look of happiness on Ida May's face. As she looks at me her eyes are shining.

'Why, Wilbur, there's nearly twenty thousand dollars here. We can go east now, just the three of us, and leave this rotten, dirty old town behind us.'

As for me, I'm grinning like an idiot, too. I've earned us a way out. Not a way most folks would have chosen, maybe, but what was the difference between this and striking gold? I'd had to prepare me just as hard as one of them prospectors, and my way was surely more dangerous. All that mattered was that we could escape now.

Of course we should have saddled up Mabel and rode out of town right there and then, but Ida May thought she should tell Lady Muldoon she was leaving, and she wanted to say goodbye to all her friends. That was our big mistake.

We stuffed the moneybag under the bed and fell asleep. We woke when Junior started fussing and lay looking at each other for a moment, before jumping up and checking that the money was really there, that it hadn't all been a dream. It was there all right, and we sat looking at it for a while before we roused ourselves. Ida May was going to pack as much as she could into one big bag, and I was going back to my lodgings to fetch the few belongings I still had there. It shouldn't have taken long.

I walk down Main Street with my hands in my pockets, trying to grin and whistle at the same time, until a couple of people turn to look at me and I decide to keep my head down and stop attracting attention to myself. I'm feeling so darn happy, though – till I turn the corner and see a fella nailing a poster to the side of a bank. I can just see the face on it, over his shoulder. The bottom of it's curled up, so he smoothes it down before knocking in the last nail and standing back to admire his work.

I feel my heart hammering my ribs like it wants to escape as I sidle up, trying to look as casual as ever I can. The picture's of me all right. Whoever drawed it has managed quite some likeness, got my squint off just perfect. Underneath it says,

Wilbur McCrum, Outlaw. Killed one man, thought to be involved in a number of robberies of stage coaches and banks. Wanted, Dead or Alive.

So that's me – an outlaw. I've never really thought of myself that way, even though I knew what I've been doing weren't exactly right. I think I figured that iffen only I could explain to people – about how I was, and how hard it was to live – then they'd understand. But seems like it's too late for that now.

A crowd's beginning to gather round the picture – there ain't much to do in towns like this, and anything new is interesting – so I figure I'd better get out of there before someone recognizes me. I turn on my heel and head straight for the joy house.

Then I hear something that makes the hairs stand up on the back of my neck: horses' hooves, a whole bunch of them. I duck into a doorway and peer out. A posse of bounty hunters is riding into town. There are five men, all of them looking awful serious, and all wearing long coats that I know are to hide their shotguns. I realize as surely as a mouse when it first catches sight of a cat that these men have come looking for me, and they won't rest until they find me – dead or alive.

I return to the joy house the back way, and find Ida May surrounded by Lady Muldoon and the other girls. Some of them are red-eyed. Big Helga's snuffling away like a sad elephant and she and all the others look up at me accusingly as I come through the door. I know there's no time to lose being sentimental, though, so I tell them straight out, 'The posse's here!'

There are gasps from some of the girls. Ida May stares at me.

'Are you sure it's you they're here for?'

'There's a poster outside the bank. I guess there'll be others going up around town.'

'What are we going to do? Can we get past them?'

'I don't think so – there's five of them, and only one road into town, and one road out. I'll have to give myself up, Ida May. They've got no reason to know anything about you.'

'No! Wilbur, we're in this together. We can get away from here, I'm sure we can.'

'But what about Junior? They might start shooting at us.'

Ida May looks to Lady Muldoon for help.

'Leave him with me, I'll take care of him. You've a better chance of making your escape if there's just the two of you. Once you get enough distance between you and that posse you can send word and I'll bring him to you.'

Ida May and me just stare at each other, not knowing what to do for the best.

'You haven't got time to wait around, you have to get out now, before they start searching. Wilbur, I'll get you a disguise.'

I'm thinking of that beard made of rope as Lady Muldoon whispers something in Helga's ear. They both turn their eyes toward me, and Helga laughs out loud in a way that makes me feel uneasy. Then they go off together to fetch something, while I wait and wonder what they've got in store for me.

By the time they get back I've got my fingernails dug into the potato in my pocket, I'm feeling so darn awkward. That's nothing, though, to how I feel when they hold up the clothes they've brought me: corsets big enough for a whale, and a great big fancy silk dress.

'We'll have to pin them up a bit, but I reckon they'll do.'

The way I feel about this plan must be showing in my face, 'cause before I can say anything, Lady Muldoon carries on, 'It's your only chance, Wilbur. They're looking for a man, not two girls. You only have to get past them and you can escape back east where no one cares what happened here. You got her into this, Wilbur – now you have to get her out.'

So here I go, letting them fix corsets round me, and lower the dress over my head. I have to own that, although I ain't too happy about wearing women's clothes, I sure do like having these women fussing round me. I ain't never had this much attention from ladies in the whole of my life, let alone all at one time. They stick a few pins in me, but then I'm used to that, what with going to school with Jonny Rose, so to tell the truth, I'm sorry when they decide they're done, and they stand back to admire their handiwork. They look eager at first, but after a moment spent staring at me, their faces fall.

'We need something else,' Ida May says, frowning.

'A veil would do it,' says Helga.

Ida May tuts at her. 'Maybe some rouge, and a little colour around the eyes. You just don't have a very ladylike face, Wilbur.'

Helga snorts at this, and I can't help feeling a little affronted. It wasn't my idea to dress me up like a woman, after all. Anyhow, one of the girls fetches some facepaint, and they get busy again, trying to make me look more attractive. It tickles, and I have to keep real still, but in the end they stand back again for another look. I see from the way they glance at each other that they still ain't happy, but they're running out of ideas now. Then Lady Muldoon pipes up, 'A hat. That's what we need – a real big, fancy hat that'll draw attention away from his face. I think I've got just the thing.'

She bustles off and comes right back with the biggest hat I've ever seen. It's got a big black brim, and lots of net stuff around it, and worst of all, two huge feathers sticking out the side, like some bird nose-dived in there and got stuck for ever.

'I thought I was trying to hide. Every darn person in town's going to turn around and stare at me wearing a hat like that!'

'Ah, but that's the idea,' says Lady Muldoon, pinching the netting and smoothing the feathers, and looking mighty pleased with herself, 'they'll be looking at the *hat*, not at you. I think it will work.' And she puts the thing on my head and pats it down.

'I'll lend you my buggy. If you drive, Ida May, Wilbur can busy himself with looking the other way as you pass the bounty-hunters. You get yourselves ready and I'll see that the horse is saddled.'

Walking in those skirts is real hard. You have to keep your legs close together, and I keep tripping on the hem. I don't know how I thought I could ever fool anyone. The corsets are real itchy, too, and it's hard to stop myself from scratching. I'm glad I wasn't born a woman.

We're just outside now, waiting for Lady Muldoon to bring round her buggy. Ida May and me are standing close together, trying hard to look like two good-time girls about to go out for the day, when I realize how thirsty I am. I've not had a thing to eat nor drink since the night before, and my mouth's as dry as a desert – I can almost feel a sidewinder slithering across it. Without saying a word to Ida May, I walk over to the well outside the saloon to get me a drink of water.

Here it is. It may be hard to watch, but I want to see what happened, being as I had my back to the action the first time around. There's a sound of hooves drumming in the dirt, but all I can see is me, stooping over as I take a drink. One thing I do notice, though, is that the hem of my skirt is caught up in the fastenings of my chaps, showing off part of my trouser leg and boot. Ida May must've noticed this, too, because I hear her voice calling, 'Wilbur!' and then I hear shots. Not one, but two – I guess they missed me the first time – and all of a sudden I feel the thud of a bullet in my back. Feel it for real, not just remember feeling it. And then it's as if I'm being sucked backward, up through the water. As I go I can hear everything again I've heard since drowning, but playing real fast, so it sounds more like musicians tuning up than folks talking, and I see flashes of bright colour. It's like some huge hand has a hold of my collar, or as if I've been caught by a twister and I'm being pulled up into the air. It feels like my head's going to burst with the noise and the lights, and the speed we're going.

And then it stops.

I'm out of the water. I try to take a breath, but I can't, and I'm still being pulled up and up, until suddenly I'm falling.

Part 2

THEY THINK I'M DEAD

That should have been it, the end of Wilbur McCrum, failed outlaw, failed son, failed husband, failed father – but it wasn't. You'll have realized by now that I wasn't much good at living; well, I guess I wasn't any good at dying, neither. Anyone else who'd been shot and then drowned would have stayed that way, but not me, I didn't manage to die.

So how did I get from there – being shot while fleeing the posse and falling into a well dressed in women's clothes – to where I am now: sitting propped up in a comfortable bed, with a fire burning in the grate, writing my story in a handsome leather-bound journal? You might say I was reborn, given another chance – a chance to make a better job of living my life. And I'll tell you what I made of it.

The first thing I knew was the sound of voices, and they didn't sound like the devils I was expecting – they weren't taunting me, just talking about me. I wanted to open my eyes but for some reason I couldn't, so I just lay there and listened, while I tried to figure out what in tarnation was going on.

'I don't know, George. It seems a strange idea to me. Once you're dead you go in the ground. Anything else just seems plain wrong.'

'But there's reasons for that, Ed. You bury a body six feet under because otherwise it'd rot and get high, or the coyotes would eat it. If only you knew how to keep it fresh there'd be no need to bury it.'

That was when I began to wonder if it was me they were talking about.

'I've been reading about those Ancient Egyptians – they did it all the time. Now *they* had a proper respect for death. When a person died they'd bury him in these underground chambers along with any manner of things he might need in the next life: food, tools, musical instruments, ready for when he woke up on the other side. Then they'd build this *pyramid* above ground, like some sort of home for him, you might say. They preserved the body, wrapped it in bandages and put it in a special kind of coffin with a face painted on it so's everyone could see what he looked like when he was alive. They took out the guts, brains too. They stuck a hook through the nostril, punched a hole in the skull, then pulled them out through the hole . . .'

'George! You ain't . . .'

'No, no, Ed. Don't you worry. I've not got the skill for anything like that. Everything will stay where it's always been. I'll just soak him in arsenic, hang him up to dry and see what happens. They did it with old Abe Lincoln, you know, to keep him fresh till they could bury him.'

'I still don't understand why you want to do this thing, George.'

'It's a kind of experiment, Ed. I figure if it works I might be able to move somewhere fancy, like Chicago or San Francisco, and set up a business pickling the dear departed of rich folks. Just think of it – they could keep Grandma, say, in her favourite chair without having to worry about the smell. If I got real good at it, she might even look better than when she was alive. The potential's endless.'

Ain't they heading for a surprise, I thought.

'I ain't sure, George. What if he's got kin who get to hear he's dead and come looking for him?'

'Then I've done them a service, keeping him fresh till they've arrived to bury him. I might even ask for a consideration to cover my expenses. You haven't got some kind of legal objection to this proposition of mine, have you, Ed?'

'Hell, George, I don't pretend to know too much about the law except that horse rustling's a hanging offence. Everything else seems kinda blurred to me – there's always an argument on both sides. You know they only made me town marshal because I'm taller than everyone else. I just thought it might be kinda embarrassing to have to explain to his Ma what her son was doing hanging from a hook in your store.'

'I have to thank you, Ed – you've just given me another idea: it can take a while for news to reach a dead man's folks. I might have a sideline in temporary preservation going. As for this poor devil – would *you* want to claim him?'

The two voices were coming closer until it sounded like they were standing right above me. I tried real hard to open my eyes, but I realized there was something heavy and cold pressing on them. Someone had put coins on my lids to keep them shut.

I wanted to open my mouth and holler, 'You just hang on there – I ain't dead! You can't do nothing to me while I'm still alive!' But something was binding my jaws together and I couldn't make a sound. I couldn't raise my hand nor twitch my toes, neither, but then I expected that, it had happened to me so many times before. Never like this, though. I can't tell you what it felt like to hear those two talking about me as if I was a piece of meat, a piece of beef jerky they needed to dry out so's it'd keep till winter.

Struggling to make them understand was like being in the kind of bad dream that makes you fall awake in the middle of the night to find your blanket's soaked with cold sweat. This was worse than being shot; that was all over too quick for me to realize what was happening, but this went on and on, and although I was desperate to make them hear me, they had no idea. To them I was just a sorry-looking corpse – one that no one would bother to claim because it wasn't worth the journey. It was like I was shackled to the bed, a prisoner in my own body, and I had no idea when it would end.

Then I heard one of the voices say, from real close, 'I wish that woman hadn't put these coins on his eyes . . .'

All of a sudden the weight was lifted from my eyelids and they sprang open. I could see again. And I can see it now, clear as day – despite all the years that have gone by.

The face just a few inches from my own belongs to an

elderly gent with a friendly expression and hair that stands up around his head like wisps of white cloud on a hot July day. He's a dapper little fella wearing a smart black suit with a watch chain, and a starched white handkerchief in his breast pocket. Judging by the wrinkles round the corners of his eyes he spends a lot of time smiling. He's not smiling now, though – he's frowning, but like he's interested, not ornery.

'Well, will you look at that, Ed – they opened by themselves. Looks like the poor fellow had a squint to add to his troubles.'

The other fella is younger by a few years, and much taller. I recognize him as the marshal I've seen around town and done my darnedest to keep clear of ever since I arrived. His big drooping moustaches are streaked with grey, adding to his mournful expression. I can tell he don't much like the look of me. He keeps on twisting the brim of his hat in his hands, and trying to keep his eyes elsewhere. But he can't help glancing back at me now and again . . .

Above their heads I can see a ceiling with cobwebs in the corner. There's a crack across it, and over George's shoulder I can make out part of a picture hanging on the whitewashed wall. I can't see the details, though, because my eyes ain't clear, as if there's water in them still.

After a while the marshal asks, 'Are you quite sure he's dead, George? Only he looks to me like he might sit up and start talking any minute.'

'Calm yourself, Ed. I've been in this business thirty years, and if anyone knows what a dead fellow looks like it's me. I can't understand why folks are so afraid of a dead man when it's the living do all the harm. I know you probably don't share my belief, but to my mind there's a kind of perfection in a dead man you don't find when he's alive.'

'How d'you mean, George?'

'Well, think about it, Ed – which one of us is perfect? We all make mistakes, from an outlaw like this fellow to the Queen of England herself. Everyone has some good and some bad in them; you don't know which will get the upper hand, the Lord or the Devil. You can't say, if you see someone riding off to try his hand at panning for gold, whether he'll make his fortune or be scalped by Indians. If you dwell too much on thoughts like that you end up pretty miserable.

'When a man's lying dead there's no more worry, no more hopes and expectations, no more disappointment. He's reached the end of his particular road, the same end we'll all come to sooner or later. Everything in his life is leading up to this, and now he's here he's achieved a kind of peace, a kind of nobility almost, and it's down to you to treat him with due reverence.'

'And is that what you're doing with old Willie here, pickling him?'

'This one here's a special case, Ed. I'm giving him a great opportunity. I'm treating him like the Egyptians treated their kings. You might say he's a pioneer.'

'Does that mean you're figuring to build one of them pyramids in Main Street? Only I reckon you'd cause a few problems with the stage when it tried to unload.'

The old man looks sideways at him. 'You think I'm crazy, don't you, Ed?'

'Hell, no, George. You're my friend an' all – it's just that half the time I can't understand your notions. What I see when I look at this fella is someone the bounty-hunters have been after for a while, and now old Bull's got him I just want to make sure he's dead.'

Bull? I wonder if I've heard right, or if the water is blocking up my ears.

'Oh, don't you worry, Ed. There's no signs of life. What d'you expect when a man's been shot and drowned at the same time? He'd have to be superhuman to survive that. Does he look superhuman to you?'

'I'm not sure he even looks human, not the way he's got up right now. Are you going to leave that gown on him?'

'Well, I'll remove all his clothing for the pickling process, but I'll probably dress him the way he was when he died, in the interests of historical verisimilitude.'

'Now hang on there a minute, George. I thought you was doing this as a kinda scientific experiment, not because you was fixing to run a sideshow.'

'But, Ed, don't forget I'm a businessman. If I can attract custom by having this fellow on display, then why not? He doesn't mind, do you, son?'

Then he punches me on the shoulder, and the dull ache I've been feeling in my chest ever since I woke up explodes like dynamite under my ribs, and the world goes black again.

AT THE UNDERTAKER'S

———⚙———

*T*he next thing I knew I was awake, but I still couldn't move. For the first time in my life I understood a steer that's all trussed up and ready for branding. You can tell from its eyes that it's desperate and mad all at the same time, but it can't do nothing about it; it's down and beat and must take its punishment.

As my eyes began to clear I saw I was somewhere different, and now there were three people looking at me: the old man, a white-haired lady and a young fella with a pinched kind of face, and ginger hair that stood up straight like a brush. The old lady looked worried.

'Are you *sure* this will be good for business, George? Mightn't he frighten people, stop them coming in?'

'I don't believe he will, my dear. Look out there – do you think it's me, or Henry, or even your charming self that those folks are taking such an interest in?'

On account of being laid down, I couldn't see what he was talking about, but I could hear several voices speaking at once, the sounds made by a crowd of people excited about something.

Then the young fella leaned in closer and stared

straight into my face, not looking pleased. 'Jesus, George! Couldn't you have found someone less ugly to pickle? Just remember, we're gonna have to look at this fella all day long.'

'I'll thank you to watch your tongue in the presence of a lady, boy. And I don't suppose you'd be quite as handsome as you are now if you'd been dead for a couple of days. You know, there are some parts of the world where they keep their dead ancestors about them, even pretend to feed them. I reckon that as Wilbur may be with us some time we should treat him like one of the family in the same way.'

'But, Mr B, the whole reason I'm here working for you is that I can't abide the sight of my family. I got outta there as soon as ever I could.'

'Less of your wise-cracking, son. Just remember that a week ago this man here was walking around, breathing the air, admiring the pretty girls, full of the joys of spring, same as you – and now look at him. You shouldn't treat life too lightly; you don't know what's waiting for you around the next corner.'

'Well, it won't be old Bull Freemantle and his posse, that much I know. I don't rob banks, and if I did, I'd make darn sure I did it properly and didn't get myself caught – 'specially not with women's skirts on.'

He had a mean look on his face – I reckoned I'd have to watch out for him – but I was thinking about what he'd just said. I hadn't heard wrong the first time – the man that got me *was* called Bull. It seemed like it wasn't just real cattle that was after us McCrums.

Next thing – and I can picture it again now, clear as

you like – I hear bolts being shot back, and George's voice, sounding antsy.

'Now, ladies and gents, I'll thank you to show a little respect for the dead. I don't suppose you'd be too eager to prod him when he was alive, would you now? He might have drawn his revolver on you!'

People start laughing at that, and someone hollers, 'That's Wilbur McCrum, mister – the safest person around when he got out his gun was the one he was aimin' at!'

More laughter, louder this time. I have to own I was a pretty lousy shot, but when you're boss-eyed it's awful hard to hit your target. The only man I ever killed in the whole of my breathing days was Nattie's husband, and that was an accident.

They carry on jeering at me, and another one calls out, 'Come on, Willie boy, come an' git me!'

I can only see the ones who are standing real close and peering over to get a good look, but I can tell things are turning ugly. I'm hoping there won't be a riot, or I might get killed again for real.

George speaks to them: 'Come along, folks. Wilbur's had a very busy couple of days, what with being killed and then finding himself at the frontiers of science and all. I figure he deserves some peace and quiet right now and, besides, we've got a business to run here.'

The buzz of the crowd moves away, but I can hear another sound now, a snuffling, like someone has a chill, or is maybe crying. Perhaps it's Ida May. I try again to sit up, or even just move my hand, but there's nothing doing. I'm beginning to feel real scared now – what if I don't come out of this fit before George pickles me?

As I'm thinking this, a big face appears, all swollen and blotched red from tears, leaning over me, and a choked voice says, 'It's all your fault! I wish you'd never set foot in this town, Wilbur McCrum!'

I can tell from her accent it's big Helga, but I'm real surprised she's that grieved. Trying to figure it out makes me tired, and I drift off again.

I CAN MOVE AGAIN

———◆———

$\mathcal{I}$ wake to the sound of George's voice, but I can't see him. There's hardly any light, so it must be night-time, and I figure the crowds have gone. I get quite a shock when George uses my name.

'What are we coming to, Wilbur? In all the years man's been on this earth we still haven't learned how to behave any differently than rutting stags over a doe. We can build railroads and palaces, write great books and compose music to make a man weep, and still we have no more sense than the common beasts.

'I mean, look at you, Wilbur – the Good Lord may not have made you the prettiest creature on this earth, but I thought from the first time I saw you that you didn't seem stupid – your face, I mean, not the way you were got up. Why, the moment I took those coins off your eyelids and you looked me straight in the eye I could have sworn you were trying to say something to me. Ed could see it, too, only I pretended not to know what he was talking about. He has a melancholy disposition, you understand, and I didn't want to scare him.

'I wonder what made you turn bad, Wilbur. Why

couldn't you have earned a decent living, like most folks? Who knows, if only we'd encountered one another a little earlier you might have been alive today, helping me with the business, answering me when I talk to you, instead of lying there. Henry is a nice enough boy – there's no real harm in him – it's just that he doesn't take any real pride in his work. For him it's all about making money, the quickest way possible.'

It sounds peculiar, given my situation, but it's kind of pleasant just to lay there, listening to George as he talks about the way he sees life. And death. He has a whole lot of interesting ideas. Then I remember that one of those ideas is to pickle me in arsenic. I think hard about moving, but I can't do it. I'm beginning to get panicked again now. What if Ma gets to hear what's happened and comes to bury me? What then? I have a truly awful thought – what if I ain't so unusual after all? What if there are people who're buried who ain't really dead, neither? Able to see and think, but not able to let anyone know, like me, and they're just buried. Do they lie there, with the weight of all that earth on top of them, feeling the worms sliding slowly over them, not able to do a darn thing about it?

The light from George's lamp moves up the ceiling, and I see his shadow for a moment. 'Well, I'm just about done here. Goodnight, Wilbur, goodnight, son.'

I hear the sound of a key scraping in the lock. I'm drifting off to sleep when I hear it again. I figure George must've forgotten something, but then a different voice speaks – it's the red-headed fella, talking quietly.

'That was close. We'd better hide this in the storeroom and get outta here.'

'I don't know what Mr B would think of this, Henry, it seems kinda dishonest.'

'The trouble with George is that he does too much thinking for thinking's sake. Which is all very well for your fancy college professors and your rich folk in cities who don't need to earn enough to keep a roof over their heads, but for us out here you need to be more practical and down to earth. That's why I came up with this idea. Re-using caskets makes a lot of economic sense, Thomas. Putting a flap at the end here instead of a fixed panel was a stroke of genius, if I say it myself. As long as you can persuade any relatives present that it'll be less upsetting for them to move away before the coffin goes in the ground, all you need is a quick sleight of hand. Tip the box up, and in he slides, right as rain.'

'But, Henry, don't you think you're cheating folk, letting them think their dear departed's being buried in a fancy casket when he's just going in the earth with nothing to protect him?'

Henry snorts like a bronco just out the gate. 'Protect him – from what? The worms will get him sooner or later. Might as well be sooner. He don't care, and they don't know, so no one suffers. Anyways, the price tag on the coffin don't say it'll be theirs to *keep*. The way I see it, it's a hire charge. Their fella gets to use it up until the time he goes in the ground, like renting a room. When a grieving relative pays for a casket they don't expect to see it after the burial, do they?'

'They might do, though, if they come back in the store.'

Henry's voice is sharp. 'They ain't to know it's the same one, are they? What we do, Thomas, is all about *appearances*. We do our best to make dead people look like they're sleeping. We straighten out their broken arms and legs, wash off the blood, rouge their cheeks and cover their scars. Same way we put them in a fancy box with a soft lining which ain't one bit of use to them. It's an *illusion*, Thomas, the whole darn thing. We're smoothing their way to their final resting place for the sake of those left behind, and if re-using caskets helps keep costs down and means they can afford a better one than they would've been able, then where's the harm? What they don't know won't hurt them.'

I have to own that although Henry might be a slippery kind of character, he sure has a way with words. Maybe he's learned from listening to George; maybe George took him on because of it. Either way he can talk the hind legs off a mule. As I'm thinking this, I realize something – my nose has just itched, and someone has scratched it, and that someone must've been me! I think about raising my hand in front of my face – and there it is, a white shape in the dim light! I concentrate on wiggling my fingers, and the shape moves, separating out into five clear shapes moving through the gloom like the legs of jellyfish through water. I grope around for the edge of my coffin and clamp my fingers over it, then do the same with my other hand. Pulling with all my might I manage to haul myself into a sitting position. I can see the two fellas now, quite clear in the light from the lamp they've placed on the floor. They haven't noticed me yet, but I know I ain't going to be able to climb out of this box and leave the place without them seeing me, and I also know that when they go they'll lock up again and I'll have to break out, which I don't reckon I'm fit to do just now. I figure, though, that on account of they're doing something they didn't ought to be, they might just let me go. Of course, they might have another try at shooting me instead, but I can't see no guns. So I clear my throat.

It was my intention to throw myself on their mercy, but I don't get the chance. Henry has his back to me, but Thomas stares straight at me, like he's seen a ghost.

'What is it?' Henry asks him.

Thomas don't say a word, just keeps right on staring, and I see a dark patch appear on the front of his pants.

Henry looks over his shoulder and jumps to his feet, kicking the used casket and making the flap swing backward and forward like the batwings of a saloon door.

'Sweet Jesus!'

While this is happening I'm trying to raise myself up onto my knees, but I'm real stiff from not having moved for so long, and the blood stirring in my veins again gives me pins and needles awful bad. Lucky for me this unbalances the coffin so it tilts and falls off its stand and I'm tipped face forward onto the floor. By the time I've struggled to my feet, tripped over my skirt and stood up again, Henry and Thomas have gone, leaving behind an open door and the faint smell of piss.

I bend forward with my hands on my knees, trying to stop the room from swaying. The wound in my shoulder is throbbing more now the blood's flowing again. I know I'd best be on my way, though, as even iffen Henry and Thomas don't raise the alarm, someone might have heard the commotion and come to see what's occurring.

I make for the door, staggering like a drunk, grabbing

on to the edges of caskets for support as I go. I wonder as I pass the lantern whether I should maybe take it, but I reckon the darkness will serve me better. As I clutch the doorframe I take a quick look up and down the street before hauling myself out and lurching away. I stick to the backs of the lots, crouching low, which pains me. All the while I'm listening for sounds of a posse getting up, but all I hear is a dog barking somewhere distant and tethered horses shuffling against one another in the street.

BACK AT THE JOY HOUSE

I reached the back of the joy house and let myself in by the kitchen door. I could see Lady Muldoon sitting at her desk, writing figures in a big ledger book with one hand and pressing a handkerchief to her crooked nose with the other. She heard me before I had a chance to say anything and looked up with reddened eyes. I moved toward her, holding out my hands, fingers spread wide, hoping to calm her. I reckoned I was lucky it was her saw me first – any other woman would've screamed the place down.

'There ain't no need to cry,' I said. 'I ain't a ghost – I had a fit, is all.'

Lady Muldoon just carried right on staring at me, but at least she shut her mouth, so she looked less like a catfish.

'Where's Ida May? I figure you should be the one to tell her I ain't dead. I don't want to scare her out her wits.'

'*How*, Wilbur? How did you manage to come out of that well alive?'

'I don't rightly understand it myself. It sure felt like I

was dying. Even when I woke up I couldn't move nor speak. I thought I might be in that fit for ever.'

Lady Muldoon stared at me some more, but I could see she'd started thinking again.

'Wilbur, it wasn't you I was crying over. It was her.'

Now it was my turn to stare. I looked at her and remembered that second shot, Helga's words about wishing I'd never set foot in this town, and put it together, hoping all the while I'd got it wrong. 'Ida May got shot? Is she hurt bad? Where is she? Let me see her!'

Lady Muldoon shook her head, and I knew what she was going to say before she said it. 'She's dead, Wilbur. When she called out to warn you they shot her dead. She didn't suffer, and she didn't see what they did to you.'

I dropped to my knees and my eyes misted over. I could hear a rushing sound, just like I was in the water again, and even though Lady Muldoon was crouched down in front of me holding on to my arm and trying to say something, I could only see her lips moving. I didn't go into a full fit, though, maybe on account of the last one being so long, and after what seemed like an age, a sound cut through the noise in my ears – a scream loud enough to wake the dead.

All of a sudden I was surrounded by skirts and a candle fell to the ground in front of me, a thin wisp of smoke coming out the wick, like a dying breath. I raised my eyes and saw Helga, hair tied up in rags, her big hands covering her mouth. Three of the other girls were peering out from behind her. 'It's all right,' I said, the words sounding like they were a long way off, 'it's really me. I ain't dead.'

'But I saw you. I saw you in your coffin at the undertaker's. You are a spirit from the other side.'

'No I ain't, Helga, truly I ain't. I'm just Wilbur, like I always was. I had a fit when I went down that well and they just *thought* I was dead, see.'

I was still on my knees, but I spread my arms wide so she could see as much of me as possible. I soon realized my mistake, for she came at me like a cannon ball, shouting in what I guess must have been her own language – cussing sure does sound more impressive in German – and I didn't have time to protect myself. So before I knew it I was flat out on the floor with Helga on top of me, crushing the breath out of me. I don't know if it was lack of air or the pain in my shoulder that sent me back into the darkness again.

I wake up in what I guess must be Lady Muldoon's private quarters. It's much plainer than the rest of the place – just the bed I'm laying on, a chair, and a small writing table. She's sitting next to me, holding a bundle in her arms and jiggling it up and down, talking softly.

'Is that Junior?'

'I brought him so you could say goodbye.'

I don't say a thing.

'You can't take him with you. Once George realizes you're gone the posse will be after you again. You can't take a baby on the run with you, Wilbur.'

I know she's right. I don't reckon I'd be much good at caring for him even iffen I wasn't on the run. I sit up slow, as I'm still stiff, and I reckon Helga has bruised a few of my ribs. Lady Muldoon puts Junior in my lap and

I cradle him with my good arm. He looks at me with his round blue eyes and I try to figure out what he's thinking. He don't know I'm his Pa, I'm just one of the faces he's seen every day since he was born, and how is he to tell the difference between me and the Chinese cook? If I go away now he might never get to know me at all, and the cook will be more of a daddy to him than I'll ever be. But then why would he want a daddy like me? Nothing I do ever turns out right, and it's on account of me his Ma was killed. My heart feels so heavy it's like it's soaked up all the water in that well, and I can hardly move my sorry carcass.

'You'll need to wash, Wilbur,' Lady M says as she takes my son from me. 'You smell like a mule in August. Don't shave, though. Your beard's coming through grey, and that'll help disguise you. I'll take a look at your shoulder when you're done.' She regards me closely, then frowns. 'I guess you'll need some help getting out of that dress, too.'

I see then that I'm still wearing Helga's skirt, streaked with dried mud and torn around the hem. I slump down on the bed again.

'Don't despair, Wilbur. Just remember, when things look as bad as this, they can't get any worse. When you fall into a pit – or a well – the only way for you to go next is up.' She comes and sits beside me. 'There's been times in my life when I could have just laid there and howled at the moon, but I knew that wouldn't get me anywhere, so I just picked myself up and started again. It's all we can do, Wilbur. There's no use in trying to figure out what life's all about. I gave up on that long ago, and I've been much happier since. Just remember that Ida May would've wanted you to carry on, so do it for her sake, and for Junior.'

'What did they do with her – after?'

'Same as you – they took you both. George didn't think it was right to keep a woman on display, so she was in back somewhere. George is a decent man, just a little crazy.'

'I've got to get her, bring her home.'

Lady M grabs my arm. 'There's no point trying. Even if you had the strength to carry her here on your own, they'd catch you. Besides, what would we do with her? She needs a decent burial, Wilbur, and until then George will look after her. It's not exactly good for business to have a dead body laid out in one of the rooms, and Helga's taken it bad enough as it is – if Ida May was here she'd be good for nothing at all. Come, let's get you out of those clothes.'

After she's helped me undress and wash, she looks at the wound and finds the bullet has gone clean through, so she bandages me up. 'You'd best get moving, Wilbur, before it starts to get light. I've saddled up Geraldine, my mule, for you – she'll be easier to hide than a horse.'

I follow her outside, and the chill of the night hits me. I guess I was too dazed to feel it before. The mule has rags wrapped round its hooves to muffle the sound, and it looks at me out the corner of its eye in a way that shows it ain't pleased to be woken at this hour. Lady M fastens a saddlebag to it, and the mule shuffles from one leg to another, in protest.

'There's some bread and a bit of cold beef in there –

and a .45, in case you need it.' I swallow hard. I feel light-headed, and my shoulder's throbbing. All I want to do is lie down and go to sleep again – I don't much care if the posse catches up with me. The woman I love is dead on account of me, our child has lost his Ma, and I didn't even say goodbye to her when I had the chance.

'Go on – if you don't want to ride her you can lead her until you're outside town.' She gives me directions to a hiding place not too far away and promises to come find me as soon as she can; in the meantime she's going to try and sort something more permanent for me – something more permanent and far away.

I try to smile at her, but a smile won't come. She pats me on my good arm and I take hold of the leading rein. I look back and see some shapes in the doorway, but none of the girls come out to say goodbye. I don't blame them.

LADY M HELPS ME ESCAPE

❧ That first day after I found out what happened to Ida May was the lowest I'd ever sunk. I have to own that I spent a long time holding the Colt, turning it over in my hands, feeling the cool metal – then I put it in my mouth. It made me gag, so I took it out again. I knew the best thing I could do was use it – even I couldn't miss at that distance – but I thought of Junior. He'd already lost his Ma, and I owed it to him to try and make something of my life, so maybe one day I could look him in the eye and see he was proud of his Pa. And Lady M had said she'd come and find me. I'd caused her and her girls enough trouble as it was, without leaving her to deal with the body of a man who was already supposed to be dead. What would she do – try to smuggle me back into the undertaker's and hope no one would notice the extra bullet hole?

The main reason I didn't kill myself, though, was on account of I already felt like I was dead, as if George had done what he said those Egyptians did, and taken out my insides, leaving me hollow.

*

Then early one morning – real early, from the commotion the birds are making in the trees – I'm woken by the sound of a twig snapping under a boot, and quick as a jackrabbit I'm up on my haunches and peering round the trunk I've been leaning against. I slide the Colt out, keeping my back to the tree for protection and trying to ignore the pain from my wound.

'Now don't you go firing that thing at me, Wilbur McCrum. You know what a lousy aim you've got, and if there's trappers in the vicinity you'll have them all over here before you know it.' Lady M comes into view, her skirts gathered over one arm, clutching on to low branches for support as she climbs up the slope toward me. I lower the gun, relieved to see her.

'Come on, Wilbur – it's time to get moving.'

When she reaches me she takes a moment to catch her breath, leaning against a tree trunk with her chest heaving. Then she untethers Geraldine. I may be fooling myself, but I believe that mule looks relieved to be moving out of the clearing where she's darn near eaten everything there is to eat. Lady M leads us both down the slope and back to the road, where Jock is sitting in the buggy. He looks at me, but don't say anything, nor make any move to greet me. I'm just wondering how all three of us are going to be able to sit up front in that thing when she takes me by the arm and steers me to the back, which is full of baggage.

'You'll have to hide in here, Wilbur, just in case someone riding out should see you. We don't want anyone recognizing you and telling the posse.'

I guess there ain't much point to arguing, so I clear a

space, fold myself up as small as I can and let her put the bags back on top of me. Lying like that don't do my shoulder much good, but I stay quiet about it.

Lady M makes sure I can breathe, and can see the sky if I look up, then she disappears and after a moment's wait Jock starts the horse moving.

'I wrote my friend Kate, Wilbur, and just heard back from her. She says she'll take you in for a while. She married some fella who set up a saloon in a place called Rock Springs, but he got himself killed in the crossfire when a fight broke out one night, so she's been taking in lodgers to keep food on the table. She's no friend of lawmen, like most of us who've had to make money in ways some folk don't consider respectable, so she's willing to help you out.'

There's silence for a while, and all I can hear is the sound of the horse's hooves, with Geraldine's in between, and from time to time some word of encouragement muttered by Jock. I take a while getting up the courage to ask what I want to ask, but in the end I find my voice.

'Did – did you give Ida May a good funeral?'

There's more silence up front, and I figure maybe they can't hear me, so I push some of the bags aside to make a bigger space. Now I can see shiny green taffeta stretched across a broad back, straining some under the arms.

'I said, how was the funeral?'

I see their heads turn slightly toward each other, then Lady M finally speaks,

'Something happened, Wilbur, something we couldn't do anything about. It's a long story – and once again it starts with you. Folks back in Vacanegra have all manner of notions about what really happened to you when you disappeared; some think it was bodysnatchers took you, hoping to sell you to a travelling show where they'd charge people money to come look at you. George Beauchamp thinks that must be what happened, because they found this peculiar coffin in his store, with a flap at one end. It doesn't belong to him, and he reckons the robbers must've been disturbed and left it behind. Then there's an old lady who's been standing outside the undertaker's all day with a Bible in her hand, telling everyone who'll listen that you're risen from the dead.'

'What does she mean by that?'

'Risen up, like Jesus. She says you died, and that you rose on the third day, and it means you're the Second Coming.'

'Any more ideas about me?'

'Oh, yes. There's a preacher in a long black coat who's taken up a place across the way from the old lady, saying you were in league with Beelzebub, and that he came to the undertaker's and breathed his foul breath into your mouth, which is how you were able to rise again. And at least three people have told me they reckon you were just too clever for the bounty-hunters, that you faked your own death and then got away.'

'They think that? There's folk think I'm clever enough to do that?'

For the first time since I heard about Ida May I'm beginning to feel alive again, and it's as if the Wilbur who staggered out of that undertaker's was a new me – smarter, stronger, better than the one who went down the well. It's like I truly have risen again.

But Lady M is still talking. 'Anyway – ever since George found that strange coffin in his store he's been obsessed with figuring out what it was for, and he took it off to show some friend of his who's an undertaker in another town. He left that good-for-nothing Henry Fossey in charge and that's when these two characters turned up, claiming to be Ida May's uncles. One of my girls saw them, and she said they were dressed mighty fine – one of them was chomping on a cigar as fat as Junior's arm. Henry said there was nothing he could do, he couldn't prove they weren't her kin, but I don't trust that boy; I reckon he planned it, took his chance while George was away, and somehow got word to these fellows he had a body to sell.'

This is all such a shock to me I can hardly speak, but I manage to get out, 'So who d'you think they were?'

She's quiet again before she answers me. 'Well, Wilbur, I believe they do run a travelling show.'

'A travelling show? You mean . . . ?'

'Yes, Wilbur, I mean a freak show.'

That's when the talking stops. I'm not sure whether it's a proper fit I go into, or whether the blackness that comes down on me is just plain despair. All I know is, I don't want to get out that buggy, but I don't want to be in it, neither. The new hope I'd been feeling is all eaten up and what I want is to die, right then and there, then maybe Lady M and Jock can get a good price for selling me to the freak show, too, and Ida May and me can be back together again, until in the end we crumble to dust.

INJUN KATE

When I open my eyes again I realize the buggy has stopped moving and it's dark. I can hear voices murmuring, and after listening to them for a while I can tell that two of them belong to Jock and Lady M, and the other to someone I don't know. I think it's a woman's voice, but it's gruff enough to be a man's. A moment or two later they get louder and I can tell they're coming close to the buggy. Then the bags are lifted roughly off me and I can make out three figures standing there, though it's too dark to see their faces. I feel fingers closing on my arms and I'm hauled into a sitting position.

'We're here now, Wilbur,' says Lady M's voice. 'This is my friend Kate, who'll take care of you for a while.'

A hand grasps mine and starts shaking it hard, which makes my shoulder smart some. The skin is rough to the touch, and whoever it belongs to has a strong grip.

'Pleased to meet you, Wilbur. You're most welcome here.'

'Wilbur's feeling a little fragile, dearie. He's been shot and drowned and risen from the dead, and he needs to rest up and recover.'

'Sorry, I forgot.'

I feel myself being pulled off the cart. I stumble some before my feet find solid ground, but with the others to guide me I make it inside. I'm standing in a small parlour, there's a fire going in the hearth, a mantelpiece with a lacy cloth on it and two brown and white china dogs with staring eyes that spook me some, a couple of stuffed arm-chairs and a number of wooden chairs that don't match. On the wall a clock with a pendulum hanging down is ticking all solemn. This establishment might not be real fancy, but it's trying to be, and it might just get there one day.

'I guess you'll need a while to settle in. I'll show you your room.'

I turn and look at the person who spoke, and find myself staring at her chest. Kate is a tall and bony woman, and in poor light she might be mistaken for a man.

I don't know how I did it, but I slept that night from the moment my head hit the pillow until Kate brought me some coffee in the morning. I don't know iffen it was the smell of it woke me, or the weight of her sitting on my bed, but there she was, looking at me steady. If she'd been a man I'd've felt scared of her, looking at me like that, but I was well used to women giving me hard stares, what with Ma and all.

'I know you've had a real hard time, Wilbur,' she said – not bothering with *good morning* or *how you doing?* – 'but you should look at it this way: you've been given a second chance. When Sam died I didn't just feel sad, I felt angry – angry that at last I'd got a good life going for me and it had been snatched away, and there wasn't a darn thing I could do about it. I could've sold up, left this place, gone back to my old life as a saloon girl, but I decided I was gonna make the best of it. It ain't always been easy – life ain't easy for a woman on her own – but I'm still here, and I'm doing OK. And most important of all – I don't have to simper at men who smell worse than their horses and have worse manners too.'

She waited, as if she thought I might want to say something, but when I didn't she carried on. 'You see, you've got the chance to start over. You can leave the robbing banks and hiding from the law behind you, give yourself a new name and go back out there as someone different.'

She stopped talking again, but I still didn't feel like saying nothing. 'Well, drink your coffee and I'll fix us all some eggs. The others'll be going soon, and I'm sure you'll want to say goodbye to them.'

I'd fallen asleep in my clothes, and I wasn't in the mood for washing, so before long I followed Injun Kate downstairs. Lady M and Jock were sitting at the kitchen table, talking low, with their heads close together. They looked up when I came in, and Lady M smiled at me.

'Morning, Wilbur. I hope you slept well. Can I fix you some breakfast?' She took a plate from the dresser and went over to the range, where a pan of eggs was keeping warm.

'What do you think of your new home? A change from your old one. Kate's a good girl and she's had a hard time herself, losing her man the way she did. This isn't the only saloon in town, and some people are particular when it comes to mixing with Injuns. She's only half Cheyenne, but that's enough for some folk.'

She kept on talking at me, telling me about Kate, and what she knew about the town, and part of me wished she'd stop and give me peace and quiet while another part was glad I didn't have to make no effort at conversation myself.

I ate as much of the dried-up eggs as I could stomach and, as Lady M filled my mug with more of Kate's bitter coffee, I realized something – she didn't want to go. I had my hands round the mug and I was looking into it. I could smell it, I could feel the heat of it through the tin. I was alive, and there was no point trying to pretend otherwise.

'I'm sorry,' I said. 'About everything that happened. You've been awful kind to me. Most folk would've handed me over to the posse instead of helping me get away. I do appreciate it.' I didn't dare raise my eyes and look at her in case the last time she saw me I was lying on the ground in a fit.

Her hand came over and patted my wrist. 'I know what it feels like, Wilbur – the guilt. I know what it feels like to think you're responsible for someone you love dying. I learnt a long time ago that we can't really govern what happens to us. We just have to make the best of it, Wilbur. Can't do anything else.'

I followed her and Jock outside, and while Lady M was taking her leave of Injun Kate I figured I'd better say something to the Chinaman. 'Thanks – for helping me an' all.'

He didn't answer, but he nodded, and gave the hand I

held out to him a little shake, like it was something he wanted to dry off. Then he helped Lady M into the driver's seat, climbed up beside her, and me and Kate watched them move away through a town that was just waking up. A woman came out of a hardware store and threw some water on the ground to keep the dust down. The nearside wheels of the cart went through it, and I wondered how long the mark they made would stay there.

ISAAC

~~~•~~~

*J*ust as soon as Lady M and Jock had gone, Injun Kate told me the plan.

'I still own the saloon, along with my husband's brother, so you can work there, cleaning tables, sweeping up and such. I've told everyone you're my cousin Isaac and you're a bit simple – that way I figured you wouldn't have to talk too much. Iffen people ask you questions you can look at them like you don't understand and they should leave you be.'

Although I had my own clothes, Kate figured they'd make me look too much like myself, and she didn't want me to be recognized by any acquaintances that happened by. She gave me some pants, a shirt and a jacket – all her dead husband's – and when I'd put them on she stood me in front of a long mirror in her bedroom. Now, like I said before, Injun Kate was a tall woman, and I reckon her husband must've been able to look her in the eye, because those pants dragged on the floor, and I had to hold them up to stop them falling round my ankles. And that wasn't easy, on account of the sleeves covering my hands. I was like a little boy dressed up in his Pa's things. The corners of Injun Kate's mouth were turned up in something approaching a smile as she stood behind me, hands on my shoulders, looking at my reflection in the glass over the top of my head.

'That's just perfect, Wilbur. If you seemed simple before, you look even more backward now.'

Her eyes were shining and I could tell she was real pleased with the result, so I didn't dare ask her how I was going to be able to do any kind of work dressed like that.

She showed me her saloon, which had a painted sign outside with a tepee and the words *Injun Kate's* in black paint. You couldn't call it a fancy place – just one long, low room, with a ceiling made of planks of wood that was just like the floor, which I figured must get mighty confusing for anyone drunk enough to fall flat on his back.

My job was to sweep up, clear away empty glasses and wipe the tables clean. I had to put down fresh sawdust whenever it was needed – which was a lot, on account of the amount of spitting that went on. If there was trouble I was supposed to help the barman out. There was a loaded shotgun ready behind the counter, but I told Kate I wasn't much use with guns, on account of my squint and the fits, and she said then I should just try to whack any troublemakers over the head with my broom.

I started work a couple of weeks later, when my wound was healing nicely. I didn't mind it too much, mostly because not one soul there took a blind bit of notice of me, except for Harry the barman. He believed what Injun Kate told him about me being her backward cousin, and I heard them talking while I waited outside, practising my simple look by staring into the sky with my eyes even more out of focus than was usual.

'But why would I need someone else to clean tables? No offence, 'cause I know Isaac's family and all, but what use is someone like him to me? When I'm busy in here I won't have time to keep telling him what to do.'

'He ain't that backward! He can remember things, just as long as they're not too complicated. If you make it plain, he'll get on with the job and won't worry you none, just you wait and see.'

As I came in Harry picked up a glass and started on polishing it real hard with his cloth. He gave Injun Kate an ornery look, but he didn't say nothing more.

For the first few days I had to be careful: I was trying to make it look like I didn't know much, but at the same time I had to show Harry I could do everything he needed me to do. There wasn't a great deal to it, but still I could see he doubted me. Every time I looked over to the bar, his eyes would shift and he'd pretend he was looking at something else – a fly on the ceiling, or a real small speck of dirt he just had to clean off the counter – but I knew he was watching me, and waiting for me to make a mistake so's he could go back to Injun Kate and say I was no use to him.

Course, that was where Ma's training came good – I'd had an awful lot of practice at chores, so I could sweep a floor clean in no time. I just had to make sure I wasn't done too quick. I took to stopping every few minutes and staring – out the window, at the wall, it didn't mat-ter – and that, and the fits when they came, helped with making me seem simple, I guess.

I JOIN A FREAK SHOW

Anyhow, I stayed with Kate for more than a year, and I reckon I might have stayed there longer iffen one day I hadn't been reading a newspaper that someone had left on the bar and seen an advertisement that made me feel cold all of a sudden.

All the Fun of the Fair. Come and see the attractions at Cullen and Baileys' Circus. Marvel at the amazing two-headed girl, wonder at Sophia, the Mule-Faced Woman, gasp at the sight of the mummy, the withered remains of the good-time girl who was once the brazen sidekick of a notorious outlaw.

That advertisement upset me so much that before I knew it I'd fallen backward off my barstool and cracked my head on the floor.

While I was drinking the whisky Harry poured for me I showed the newspaper to Kate.

'It's her. I know it's her.'

'Now don't go getting your hopes up. There's a lot of circuses and freak shows have mummies in them.'

'But how many of them are women? And it says she was an outlaw's girl.'

'They'd say that even iffen she was just some poor soul died in a threshing accident. It sounds better than she was a girl died on her Daddy's farm.'

'All the same, I've got to go, Kate. Iffen I didn't at least go see I'd never forgive myself. I'd always believe it was her.'

'And just suppose it is. What're you gonna do – march right in there and say to them, I'm the notorious outlaw you're talking about, and I want my woman back? They'd tie you up and call the marshal before you could draw another breath. It's too dangerous.'

'I don't have to tell them who I am – I could maybe pretend to be her brother. I need to go see for myself whether it's her. Then I can decide what to do next.'

Kate stood in front of me, arms folded over her flat chest and an anxious look in her golden eye. But she knew it was no use trying to stop me, and I lit out right away for the outskirts of town.

I could see the circus from some way off – a big tent pitched on waste ground with a bunch of smaller tents ranged alongside – and as I got closer I could hear it, too. If I close my eyes now it's as if I'm back there again.

There's hurdy-gurdy music coming from somewhere, but you can't hardly make it out above the noise of all the fellas standing outside the little tents, trying to get you to pay to go in. Each one has a man hollering his lungs out:

*'Come see Lionel, the Spider Boy. You ain't never seen
   anything like it . . .'*
*'Don't miss Sophia, the Mule-faced Woman, the ugliest girl
   you'll ever see . . .'*
'Roll up, roll up, for Mary-Lou, the two-headed girl . . .'
*'See the family of midgets, so small they can live in a doll-
   house . . .'*

My head's reeling, listening to all of this, and it ain't
just the noise of it – there are things to look at, too.
Standing outside the big tents are three fellas holding
ropes attached to the muzzles of some of the strangest
creatures I've ever seen – two great big hairy things with
humps on their backs and legs that seem too spindly to
hold them up, which I know are camels, and a smaller,
darker, woollier thing that looks like a cross between a
camel and a horse. One of the camels is staring at me, so
I stare back. Its eyes are real big, with eyelashes longer
than any girl's, and it's chewing on something. I don't
like it, and when it makes a sudden bellowing noise it
sounds too much like a cow, so I move off pretty quick.

Each tent has a picture of whatever's in there: the
spider boy is crouched low on the ground, grinning at
you in a mean kind of way; the two-headed girl wears a
fine dress and waves a fan in front of both of her faces;
the fat lady smiles next to a tiny little man who don't
look too pleased at being squashed to one side of her.

I walk up and down, taking no notice of all the
invitations to 'step inside, sir,' until something stops me.
The last tent in the row has a picture of what appears to
be a real old woman, propped up in a coffin. It's starved-

looking, and the skin on it is shrivelled and brown. Next to it, and too big, is a mean-looking individual, stooped, with his drawn gun pointing straight at me. He's wearing a spotted bandanna round his neck and his teeth are bared, either in a snarl or 'cause he's chewing on the cigar clamped between them.

Although it's hot and dusty I feel my sweat go cold and the skin of my armpits begin to prickle. This is it; now I'm going to find out whether it really is her. I hardly look at the fella who takes my five cents and holds open the tent flap to let me through. Before I have time to think about it I'm staring at a face that's horrible to behold. There's no flesh left, so the skin is stretched tight over the bones. The eyes are sunken and it looks like one of them has gone. There's a small hole in the middle of the forehead, and over the top of the low-cut dress the mummy's wearing you can see two small, shrivelled breasts. The mouth is open in an O-shape, like she died crying out, and two of the teeth are missing.

When I see that, I imagine I can hear in my head the cracks of two gunshots and I have the same feeling as when I was pulled out the well, like I'm being sucked backward into the dark. And the worst thing is it happens again and again. I wake, see that horrible figure and pass out again, until one time I open my eyes and I can't see her no more on account of the legs of all the people gathered round me.

There's a big fella squatted down right by me, and it looks like squatting ain't something he's used to doing, 'cause his round face is getting more and more like a beet as he speaks to me.

'Well, that was quite impressive, boy. I ain't seen a turn like that round these parts, but I know they have 'em out east. In India they have people who can do all manner of things while in a trance – stick daggers through their cheeks, walk on hot coals . . . They're mighty clever, some of those boys. I've heard about an act where a fella charms a rope out of a pot and a lad climbs up it and disappears into thin air.'

I don't like the sound of all this, nor the way he's looking at me as if he's cooking something up, but I can't really get away, lying there like I am in the dirt in the middle of a crowd of people.

'What are you thinking, Nat?' Another man squats down beside the fat one, and he begins staring at me, too. He's a skinny fella, with a weak chin and watery eyes. He has a droopy kind of face, like a puppy that's just been kicked.

'I was thinking, Joshua, that we might offer this fella a job. We need someone to replace Edna, now she's decided to shave off her beard and marry that darn cowpoke.'

I don't much care for the way they're speaking, as if I ain't able to understand them, but iffen they're willing to give me a job I'm not about to refuse. Iffen I want to get Ida May away from them I'll need to stay close.

Nathaniel holds out his arm and Joshua hauls him to his feet, which takes a while, and then helps straighten him out. No one thinks to help me, so I just get myself up and dust myself off as best I can. When he's done pulling his waistcoat back down over his belly, Nathaniel turns to me and says, 'Five dollars a week suit you, boy? Food and a bed thrown in, of course.'

It's less than Kate is paying me to work in her saloon, but I don't need much apart from feeding and watering, and iffen it means I can stay near Ida May, I ain't going to argue with him.

Having made his bargain with me, Nathaniel spreads his arms wide and begins to shoo everyone out the tent. 'All right, folks, you've seen all there is to see here. There are plenty more sights to amaze and delight – even terrify you. So move along now.' Then he turns his head and says over his shoulder, 'By the way, what's your name, boy?'

I nearly say 'Wilbur', but just in time remember I'm Isaac now.

'OK, then, Isaac. Joshua here'll take care of you until the show's over. Then we'll introduce you to all the fine people you'll be working with.'

Joshua looks at me like I'm a rattler, so I just pick up my hat and follow him. He takes me to where a number of wagons are circled, away from the tents. We climb inside one, and it's quieter there. You can still hear the music and the hollering, but it's distant enough not to trouble me. The wagon is covered, so it's cool and gloomy in there, which suits me fine. Joshua too, I think, on account of he don't really want to look at me.

He takes out a small, leather-covered book and a pencil, licks the end of the pencil, and starts asking me questions.

'Full name?'

I haven't thought to give myself a second name before now, so I start looking around, trying to think of one. The only words that come into my head are no use to me at all – 'circus' and 'tent' and things like that, and I'm starting to sweat again, until I glance down at the floor and say, 'Boot, Isaac Boot.'

Joshua has his pencil on the page, ready to write, and his eyebrows go up when I say that, but he just repeats my name. 'Isaac *Boot*. How old are you, Isaac Boot?'

This one has me thinking, too. 'I reckon I'm around thirty, sir.'

'You don't know how old you are?'

'Not exactly, sir, no. My Ma would know, but I ain't seen her in years. Don't rightly know where she is nowadays.'

'I see, well, thirty will do, I guess. You're not from around these parts?'

'No sir. My family's from Independence.'

That ain't exactly a lie, 'cause that was where Ma and Pa started out from.

'Ever worked in a circus before, Isaac?'

'Can't say as I have, sir. Mostly I've done odd jobs. I helped my Ma when she had a farm, I worked in a smithy and in a sawmill, then in a saloon. I can turn my hand to most things.'

'And these fits of yours – how often do you have them?'

'All depends. I get 'em if I'm upset or agitated, and being stared at by a crowd's likely to get me pretty agitated most of the time, I reckon.'

'But can you bring a fit on when you need to?'

'I ain't never tried before. Mostly I've tried not to have them, but I reckon I could, iffen I needed to – or at least I could fake it.'

'That's what I like to hear. That's what this profession

is all about, when it comes down to it, faking. We pretend
to be showing folk a boy whose mother was frightened
by a spider when she was carrying him, but he's really
just a poor cripple who's learned to walk on his hands.
The two-headed girl, Mary-Lou, is really Siamese twins,
Mary and Louisa; Baby Sue ain't a real baby, she's a
three-hundred-pound woman in a short smock and a
white bonnet; the midgets ain't fairy people, they're just
plain midgets. If I know Nathaniel, he'll make you out to
be someone possessed by the Devil, or some such, and if I
was you I'd just go along with it. Nathaniel likes to get
his own way, and I've only managed to work with him
this long by letting him, most of the time. He's got good
instincts, though, I'll give him that. He's a showman
through and through, so I mostly let him deal with the
acts, while I deal with the money side of things. I don't
always agree with him – I don't agree with having
mummies around, for one thing – but he knows what'll
draw the crowds.'

I see my chance then, and decide to ask about Ida May.

'That mummy – the girl – where'd you get that?'

'Oh, that was one of Nat's bargains. He got it off some
undertaker's assistant in a little town somewhere. The
fella must've heard about us, 'cause it was him sent word
that he'd got something to sell. At first he said he'd got a
pair – the girl and her outlaw – but the outlaw got stolen
somehow, so we ended up with just the one. Nathaniel
was mad at that, you bet. Got the price down as low as
he could.'

I sure am glad it's too dark in that wagon for Joshua
to see my expression, for then he'd surely suspicion me.

I MEET A MULE-FACED WOMAN

When Joshua was done asking me questions he said I could wander around some, get my bearings. Although it was only a couple of hours since I'd arrived there, it was strange how different the circus seemed once I was a part of it. Instead of looking at the sights I found I was watching the crowds. There were more people arriving now that dusk was falling and the working day was done. These folk had come to be entertained, and I could see the eagerness in their faces. Life back then was hard, but it was dull at the same time. Bad things happened – sickness and gunfights and prairie fires and freezing snows and plagues of grasshoppers – but good things didn't come along too often, so if ever folk had a chance to lose themselves they grabbed a hold of it with both hands.

So there I am, I watching them coming now, strolling a tired evening stroll, and seeing how, as they get closer, they most of them speed up till they're almost running, like they don't want to miss nothing by being tardy. The womenfolk stand on their tiptoes, moving their heads from side to side to see better over the shoulders of the men in front; the children who've been brought along for a treat forget to be fractious as they're lifted up by their pas; the other men mostly stand with their hands in their pockets, leaning back over their heels, trying to look like they've seen it all before, pretending they ain't as excited as the rest.

I like watching the crowd, thinking that I'm going to be part of this show, and help make these folk forget their cares for a while, when I'm interrupted by a tap on the shoulder. I turn around, and I'm so taken by surprise at what I see I'm ashamed to say I gasp out loud.

The person standing in front of me is a woman, but I can only judge that by the way she's dressed – in a fancy white gown with lace at the collar and cuffs. Her face ain't like nothing I've ever seen – leastways, not on somebody still living. It's real long – more like a muzzle than a face – and it's kind of grey, as if it's covered in hair. Her nose is long and flat, and her eyes have big dark patches under them. She's seen my surprise, and there's a look in those eyes that makes me feel real sorry. She hides that look quickly, though, and says,

'You're Isaac, aren't you? I saw what happened earlier in Belle's tent, but I didn't get too close. I didn't want to scare you. I'm Sophia.' And she holds out an arm that's covered in wiry hairs.

'Sophia the . . .'

'. . . Mule-faced Woman, that's me.'

I look down at the ground, embarrassed, but Sophia ain't going to let that stop her. She puts her arm through mine and leads me around, telling me people's names and their jobs.

'Some barkers are real mean and hardly let their poor freaks have a break during the day. Thank goodness mine's not like that, I couldn't abide it.'

'What's a barker?'

'Not *what*, silly, *who*. The barker is the person who stands out front and tries to attract attention to his sideshow. They take a share of the entrance money, so the more folk they can attract, the more they make. Mine's called Lonnie, and he's got the most beautiful blue eyes . . .'

I GET PAID TO HAVE FITS

That night I sleep under one of the wagons, which ain't so comfortable, and means I'm up bright and early the next morning when Joshua comes to find me, followed by a fella who don't look happy.

'Isaac, this is Zeke. He's your barker. He's the one who'll get the customers in to see you. Zeke's one of the best in the business, so I'm sure you'll do well, between you.'

Zeke's chewing on a piece of straw. He glares at me from under the brim of his Stetson, eyes all screwed up like he's staring at a fire. He don't say nothing.

'Now, come on, Zeke, don't be sore. It's not Isaac's fault he ain't a bearded lady.'

He turns to me. 'Zeke worked with Edna, and she was real popular with the crowd. Used to let the smaller children come up and tug her beard, just to prove it wasn't fake. Of course, your bearded lady is unusual among the freaks, on account of she can up and decide she don't want to be a freak no longer, and that's what Edna did: shaved her face and left the circus.

'It's like I told you, though, Zeke – oftentimes they get bored. Life outside the circus is just too dull for them.

They miss the travel, the appreciation of the crowd. The lure of ordinariness wears off after a while. I shouldn't be surprised if she came back.

'Not that I'm saying you won't attract the crowds, too, Isaac.' He's having a hard time trying to keep both me and Zeke happy. 'It's just that Edna was a hard act to follow, if you understand me.'

Joshua gets out his pocket handkerchief and wipes the sweat off of his face. He looks from Zeke to me and back again, hoping we're about to become friends.

Now, I'm prepared to be neighbourly with just about anyone, but I don't believe Zeke feels the same way. He's still staring at me with slitted eyes, which is a look more fitting for a person sizing up his opponent in a gunfight than someone he's got to work with.

I hold out my hand. 'Isaac Boot. Pleased to make your acquaintance.'

Zeke looks down at my hand, then back up at my face. He stares at me so long I feel the world begin to sway and blackness comes.

Next thing I know, I'm looking up at the two of them, and they're looking down at me. Zeke's still chewing, but his eyes ain't all screwed up no more, and his hands are by his sides, not on his hips.

'There you are – you see? I reckon that'll draw the crowds. Nathaniel's trying to get an angle on it, can't quite make up his mind if he's possessed by devils or speaking in tongues, but I'm sure he'll think of something, and with a gaudy enough picture outside the tent I reckon he'll do well.'

Zeke just turns and follows Joshua without saying a

word to me. Neither of them offers to help me up off the ground.

That afternoon I face my first audience. No one's told me what I'm supposed to do. I just sit on a stool in the middle of a tent, listening to Zeke calling to the crowd, trying to get them to come have a look at me.

Nothing much happens for a while, and I begin to feel drowsy. I can hear Zeke crying out, 'Come and see the man possessed by the Devil. See him *writhe* as the evil spirit torments him. Hear him *prophesy* wars and tempests, *famines* and droughts, all the *disasters* his master will bring down on us if ever he gets the upper hand over our Good Lord!'

It sounds fearsome the first few times, but after a while that and the cries of all the other barkers, repeated again and again, helps to make me nod forward and almost fall off my chair. I try clenching my fists and driving my nails into the palms of my hands to keep myself awake. It won't do to have my first bunch of customers find me lying snoring in the dirt.

I don't have to wait too long, though, before the tent flap opens and Zeke shows in a small group of people. They stay as far away from me as they can while still being inside the tent, mostly standing sideways, like they're giving themselves a chance to get out of there iffen I turn nasty.

They look at me, and I look at them. There are three women, five men, two little boys and a girl about twelve, maybe. All of them waiting for me to do something. I know what it is they want me to do, but I just can't.

Zeke's staring at me, too. He's got that look again, like he's about to draw a gun on me, but even that ain't enough. The silence is getting uncomfortable, and I don't want them to start asking for their money back, so I try thinking of bad things that might set me off. I start with Jonny Rose, remembering how he used to stick those pins in me and laugh, but it's no good, I got the better of him in the end, so he don't scare me no more. I try thinking of Pa, and of Ma, but nothing works.

The crowd are starting to shuffle their feet and clear their throats. I see the girl look at Zeke, like she's expecting him to do something, and I wonder iffen he might take out his gun and start firing at my feet, just to get me going. Then I hear something that makes me remember why I'm here – carried on the wind I hear a barker call out the word *Mummy*, and all at once I see Ida May again, as she was when I clapped eyes on her in that tent the day before, and I don't remember any more after that.

When I open my eyes again I can see a tan pair of boots, and above them is Zeke, sitting on my stool and counting money. I wipe my face with my hand.

'How'd we do?'

'Not bad, not bad at all for a first-timer. Reckon I might have been wrong about you. Carry on like this and we'll make a good team.'

Zeke quit staring at me after that.

As the last of the paying customers wandered away into the night, the circus acts and freak-show workers would begin to gather around the chuck wagon. In my time

with the circus, these were the best hours for me – when
we'd finished for the day and could please ourselves. We'd
sit around eating and talking if we felt like it, being quiet
iffen we didn't.

It was Sophia's favourite time of the day, too.

'When I was a little girl I knew when the sun started
to go down it was almost time for me to go out and play.
Ma only ever let me out after it got dark – I guess she
was scared people might throw stones at me iffen they
saw me. Darkness was my friend 'cause in the dark I was
just the same as everyone else. Stupid, ain't it, that you
can only take someone for what they are when you can't
see their face?

'In the dark I can feel like a princess, like the most
beautiful girl in the world, and sometimes I imagine I'm
in a ballroom, with the biggest crystal chandeliers you ever
saw, and I'm dancing, held in the arms of a duke or a
prince, and you can be sure he's the tallest, handsomest
man in the room, and naturally he falls in love with my
pretty way of talking and my bell-like laughter ... And
then the sun comes up, and I'm a freak again and the only
reason anyone would want to look at me is to make themselves laugh, or feel lucky they're not the same way I am.'

One of the things I liked about Sophia was that she
was always dreaming. Most of the freaks had learned that
life was pretty darn hard, but somehow she was able to
forget the names she'd been called and all the mean looks
she'd gotten over the years and take herself off to that
other world of hers where she was Princess Sophia, and
everyone loved her.

It was Sophia, though, found out my secret.

I TELL THE MULE-FACED
WOMAN THE TRUTH

The sight of Ida May had affected me so bad I didn't want to go back there at first, but I knew I must. I waited until most people were gathered around the chuck wagon, and her barker, a half-Cherokee fella called Tash, was in the middle of a card game with Nathaniel and some of the others. He was a man who liked his drink, so I'd no reason to suppose he'd come back to the tent before morning.

I stood outside, breathing deep, and turning a potato over and over in my hands, scraping away at one of its eyes with my thumbnail. After a few minutes of this I was almost in a trance, and I took one more big breath, lifted the tent flap and went in.

Just like before, I'd only been looking at her for a moment when I hit the ground, and as soon as I came round I'd see her and be gone again.

Eventually, though, it subsided – the shock and the horror must've worn off a bit – and I found myself staring at her. Her skin looked as dry as parchment; her hair – the same hair I used to love playing with – was the thing that had changed the least about her, as if to mock her shrunken body.

She was my honey, my love, my darling. She was my dove with the dusty wings – and now the sight of her turned my stomach. Iffen she'd never have met me she'd have been alive now. She might have married a fella who came to the joy house, or saved up enough money to move on, and settle down with some cowboy. She'd maybe have had babies and grown fat and homely and learned how to bake and keep house.

Instead she was in a coffin in a freak show, on display for the whole world to see – the whore who got shot by the posse looking for her outlaw sweetheart. Preserved forever in her best dress as it faded to rags on her leathery skin. Shrinking slowly in her decaying finery, nothing more now than a bag of bones held together by a covering of parchment.

She was the finest, the most beautiful thing in the world to me one time, and now I couldn't bear to look at her.

I visited Ida May as much as I could after that, and one thing I've learned is this: a man can get used to anything with time. When you stare at something day in, day out, week after week, it don't matter how terrible it was to you at first, a man can't stay horrified for long. And it's almost worse, knowing you can come to accept something that once would've made you run screaming, would have driven you mad, and the memory of it woken you sweating in your bed every night.

I couldn't help but ask myself how much I really cared for Ida May if I could look at her every day and see how she was, and know it was me killed her. Those were some of my darkest times, and I only got through them by fixing in my mind that I was going to get her out of there, get her away from the crowds that came to gawp at her, to snicker and point, to turn away in disgust, or stare at her with pity in their eyes.

It's while I'm sitting with her one evening that Sophia finds me out.

'I'll think of something, Ida May, I promise I will. Maybe if I put by enough money I can buy you off Nathaniel . . .'

It's her breathing gives her away. Something to do with the shape of her face, I guess, but Sophia breathes real loud – so I know she's there. I stop talking and look round.

She laughs at me, first off. 'What are you doing, Isaac? Why are you talking to that old mummy? And why were you calling her Ida May? Nathaniel told us her name was Belle.'

When I don't say anything she stops smiling. 'Isaac, did you know her when she was alive?'

I still can't speak for a while. Then I say, 'I did, Sophia. I knew her well. Ida May was her real name, and she would've been my wife.'

Sophia bears her teeth in a grin again, but it's less certain this time. 'Your wife? But I thought she was an outlaw's girl. I thought she died with him.'

'He didn't die, Sophia. They just thought he was dead,

but he wasn't. He was in a fit, is all, and when he woke up he was in a coffin. The only thing he thought about was getting away, he never knew she was dead.'

Sophia ain't smiling no more. '*You*? *You* were the outlaw? They said he was the most evil man ever climbed on a horse. They said he killed without thinking and that after he died the Devil himself snatched his body, so's they could ride out together. That was *you*, Isaac?'

'My name ain't Isaac, it's Wilbur – Wilbur McCrum. I'm pretending to be someone else so they don't come after me. I ain't what they say I am, Sophia. You're only a mule-faced woman because that's what Nathaniel decided to call you – same for me: I wasn't really an outlaw; I just made a few mistakes trying to make a living, is all. I only ever killed one man, and that was an accident. And he deserved it, anyhow. All the rest has been made up by the sheriffs and bounty-hunters, and people who like to tell tall tales. You've no reason to fear me, Sophia.'

'But ain't it dangerous to be here with her, if they're still looking for you?'

'I had to find her. I couldn't just leave her to be bundled up in a carpet, stowed away in a wagon and then unrolled in the next town for more crowds to stare at. She's the mother of my child. She deserves a decent burial.'

Sophia's watching me, standing sideways-on like the paying customers often do, and holding up the hem of her skirt and rubbing the lace between finger and thumb. I wonder if that's the same for her as holding a potato is for me.

'I ain't going to hurt you, Sophia. I ain't never hurt anyone – leastways, not on purpose. I came here so's I could get Ida May back, but I couldn't do that if they suspicioned who I truly was. Nathaniel'd get the bounty-hunters here as soon as he found out. Will you help me, Sophia? Will you keep my secret?'

She keeps on looking at me, clutching at that lace. I can see she's considering what to do, and it ain't easy for her. I reckon I've said all I can, though, so I keep my peace and wait.

Then Sophia shifts her gaze to Ida May. 'What did she look like, Isaac – when she was alive?' she whispers.

'She was real pretty – well, I thought so. She was a spirited kind of girl, that's how she was killed – I told her to stay put, that the posse was only after me, but she wouldn't listen. She saw them before I did and tried to warn me. So they shot her.'

Sophia's crying. The tears leave tracks in the grey fur on her cheeks.

'So she died for *love* ... It's not fair, Isaac! She died because she loved you and she's ended up like this.'

'Will you help me – help us – Sophia?'

She looks back at me again. 'Yes, I'll help you. I'll do whatever I can, Isaac. I suppose I should really call you Wilbur now, when no one else is around?'

'I reckon it'd be better if you stuck to Isaac, in case you forget.'

So that's how Sophia became my partner, and I trusted her to keep my secret till she died.

HEAD IN THE CLOUDS

We carried on, quite content, and things seemed settled, leastways for me. Then one evening as I was sitting by the chuck wagon, chasing the last dumpling around in my beef stew, Nathaniel rolled by in a gig, stirring up the dust as he reined in his horse. It's funny, ain't it, how you can recall events from years ago in such detail, when you can't even remember what you did yesterday . . .

'Help me with this, will you, boy?' he says, as he climbs down, presenting me with a view of his substantial backside.

Since he calls just about everyone who's not female 'boy' I ain't clear he's talking to me, but when I look about and see no one else is paying heed, I put down my billycan, wipe my hands on my overalls and go over to see what he's got.

As soon as I look in the back of the cart and see the blanket I know: he's found himself another mummy.

'You take the legs and I'll take the head. Careful, now. That's right, be real gentle. These things ain't so easy to come by, and this here's a particularly fine specimen. It's only thanks to a canny jailer that I managed to get it.

Hung on to it after the fella died, thinking to sell it if the opportunity presented itself. There! Let's take a look at the goods, shall we?' And he bends down with some effort, and pulls the blanket back.

Everyone who's there – freaks, circus acrobats, barkers – gathers round to see what Nathaniel has got, and it sure is an awesome sight: it's one great big Injun – must be well over six foot tall when he's stood up. He has those cheekbones that Injuns have, and they're sticking out even more now he's dead, and the flesh on him is shrinking. He's got a big Sioux headdress on him, and what with the black brows and the piercing eyes that still seem able to look right through you, altogether he's a fearsome spectacle. I have to own to feeling just a bit scared of him.

'This here's Head in the Clouds, and I think you can see why they called him that. Got killed in a bar-room brawl, and ended up in a spare cell in the local jail, as the marshal didn't know what to do with him. When the jailer heard the circus was in town he came and asked me if I'd like to take him off his hands.'

I hear scuffling behind me, and I glance round to see Joshua pushing his way through the crowd to take a look.

'You might have consulted me, Nathaniel, before you went and bought another mummy!'

'For a man who runs a freak show you've got mighty delicate feelings, is all I can say, Joshua.'

'Well, you know my opinion, Nat – there's nothing wrong with a good honest-to-God freak, but it's the mummies I can't abide. Turn my stomach. Ain't natural to have a body around so long after it's died. Seems dirty to me.'

'Well, you ain't too proud to take your share of the money they bring in, are you? They pull in the crowds – they're a little bit of history, and they're kind of frightening, too. It's a fact of life that people like being frightened – just as long as they know they're really safe, of course.'

'If you ask me, you're tempting fate, keeping these mummies.'

'If I didn't know better, I'd say you was superstitious, Joshua.'

'T'ain't superstition, Nat. I'm just a God-fearing man, is all. Besides, don't he look to you like he can understand every word we're saying? Gives me the shivers.'

Of course there was a lot of talk about the new arrival after that. Most of the freaks agreed with Joshua that they should stick to live attractions. They knew mummies were cheaper for the freak show, on account of they didn't need feeding and they never got sick and took to their bed for a few days – nor ran away to the normal world. But at the back of their minds I think there was something else bothered them: they didn't mind being on show when they was alive, as they had to earn a crust somehow, but they sure as hell didn't want to be used as exhibits after they was dead.

WHAT HAPPENED
TO NATHANIEL

Now, even though I didn't much like Nathaniel's way of doing business, I wouldn't have wished him to end up like he did.

On account of Grandpa's experience, I'd always tried my best to keep away from Injuns – Kate was a half-breed, so I didn't count her – but after Head in the Clouds had been with us a few days I decided nothing bad was going to happen to me just because of him. When I thought about it, him and Ida May weren't so different no more: the main thing folks took notice of wasn't that they were a white woman and an Injun, it's that they was both dead. Whatever had happened in their lives, death had brought them together to be gawped at by crowds in small towns all over the West.

Then something happened to make me realize they weren't the same, after all.

One afternoon a group of Injuns shows up looking mighty ornery and making such a commotion that Zeke and me, along with most of the other freaks, come to see what's happening. I might not be able to understand what they're saying exactly, but I get the picture: they don't like one of their own being put on show that way.

Of course, Nathaniel has come to investigate, too. At first, he tries to laugh it off, like it's all a part of the performance, but I can see people in the crowd are getting anxious, and they start to edge away from the Injuns until there's quite a space around them.

Soon most people have moved off, with just a few rougher-looking fellas left hanging around like they're hoping for a fight. Nathaniel gives up pretending the Injuns are a part of the show and asks in a low voice iffen any of them speaks English. When one says yes they walk away with him, and that's the last I hear of them until the evening, when Sophia tells me about the discussions they've had.

'Did you see it, Isaac, all those braves who came looking for him, trying to argue it out with old Nathaniel? Some of them were real handsome, too. They want him back. They say it ain't dignified to put a man on show once he's dead, and more important than that, he can't enter the spirit world with his body still in this one.

'Course, Nathaniel ain't having none of it. Joshua said that maybe they should hand him over, 'cause after all, a body's supposed to go to the next of kin, and them Injuns are as near as damn it. But Nathaniel said, *Over his dead body* – that Injun's a crowd-puller. Then Joshua said, *Don't talk like that, Nat, not even for a joke*, and Nathaniel said he was a superstitious old fool and if he was so darned scared of what might happen then he should stay home, knitting by the fire.'

She finally stops to get her breath. I can tell Sophia's enjoying this excitement – her black eyes are sparkling and she's parading up and down, sticking her chest out as she pretends to be Nathaniel and looking scared and beat when she's Joshua.

I have to confess I thought Joshua was right about giving that Injun back to his brothers. I know trouble when I see it. Nathaniel didn't agree, though. A couple of nights later I was sitting in Ida May's tent, having a quiet smoke and looking out at the rain, when Nathaniel drove by in his gig, with the old Injun propped up next to him. I thought he made a strange travelling companion, but I guessed Nat was keeping Head in the Clouds safe in case those braves tried to steal him away.

There was a fierce storm that night, I remember. I fell asleep only to be jerked awake by the thunder rolling above us, and I peered sleepily through the gaps in the canvas that covered my wagon, to see the tents straining at their moorings, lit up by flashes of lightning. It was a restless night, 'cause once I was awake I tossed and turned, not able to get to sleep again for the longest time, and knowing when I did I'd be woke again soon enough in any case.

Come the morning, everyone seems low, dragging their feet, half-heartedly pushing with brooms at the sheets of water that still lie on the ground. I'm washing myself, making use of a puddle that's gathered on the side of Ida May's tent, when Joshua gallops over on an old bay mare, looking all shook up. As none of us have seen him since the Injun braves kicked up the fuss about Head in the

Clouds – he's been laying low – all the freaks and barkers and circus hands gather around to find out why he's come by now, and in such a hurry, too.

Joshua looks like he hasn't slept much, neither. His moustaches are drooping even more than usual, and the pouches under his eyes look like saddlebags.

'Folks, I have something to tell you.' His voice is breaking, like the words he's saying are too heavy for it. 'Nathaniel – Nathaniel went into town last night to play cards at the saloon and, well, he didn't come back.'

Some of the freaks start whispering to each other and I hear Sophia cry out.

Joshua holds up his hands for quiet, and when the noise dies down he carries on.

'For reasons I can't understand, Nathaniel took the Injun mummy with him, maybe to bring him luck, I don't know. It looked like he might have been right, as he won a fair sum of money and started back a happy man, according to people who saw him leave. Something happened on the journey home; no one is sure exactly what, but it seems the most likely thing is that the cart was struck by lightning.' Old Joshua swallows hard, and I look at the faces around me. They're all staring at him, quiet and still.

'What we do know is that Nathaniel – that Nathaniel's body – was burnt real bad. As a mark of respect, there will be no show tonight. Now I need some time to consider my position – I'm sure you understand.' And he turns his horse and rides slowly away with his head bowed low.

I'm watching him go when I'm distracted by a mighty

thud, which is Baby Sue keeling over from the shock, just missing three of the midgets, who have to run to keep from being squashed.

Of course the whole place is buzzing with the sound of us all talking at once. No one much liked Nathaniel, but he understood what people wanted to see and he wasn't afraid to give it to them. We know it was him kept the circus together.

Mary and Louisa walk by, taking it in turns to speak. 'But what if he decides to close the circus altogether?' – and before the first even finishes the other one begins – 'And what would we do then?' 'What's to become of us?' 'Where will we go?' 'How shall we live?'

I reckon we're all thinking pretty much the same thing. I wasn't much good at earning my keep in the ordinary world; what chance do the rest of them have?

That night Sophia comes to find me to tell me something else she's heard.

'You know what Lonnie said?' She don't wait for an answer. 'He told me there was only one body in that gig. Head in the Clouds was gone. No one believes what happened was an accident; they think Nathaniel was ambushed by the Injuns, and that they took Head in the Clouds away. Course, the other idea is that he came back to life, killed old Nat himself and returned to the spirit world.' She sniffed, and smoothed down her skirt. 'But I don't believe that – it seems a bit far-fetched, don't you think?'

Sophia goes on some more after that, but I stop

listening – not on purpose; I'm just finding it hard to concentrate, on account of I can hear Tash, Ida May's barker, talking to Zeke, and he sure sounds upset. I walk over to them and he's saying, 'He's a crazy old fool! Freaks are good business, but folk like variety. Mummies spook them in a different way to freaks, and they ain't that easy to come by. Why would anyone give one up?'

'You know why – he thinks they're cursed, thinks if he don't get rid of the other one, the same thing'll happen to him as happened to old Nat.'

'Nat went out in a thunderstorm and got struck by lightning!'

'But what happened to the Injun's body?'

'I guess it was so dry it burned to ash. Even iffen it didn't, iffen Nathaniel was killed by the Injuns, they've no reason to come back and trouble him over some saloon girl. They got what they wanted; now they'll leave us alone.'

'Try telling that to Joshua. He's hiding away in town somewhere and he's got your saloon girl all wrapped up and hidden away in one of the wagons while he figures out what to do with her.'

'And what about me? I got nothing to do now. Seems to me he should pay more heed to the living and fret less about the dead.'

They stop talking when they see me coming, but I ain't about to pretend I haven't heard them.

'Do you know where Joshua is right now?' My heart's beating so hard I think they'll be able to hear it. This could be my chance: iffen I speak with Joshua while he's still scared out of his wits about having a mummy in his show maybe I can persuade him to lay poor Ida May to rest.

'Old fool's spending most of his time holed up in his lodgings – you could try looking for him there – iffen you find him, tell him this from me,' and Tash turns his head to the left and spits neatly in the dirt between us.

I GO SEE JOSHUA

I borrowed a horse and rode into town. I found where Joshua was staying soon enough – seemed everyone knew what had happened to Nathaniel, for as soon as I asked a fella in the street to direct me he said, 'Are you with the circus? Is it true that Injun mummy disappeared? I saw him, you know, in the saloon the night it happened. The circus fella had him propped up against a chair with a glass of whisky in front of him. Thought it mighty funny. He ain't laughing now, though, is he?'

'He sure ain't. Now iffen you could just tell me the whereabouts of Mr Bailey?'

I didn't want to seem unmannerly, but I didn't want to waste time visiting, neither. The fella looked disappointed, but he showed me the place where Joshua was staying. As I walked toward it he called after me, 'Is it true, about the Injun? There's a fella says he saw him, walking the road away from town, not looking to left nor right. Is it true, you reckon?'

I didn't like the attention this business was attracting, so I was mighty glad to get indoors. Joshua's landlady was a short, plump woman with pink cheeks and her sleeves rolled up, showing her dimpled elbows. She laughed when I said who I'd come to see.

'Well, I'm glad Mr Bailey's proving so popular that folks'll come to see him, for he certainly isn't in the mood to go visiting.'

'You think he'll talk to me, then?'

'Well, I dare say he will. He let the other gentleman in, and they weren't even acquainted. Although, I must say he's quite the most nervous person I've ever had staying with me – my daughter dropped a cup last evening and he nearly jumped out of his skin at the noise.' And she threw back her head and laughed again.

I was about to ask about this *other gentleman* when I heard a sound on the stairs: the wood was creaking like it was under fearful strain, and before long I learnt why. The fattest man I'd ever seen outside of the freak show was coming slowly down the stairs. Everything about him was fat: his cheeks, which seemed like he was storing food in them for later; his lips, which were thick and wet-looking; even his eyes, which bulged like he was real angry about something – even though his big mouth was fixed in a smile that said he was mighty pleased with himself. Only his nose was small, stuck in the middle of his face like it was the last bit of him to be made, and there wasn't much flesh left after all the rest came out so over-sized.

I got the feeling he wasn't just walking slow on account of being so fat, neither; he walked slow 'cause he thought he was an important person who mustn't be hurried. Soon as I saw him I took a dislike to that fella.

So there I am, seeing him and not liking him, not one

little bit. He don't pay no heed to me, though. Don't believe he even sees me. When he reaches the bottom of the stairs he calls over his shoulder, 'Tomorrow, then, Mr Bailey. I look forward to it.' Then he turns to the landlady, takes hold of her hand in his two fat ones, and smiles a smile that makes me wonder if he ain't about to eat her. She don't seem to mind, though. She laughs again as he says, 'Madam, I thank you for your hospitality. I hope you will consider attending one of my services; it would be a *pleasure* to see you there,' and he pulls a card from his waistcoat pocket with two fingers whose nails are so white and polished they look like fat grubs hanging there.

'The Reverend Cornelius Smith, at your service, my dear.'

I feel uneasy making my way up those stairs to Joshua's room. Who was that man, and what did he want?

Joshua seems more cheerful than he's been for some time, and I wonder iffen he's gotten religious as a result of what happened to his partner. There's a spot of colour on his cheeks and his shoulders are almost straight.

'Who was that?' I ask him, before I even say hello.

'Him?' Joshua's eyes dart around the room, looking anywhere but at me. 'He's a travelling preacher – you know, one of those fellas goes round converting folk, baptizing them in the river and suchlike.'

'So why was he here?' I can tell from Joshua's face he's feeling bad about something, and he's making me feel uneasy too.

'He had – well, you might say it was a *proposal* he had to put to me.'

He clearly don't want to tell me the whole story; I'm going to have to drag it out of him.

'What kind of proposal, Joshua? What would a preacher want from a freak show?'

'What he wants, Isaac – well, he wants to buy Belle. To use her in his work.'

'Use her? What for? What use would a preacher have for a mummy?'

I'm feeling sick, and the edges of my vision are going dark. I can't believe that having found Ida May I'm going to lose her again.

'He wants to use her as an example – a bad example – of what can happen iffen you stray from the path of righteousness. You got to admit she's pretty shocking when you first set eyes on her. Should work a treat, I reckon.'

I don't wait to hear no more. I run down those stairs two at a time, past the surprised-looking landlady and out into the street. I'm mighty glad, then, that the Reverend Smith moves so slow, 'cause I can still see him, walking down the dusty road, flourishing his cane with each step, like he's a procession all by himself.

'Wait up!' I holler after him. 'Reverend Smith! Wait for me!'

I see him stop, but it takes the fella an age before he turns around, like a paddle steamer, by degrees. By the time he's facing in my direction I've just about caught up with him.

'Would you, by any chance, be addressing *me*, young man?' He looks like he's just eaten something bad, but he waits for me to reach him. Only trouble is, each step I take I can feel my legs growing weaker, and I start to stumble. I fall to my knees in front of the fat fella, my arms outstretched, and then the world turns black around me.

Next thing I know, I'm lying face down and my mouth is full of dirt. It seems to be dark, but when I roll over I see that's because the Reverend Smith is standing over me, blocking out the light. I'm surprised to see he don't look disgusted no more – he's smiling, his lips curled back like a toad's. 'Well, well, I've never seen anything quite the same as *that* before!'

'Excuse me, sir,' I say, trying to spit the dirt out of my mouth without him seeing. 'It was just a fit. Had them since I was a boy.'

'Please don't apologize, young man. Have you ever thought that your affliction might, in fact, be a gift from the Almighty?'

This is such a peculiar suggestion that I just stare at him.

'He moves in mysterious ways, as we all know, and everything He does has a purpose. I have a feeling in my waters that He has sent you to me to aid me in my mission.'

'Pardon me?'

'It is not for *me* to pardon you, sir, only our *Lord* can do that, and I think He is at this very minute offering you a *way* to gain His pardon.'

I don't know iffen it's his strange manner of speaking, or on account of I've just come out of a fit, but I can't make head nor tail of what he's saying to me. He must be able to see my difficulty, because he begins to talk loudly, making big shapes with his fat lips, like I'm either deaf or an imbecile.

'How would you like to work for me, young man? Would you like to dedicate your life to the service of the Lord – and get board and lodgings, too, of course?'

I understand that, all right.

'You offering me a job?'

'That's right!' he says, nodding his head, in case the words ain't enough on their own. 'If you think you can have those impressive fits on stage, I am indeed willing to employ you. This has been a most fruitful day! I am truly thankful that the Good Lord brought us to these parts!'

This was such a turnaround, from my fear of losing Ida May to being offered the chance to stay even closer to her than before, that I felt quite drunk as I rode back to the circus. I reckoned I was lucky to have borrowed a docile horse; iffen it'd been Mabel I don't know where I might've ended up.

I still couldn't understand how things had worked out quite as well as they did. I hadn't decided what I was going to say to the Reverend when I chased after him, but I guess I would've asked him iffen he truly wanted to buy Ida May from Joshua. I'd never have thought to ask him for work.

It was only when I got in sight of the Big Top that I started to think about leaving my new life behind. I'd enjoyed my time with the freaks and the circus folk, and it was going to be real hard to say goodbye to some of them, especially Sophia, but I knew I had to go with Ida

May. I was the one got her killed. I couldn't do nothing about that now, but I could see to it she got a decent burial. She deserved a grave as much as any fine lady, and then I'd have somewhere to bring Junior some day. He might never be able to meet his Ma, but at least he could see her last resting place.

Sophia can see from the look on my face that something has happened.

'You look sad, Isaac. What's troubling you?'

'I've got to leave the circus, Sophia.' Her eyes fill with water when I say that. 'I don't want to, but I've got to.' And I tell her about the fat preacher wanting me to be a part of his travelling show, and how it's the only way I can stay close to Ida May.

'Well, then, I guess you have to go,' she says, wiping tears from the end of her muzzle with her wrist. 'Nothing should stand in the path of true love.'

She makes it sound like a romantic story. I know that ain't exactly how it would seem to most people, but it's Sophia's way of consoling herself, so I let her be.

'Anyway, we none of us know what Joshua's plans are. It may be we all have to look for work someplace else.' She gives me a watery smile.

'Oh, I don't reckon that'll happen. Joshua's sure to calm down once Ida May has gone. He was always wary of mummies, and the whole Head in the Clouds business made him worse. He'll be fine when it's just the circus performers and the freaks.'

After speaking to Sophia, telling Joshua I was leaving was easy – and anyhow, I was ready to get going by then.

I felt like I was closer to being able to claim Ida May back. Surely a man of the cloth would understand why I needed to bury my sweetheart. All I had to do was bide my time until I felt I could talk to him about it.

I FIND EMPLOYMENT

$\mathcal{I}$ left the circus real quick after that. Joshua wanted rid of Ida May as soon as possible, and the very next day he rode in with the Reverend Smith and two other people I'd not seen before, a man and a woman. I could see they were brother and sister. The girl had a kind of blurred look to her, as if she'd gotten damp and her features had smudged. Her eyes were a watery blue, and she looked worried, like she didn't really want to be there. The fella had the same fine blond hair as the girl, with a wispy lock that wouldn't stay combed back, but kept falling over his forehead. Although he was young, his hair was already thinning. I was mighty surprised to hear the girl call the Reverend *papa*. I guessed their Ma must be a bony sort of a woman, 'cause they sure didn't favour their Pa none.

As soon as they dismounted, Joshua shooed away the crowd of freaks and circus folk who'd gathered, and grabbing me by the elbow, hurried me along to Ida May's tent with the visitors following behind.

Tash was nowhere to be seen, and Ida May was lying in her coffin in the middle of the tent. The Reverend went over to her at once, but the other two hung back. He looked down all solemn, his hat in his hands, but I fancied I could see a gleam in his eye when he said to Josh,

'She'll suit my purposes admirably, Mr Bailey, but you understand that as a man who has dedicated himself to spreading the word of our Lord I have very little by way of worldly wealth – although of course in spiritual terms my cup runneth over . . .'

'Oh, I don't want money, Reverend. I just want to dispose of her the best way I can. If I had the right to bury her, I'd lay her in the ground, but I figure only her kin could do that, and she don't seem to have none, else they'd have claimed her from the funeral parlour where my partner found her. If she can be at all useful to you in doing the Lord's work, then I'm happy to hand her over to you.'

The fat man's eyes moved sideways in a suspicious glare that Joshua didn't seem to notice. He really did look like an old toad, searching for bugs to catch with his tongue. I didn't reckon I liked the idea of him having Ida May one bit, and I had to stop myself saying something I'd be sorry for.

'Excellent, excellent. You understand my position – as a man of God my needs are simple, and I live modestly on what the Lord in His goodness sees fit to provide—'

Joshua interrupted him, 'Like I said, I wasn't expecting payment, Reverend. I'd be glad for you to take her away. I'm happy for her to become an instrument of the Lord. Might make up for the way me and my late partner have been using her. To tell you the truth, I wonder whether what happened might not have been meant as a punishment.'

This time the fat man lowered his head and nodded, like he was real serious, but I could still see that glint in his eye that didn't match up with his manner.

'Far be it from me, sir, to condemn a fellow man for his conduct, but it seems you could indeed say that your unfortunate partner reaped his reward. You're very wise, sir, very wise, to make atonement in this way.'

Joshua had his eyes fixed on the Reverend, but I saw the other two exchange glances. Maybe they were wondering the same thing I was – what in Hell's name would a preacher want with Ida May? Iffen he *was* a preacher. He seemed mighty pleased with himself. He was dressed in black, right enough, but gamblers often dressed like that, too. Perhaps I'd been a bit hasty, agreeing to go with him when I didn't know a thing about him; but then what else could I do? Iffen Joshua was set on handing her over to him I had to go too – I couldn't stop him, on account of iffen I claimed her as next of kin I'd have to tell folk who I really was, and I'd as like as not be hanged before I got a chance to bury her.

Tash appeared and wrapped Ida May real careful in a blanket, just like a mother swaddling a baby. Gentle though he was with her, he looked mighty riled and wouldn't meet anyone's eye.

So we take our leave, riding away in a covered wagon, with the Reverend at the reins. Sophia runs alongside for a while, looking up at me with her big sorrowful eyes.

'You will write me, Isaac, won't you? Tell me what happens – to you both?'

'Of course I will. You've been a good friend, Sophia. I'll never forget you.'

I don't have the heart to ask how she thinks my letter would ever find her when we're both on the road.

The Reverend won't let me drive, being afraid I'd have a fit and we'd all end up in a ditch, but after a couple of hours he hands the reins to his son and goes in back with his daughter. He hasn't bothered to introduce me to them, but I learn from hearing them talk that they're called Leonard and Adeline. I settle down in my seat with my hat over my eyes, like I mean to sleep, but what I'm truly intending to do is listen, and see what I can learn.

Adeline don't wait around: straightaway she says to him, 'But, Father, are you sure this is the Lord's will? Isn't it a sin to leave a woman unburied like this? How can we be sure her soul has travelled to Heaven if her body hasn't been laid to rest?'

'Now, Adeline, my dear, I suggest you leave matters of theology to me. You are of the weaker sex, and if God had meant for you to think, he wouldn't have given you the duty to bear children – it stands to reason that the two don't go together.'

Adeline falls silent and after a while I truly do drift off to asleep. The next thing I know the wagon has stopped, and from the way it's rocking I guess the Reverend must be climbing out.

I raise my hat and see it's dark. We've stopped outside a boarding house, and the others are going inside without saying a word to me. Leonard's carrying Ida May, still wrapped in her blanket. As I jump down and follow them I see him knock her head on the doorframe.

'Careful, boy, careful.'

The young fella starts to speak. 'Father, I hardly think—'

'I'm aware of that, Leonard. That is the reason I do all the thinking there is to be done in this family. With your sister being of the weaker sex, and you of the weaker mind, and your mother – God rest her soul – having long departed this earth, the burden of responsibility for keeping our little bark afloat in this sea of woe that we call life rests on my – fortunately ample – shoulders.'

We're inside now, and I can see his smug face. His son's tells a different story, though. He darts a look of pure hatred at his Pa.

The owner of the boarding house was quite old – leastways her hair was grey, although her skin was pretty smooth. She looked alarmed at the sight of the bundle in Leonard's arms.

'Why, whatever is that?' she asked, clutching the cross she wore on a thin chain around her neck.

The Reverend waved his hand as though dismissing her. 'It's nothing, dear madam. Just something I use to aid me during my sermons.' He came up real close and took her hand from the cross, bringing it over to his bosom instead.

'The mass of common people are so *ignorant* of spiritual matters, they have *neglected* to feed their souls for so long, that I feel I must help them along as much as possible. A little visual aid does wonders to clarify their understanding, I find.' He simpered at her. 'Of course, dear lady, I can see that you are *quite* different. You are clearly a person of refinement and delicacy who has no need of such coarse worldly apparatus, but what can I do?' And he dropped her hand and turned away as if he was done with her.

The poor woman frowned, confused and anxious at the same time, but I was beginning to understand that the Reverend was the kind of man who got whatever he wanted, just by ignoring any point of view but his own. She lifted the corner of her skirts and led us upstairs.

Adeline had a room to herself, being the only lady in the party, and the Reverend got his own, too, but Leonard and me had to share. When he heard that, he opened his mouth to say something, but his Pa held up a fat hand. That silenced him, so he just gave me a look like he wanted to kill me instead.

That evening, after we'd eaten, the Reverend summoned us all to tell us how he wanted things to go the next day.

'Now, Isaac, I need you to attend most carefully, as your part in the proceedings will be of great importance. You are to wait near the back of the crowd, doing your best to appear to be one of them. Perhaps you could turn to one of your neighbours and express your curiosity about what is going to happen. Whatever you choose to do, when I say the words *"The Lord is my shepherd,"* you are to begin to shout and rave, and to push your way through the *throng* until you reach the platform on which I am standing. You will continue your *gibberish* while I summon you to join me, whereupon you must fall into a fit. I shall respond by calling upon the Lord to cast out the *demons* that possess you and leading those present in prayer.

'I imagine the spectacle of you, writhing around and screaming – and you have my permission to use whatever *profanities* you can summon from the depths of your memory – will *excite* the crowd. When I unveil that wretched mummy I shall bring them to such a *pitch* of excitement that they will be only too eager to *repent* their sins and accept Our Lord into their hearts.'

His lips widened in a smile. I could see he was mighty pleased with himself.

'But, Father, where is it now? I don't see it anywhere.'

'I thought it best to stow the thing under the bed, Adeline, my dear. Our landlady seems a nervous creature, and I wouldn't want her to face the temptation of un-wrapping it and receiving the shock of her life.'

'But how will you sleep, knowing what lies beneath you?'

'I am a man of the cloth, my dear. I have always known what lies beneath me – the fires of Hell and all the devils within – but I have nothing to fear. The Lord protects his own.'

I felt quite sick at the thought of poor Ida May lying in the dark under a bed that creaked every time the Reverend shifted his great bulk. I had to try mighty hard not to fall into a fit.

THE REVEREND CORNELIUS SMITH
MAKES MONEY FOR THE LORD

———⸺⸺⸺———

*L*eonard is so angry at having to share a room with me he don't speak a word as we prepare for bed. For him that means unpacking a wash bag, shaving kit and a Bible, turning his back on me while he changes into a flannel nightshirt, then kneeling to say his prayers. For me it means taking off my boots and my jacket and getting into bed.

I'm feeling bad, which might have kept me awake, if the Reverend's snoring hadn't already taken care of that. The noise he makes sounds more like a walrus blowing out air than a person; there'll be a blast, then quiet for so long you'll think he's stopped breathing altogether, then another blast, which somehow sounds even louder than the one before.

Although I'm not too happy about the notion of trying to have fits in front of a crowd of people, I'm glad when at last the morning comes. There's a big grey cloud over to the east, and it's soon joined by more. I begin to hope it'll rain, and that the Reverend will decide not to hold his meeting, or iffen he does, that folk won't come.

I don't get my wish, though. The Reverend eats a mess of eggs, four sausages and five pancakes; Adeline has some pancakes, and Leonard and me just drink coffee. I might've been able to eat something, but just as the sound of the Reverend sleeping kept me from being able to sleep, the sight of him eating stops me from wanting to eat. For a man who's always saying how little he cares for worldly things, he makes sure he gets more than his fair share of food. His clothes are smart, too, and pants, a jacket and a vest for a man of his size takes a whole bunch of cloth to make. He has a fine watch chain and a real good pocket watch, and those nails of his are unnatural clean for a man.

When the Reverend has finally had his fill, we set out. The first thing to do is tell the townsfolk we're here. We hand out pieces of paper to people in the street, the stores, the saloons, telling them there'll be a big prayer meeting that afternoon. The Reverend has been busy – the notices are all fresh ones that say we have something spectacular to show them, something that will convince them to follow the way of the Lord.

No one shies away from us when we come up to them; they take the papers, and some stand and read them. I've never known for sure what I think about God, but it seems to me people divide into the ones who don't believe he exists on account of all the bad things happen in the world, and those who believe in him for the exact same reason, and want something to cling on to, the way someone who's drowning clings to a piece of wood that's drifting by. Anyhow, it seems like a fair number of people are curious about our meeting. I guess it's something new for them to do.

As I pass Leonard I ask him iffen he thinks many people will come and he says, 'Oh yes, my father has a way of attracting people. They flock to him like moths to a flame. For some reason they seem to find him quite irresistible.' And he laughs in an unpleasant kind of way.

Later on – after the Reverend has another go at trying to fill his enormous belly – we set off in the wagon to the crossroads just outside town where he's going to hold his meeting. Leonard and me unload the platform he uses to raise himself above the congregation – it's like a bunch of trestle tables all laid alongside each other, and I ain't sure they'll be strong enough to take the Reverend's great weight.

I look up and see the storm clouds rolling in, but people are already arriving, so I know the Reverend ain't likely to cancel the show now. Leonard sees me and says, 'He won't let a little bad weather stop him – he'll bring it into his sermon, make out it's God speaking to the sinful. If there's one thing you can say about my father, it's that he's very resourceful.'

More and more people come, and before long there's a small crowd. I make my way to the back of it, and when I glance over my shoulder a few minutes later there are as many faces behind me as there are backs of heads in front.

All this time the Reverend is sitting to one side of his stage on a stool, knees apart, sipping on something and gargling. He looks like a prizefighter getting ready for a fight, and I can see this is all a part of his act. After a while he glances up from under his brows, and he must judge there are enough people for him to start. He gets to his feet and walks to the middle of the stage. Then he just stands there with his head lowered. There's been a lot of excited talk going on, but before long silence falls as everyone waits to see what he's going to do. Then the Reverend lifts his mighty arms, slowly raises his head and hollers, 'Brothers and sisters, we have gathered here today in the sight of the Lord for a *purpose*, and that *purpose* is to examine the state of our souls.'

He's pacing from one side to the other of his little stage now, and I can see how it's lucky for him, being such a big man; someone like me would be lost in front of a crowd. And he sure can make a lot of noise, too. I reckon there are maybe a hundred people there, and he's loud enough to be heard by all of them.

All of a sudden I realize it's nearly time for me to join in. The Reverend is saying, 'Yea, though I walk in the valley of the shadow of death, the Lord is my shepherd...' and I begin to elbow my way toward him. I try to cry out, but at first I hardly make any sound. I try again, and this time I see people ahead turn to find out where the noise is coming from. 'Let me through, let me through!' It gets easier the more I holler, and the more I holler the more folk try to make a path for me, fearing I might be a dangerous lunatic, I guess.

As I reach the front and stand looking up at the Reverend I kind of lose my nerve, but he takes over. 'Have you come to make confession, son?' he asks me.

I stare up at him, without saying a word. I can hear

the rushing sound in my ears that I sometimes get when a fit is coming. The Reverend must see it in my eyes, because before I know it a large hand has reached down and grabbed my arm, and I'm being hauled onto the stage. The Reverend is so much heavier than me that I fly toward him and kind of bounce off of his belly, and before I know it I'm on the platform at his feet, taking care to turn my head away from the crowd, so I can open half an eye and take a look at what he's doing.

From somewhere above I hear him roaring, 'You see, brothers and sisters, how he *writhes* upon the ground as if *possessed*, speaking in *tongues* and muttering *oaths*.' He gives me a nudge with his toe, to remind me to writhe some. 'The Devil has a hold of this poor *sinner*, brothers and sisters, and with your help I will free him from the foul fiend's *clutches*. Will you help me?'

There are a few half-hearted cries of 'Yes!' from the crowd, and the Reverend cups his hand around his ear, leans forward and calls out again, 'I say *will* you help me?'

This time about half of them answer him with a louder 'Yes!' He still ain't happy, though, and he turns his back, pounds to the back of the stage, making the trestles bounce something alarming, then wheels around and hollers even louder, '*Will* you *help* me?'

Now pretty much all of them join in with the 'Yes!' and he seems content, because he comes back, and I hear his knee joints cracking as he lowers himself slowly down beside me and lifting my head, lays a clammy hand on my forehead and the other underneath my hair. He starts the Lord's Prayer, saying it slow so they can chant it along with him, and I begin to feel more calm. I ain't going to have a real fit after all. As he gets to the end he pulls the uppermost hand away with a flourish and lays my head back as gentle as if he's putting a baby down to sleep.

'Now I shall count backward from five, and he will awaken and find himself bathed in the light of our Heavenly Father. He will no longer be able to remember what just happened to him. Five, four, three, two, one!'

At that I open my eyes, and get unsteadily to my feet, doing my best to look mighty bewildered at the sight of all the people.

'Do you know where you are, son?'

I shake my head.

'Do you know what just happened?'

I shake my head again.

'You,' he says, clapping a hand on my shoulder so hard that my knees bend, 'have become an instrument of the Lord.'

I look around the crowd again, and maybe I overdo it some, because I hear laughter, and a man's voice calls out, 'Some instrument!'

The Reverend presses down even harder on my shoulder and glares out, like he's trying to see who spoke.

'The Lord moves in mysterious ways, His wonders to perform,' he declares sternly. 'Now, young man, do you accept the Lord into your heart?' This is the moment I'm supposed to drop to my knees, but I'm a bit slow, so he pushes me down, lays his hands on my head and begins muttering under his breath. To the crowd it must look like he's giving me a blessing or some such, but I make out the words 'Damn fool' and 'Heaven preserve me from this idiot,' and a few things I can't repeat.

While he's doing this I have to put my hands together and say a prayer, as if he's driven the badness out of me and let the goodness in, then he helps me to my feet again and I stand smiling, trying as hard as ever I can to look like a bad man turned good.

There are a few gasps from the onlookers, then people begin to clap their hands. The Reverend does as much of a bow as his belly will let him, then leads me off to the chair he was sitting in before the show started. From then on I can rest and watch the performance.

The Reverend walks to the front of the stage and says in his booming voice, 'Now, brothers and sisters, if you think this poor sinner was a pitiful sight before I laid my hands on him and cast out the devils that tormented him, let me show you what can happen to someone who has strayed from the path of righteousness and leaves it too late to repent. You may be wondering, brothers and sisters, "What's the worst that can happen to me if I carry on with my sinful ways?" Life is short and then you die, so make the most of it while you can – is that what you're thinking, sir?' And he points at a man in the front who's standing with his hands in his pockets, trying to show by the look of him that he ain't scared by this kind of talk.

'*Is* that what you've been thinking, sir?' The man looks down at the ground, and his shoulders come up closer to his ears, like he's trying to hide them. 'Well, I have something here that might change your mind.'

The Reverend walks to the other side of the stage and stops beside a sheet that's draped in front of something.

Very slowly and carefully he winds a corner of the sheet around his arm, then looks at his audience and waits. It's as if you can hear the whole lot of them holding their breath. Then he tugs the sheet away with a flourish that wraps it around him like a cloak.

'Behold!' There are gasps, and even a few cries. Out the corner of my eye I see one woman tip backward as if she's fainted clean away. The people on either side hold her up and fan her, trying to bring her round. What I'm looking at, though, is Ida May.

The Reverend has propped her against an easel to hold her upright, so's people can get a better view of her. Even though I thought I'd gotten used to her like she is, the way he shows her off still gives me a shock. I guess she don't look any different than she did in the freak show, but in the tent she was in shadow; out here, even with the storm clouds overhead, you can see the wizened skin and the lips shrunk back from the teeth.

I want to stand up and say to those people, *Ain't you never seen a dead person before?* But of course I know that most people are put in the ground a good long while before they get to look like that. I want to shout at the fat man in his fancy suit, *What are you doing? You're supposed to be a man of God. You should be burying her, not showing her off!* But of course, I don't say a thing.

'This, brothers and sisters, is the fate that awaits the unrepentant sinner. This woman was a common prostitute. She took her liquor like a man – and fornicated like one, too. She threw in her lot with an infamous outlaw and died with him at the hands of a posse. The Lord guided the hand of the man who shot her, and it was the

Lord who preserved her in this remarkable state until she passed into my hands, to be used to help spread His word.

'Brothers and sisters, I urge you now to make a decision, the most important decision you will ever make. I *urge* you to renounce the Devil; I *urge* you to denounce the demon drink. *Surrender* yourselves unto the Lord, brothers; sisters, follow your menfolk. Be reborn, free of sin in *readiness* for the Kingdom of God. And as you open your hearts, open also your *pocketbooks* – give to this mission the money you might otherwise have spent on *poisoning* yourselves with liquor, with tobacco, with ladies of the night, so that I might be able to move on and continue my work in some other town that needs me.'

He's frothing the crowd up into a frenzy now; I can see people with their eyes closed, swaying from side to side, others with their hands raised, palms upward. Some of the women are crying, and I'm wondering whether we're safe up here.

Then the Reverend calls on them, '*Say* it, brothers and sisters, say, "I renounce the Devil!"'

The crowd says the words, but not all at the same time.

'I can't hear you, brothers and sisters. Say it again, say it louder!'

'I renounce the Devil!'

'Again!'

They're getting hysterical now – I can hear some woman sobbing, 'I renounce the Devil!' over and over, like her life depends on it.

Then all of a sudden the crowd surges forward as folk run toward the stage, holding their dollar bills, eager to be the first to buy their place in Heaven. Do they really believe that old windbag means what he's saying? He's a clever old fox, all right, and I ain't convinced he cares at all for the state of their souls.

The crowd don't see it like that, though. I notice Leonard wading in to rescue a woman who's been knocked off her feet in the crush, and Adeline has joined her father, who's busy taking bills from the outstretched hands. Iffen I'd suspicioned it was this easy to part folks from their money then maybe I could have found some way to get by without robbing banks.

It's all too much. It's growing darker, inside and outside my head, and just as a great fork of lightning hits the ground behind the crowd I fall to my knees and topple forward off the stage. The last sound I hear is the thunder rolling overhead.

A COW BY THE RIVER

———◦◦◦———

$\mathcal{I}$ reckon I was in that fit a while on account of I was wet through when I woke up, as wet as when I came out the well. I was laying face down, and when I raised my head some I could see the crowd was gone. The sky was still grey as rock, so it was hard to tell whether it was getting dark. I realized there was something stuck to my cheek and when I pulled it off I saw it was a torn page from a newspaper. I was going to cast it aside, but there was a picture on the page that looked real familiar. I turned it around until I could see it properly, and then I read what it said underneath:

Wilbur McCrum strikes again.

Infamous bandido Wilbur McCrum robbed a bank in Morristown yesterday, escaping with $3,000. The scoundrel, thought to have been responsible for the deaths of at least 10 men, also made off with the pocket watch belonging to Ivor Beech, the Chief Teller. Mr Beech said the outlaw had 'A real menacing look in his eye. Before he left he pointed his gun directly at my heart and threatened to kill me if I raised the alarm.' McCrum left behind his usual calling card, a potato, thought *by some to be a reference to the fact that his family hailed originally from Ireland.*

As soon as I'd finished reading, I went back to the beginning and started again, but the words remained the same. Then I wondered whether I might not still be in my fit, or maybe I'd hit my head when I fell. How could I have robbed a bank when I was on the road with the Reverend? And what did they mean about killing at least ten men? I'd never killed anyone but Nattie's husband, and that by accident. I couldn't make no sense of this at all, so I stopped trying. I folded the damp paper as well as I could and put it in my pants pocket, then went to find the Reverend.

The next morning we moved on to another town and went through the whole performance again. The faces in the front row might be different, but the way the Reverend worked the crowd was always the same: he got them thinking they were the worst, the wickedest folks that ever lived, then he held out the chance of salvation. The catch was they needed to part with their hard-earned money to buy it, only they didn't seem to care about that. He whipped them up into such a frenzy I reckon most of them would've give him the clothes off of their backs and run around buck naked without shame, iffen he only asked them to do it.

I have to own he was a clever fella, that fat preacher. He made a good living out of just talking, and there ain't many can do that – leastways, not round these parts.

*

We travelled like that for eight or nine months, stopping in small towns all around the Midwest, taking cheap lodgings some nights, sleeping in the wagon others. The Reverend treated me like his servant – I had to bring him coffee and vittles whenever he wanted, oftentimes in the middle of the night, make sure his suits were brushed and hung up, even help him in and out of his bath, which wasn't easy, I can tell you.

The only way I kept myself from feeling lonely was to creep in and speak to Ida May when the Reverend wasn't around – which wasn't hard, seeing as so much of his time was taken up with eating.

I remember one evening when we'd taken lodgings in Vernon. The three of them were having dinner in a hotel because it was Adeline's birthday. So there I am, free to visit Ida May. I lay down on the floor next to the bed and turn my head to look at her. She's all wrapped up, of course, but I can just make out the shape of her. The Reverend has gotten a coffin for her now, to make it easier to transport her from place to place, but for some reason he still likes to stow her under his bed each night – perhaps he's afraid someone will steal her otherwise – and there's never room for her and the coffin both, so he has it on the floor by the desk.

'It's me, Ida May, it's Wilbur.' It feels strange to use my real name, when I've gotten so used to folks calling me Isaac. 'I hope you're doing all right. I promise this won't go on forever – as soon as I can get you away from the old toad I will, and we'll have a proper funeral. I've got some money saved up. He don't pay me much, but I don't need to spend much, neither. I figured maybe we could get George to do it. You remember George? He took care of us after we was shot. Although it might be difficult to do, with me supposed to be dead, too, and there being a price on my head.'

As I'm saying the words, it starts to seem kind of hopeless, and it makes me feel so bad I begin to cry. I ain't sure whether I have a fit or just fall asleep, but next thing I know, I hear the door opening and feel the floorboards moving underneath me. I can tell it's the Reverend who's come in on account of the weight of him as he moves, and the noise he makes breathing.

Quick as I can I slide myself sideways underneath the bed, pushing Ida May across some. He walks over to the window, and he must light the lamp on the desk, because there's suddenly more light in the room. I turn over real careful, so I'm on my side with my back to Ida May; that way I can maybe see what he's doing.

I can't make out much, just his back as he sits looking at something. The light shows up the rolls of fat on his neck. I can see a glass at his elbow and judging by the colour of the liquid, it ain't lemonade he's drinking. Whatever he's looking at pleases him, because he's chuckling and it turns into a cough. When he's gotten over that he begins muttering to himself, 'Why, you're a beauty, and no mistake! I like a woman with a bit of flesh on her.'

I've had my doubts about the Reverend's godliness from the moment I first clapped eyes on him, but this is something new. I lay there watching him for maybe half an hour. I can smell his cigar, but there's another smell, too, coming from Ida May. She smells like apples left to rot, and I have to keep swallowing down the bile that comes into my gullet.

Then the Reverend decides to turn in. He seems to be wrapping up whatever he's been looking at, and he bends down and puts the parcel in Ida May's coffin. As he does it his face is almost on a level with mine, and I hold my breath so he won't hear me, but bending is hard for him – he has to steady himself with one hand on the back of the chair – and he hauls himself upright as soon as he can.

He brings the lamp over to the little table beside the bed and sits down. All of a sudden the springs are nearly in my face. I keep still, though, and listen to him huffing and puffing as he undresses. I think for a moment he might kneel to say his prayers, but I needn't have worried about that; he just gets into bed and turns down the wick of the lamp until the room is dark, 'cept for the moon-light.

I lay there some more until I hear his breathing get slower. When the snoring starts I ease myself out and slide across the floor to the coffin and feel about inside it with one arm. I soon touch something wrapped in cloth, and I lift it out. I sit crouched low and undo the cord that's tying up the parcel. Then, in the thin silvery light of the moon, I take a look at what I have in my hands. A bunch of pictures of naked women! They're in a studio, sitting on fancy chairs or some of them laying on a sheepskin rug, but none of them's wearing anything but stockings and garters, and all of them have saucy smiles on their faces!

My hands are shaking now, so it's hard for me to tie

the parcel up again, but I manage as best I can and put the bundle back where I found it. Then I lay down on my stomach and pull myself to where I think the door is. I feel for the handle and turn it real slow. Then I open the door and scoot out as fast as I can.

Leonard is already in bed when I get to my room, but he makes me start by saying, 'And where have you been, Isaac? Out with some floozy?'

I can tell by the way he says it he don't believe it, so I just get into bed without answering.

I couldn't get to sleep that night for thinking about what I'd just seen. The smell of Ida May, mixed with the smell of cigar smoke, stayed with me, and I could hear the old man's throaty laugh as he looked at those pictures. I was pretty darn certain by then that the Reverend was a fake. The money he was taking from people wasn't to save their souls, it was to make him rich, so's he could go to joy houses and meet girls – girls like Ida May that he said were sinners going straight to Hell.

I must have slept in the end, because I had a real bad dream where I came into a room and saw Ida May alive, but pinned down to a bed by the Reverend. I woke with a jolt to find I was being shaken by Leonard.

'Come on, no time to laze around in bed. It's a special day today – he's doing a mass baptism.'

The way he drawled it out I could tell he wasn't too eager to go himself. I was pleased, though; the Reverend had done a couple of these events since I'd been with him, and my services weren't normally required. The folk who came to be baptized had already made up their minds to seek the way of the Lord, so they didn't need me writhing around in the dirt to convince them. I still had to go along, though, as the Reverend expected a donation in exchange for his services, and he wanted us all to be there so that no newly redeemed soul missed a chance to be generous.

We set out bright and early. It was a beautiful June day and the sky was blue as Pa's eyes. It was warm, but there was a breeze moving the branches of the trees, so we could hear the leaves rustling by the side of the road as we went by. I sat at the front with Leonard and put my face up to the sun. I felt real happy, the way you do when the sun warms your bones. It's the way people are, I guess; we forget, sometimes, how life has treated us.

After we've been going for half an hour or so I begin to smell water, and as we get closer to the line of trees that hide the river from the road I see there are already people waiting patiently by the shore.

We don't need to unload the trestles and make up the stage, but Leonard takes the little table and a couple of chairs so Adeline can sit and collect money, and the Reverend will have somewhere to rest when he needs to. He tells me to help him lift out Ida May and her coffin, too. 'He reckons on fine days people are more likely to be tempted by sins of the flesh, so he thinks we should put the mummy on display to show what that can lead to. You can quite lose your taste for fornication if you see a sight like that.'

I'm quite happy to prop Ida May's coffin up against a tree and sit on the grass beside her, watching what goes on. I know it's foolish, but it feels good that she's outside, enjoying the sunshine, instead of being left in the dark, underneath the old man's bed.

The Reverend takes off his coat and shucks the braces off his shoulders. He begins his usual speech about renouncing the Devil while he's still walking down to the riverbank. He don't want to waste time. He gets all the waiting people to kneel and pray with him and then he wades into the shallows.

A young girl is first in line and she moves slowly through the water toward him. He mutters something to her while making the sign of the cross on her forehead with a finger and thumb. Then he quickly grasps her by the shoulder and dips her under. This is a risky thing to do: once she's down there the Reverend can't see her no more on account of the size of his gut, so she could be drowning for all he knows.

She seems happy enough, though. She comes up with water streaming down her face, but with a dazed expression, like she's in a trance. She stumbles back to the shore, and Leonard grabs a hold of her arm and hauls her back on dry land.

The Reverend's had plenty of practice at this, and the line goes down real quick. Soon as one is on the way back another starts out and passes him. I notice how he takes more time with the women, though, especially the pretty ones. He holds them down for longer, and keeps one hand on their backs and another on their bellies after they come up, like he's taking care they're steady on their feet before he lets them go.

On and on it goes, and I must doze off. I don't know how much time has passed before I sit up with a start.

Maybe I've had a bad dream, but something makes me sense trouble.

The line has gone down some, but the Reverend is still in the water and he's gotten so wet his under-vest is clinging to him, showing off his women's titties and the great dome of his stomach. Leonard is helping an old man out the water, and he keeps slipping where the grass has been churned up.

Something else catches my attention, though, and I turn my head sharply: a boy in cut-down overalls has brought a big brown and white cow to the opposite bank to drink. The boy's more interested in what's going on in the river, and ain't paying much attention to the beast. He's even let the rope trail in the water while he watches the proceedings.

Now that makes me feel real uneasy. The cow clearly don't like the commotion of all the people calling out 'Praise the Lord!' every time someone goes under the water. And some of them are getting real excited, too: holding their arms up and rolling their eyes Heaven-wards.

Meantime the cow is rolling its eye, too, and starting to paw at the water. This is shaping up bad, as far as I can see, but the boy don't seem to notice nothing amiss as he stands watching the Reverend baptize a pretty girl with a long pale braid.

The cow is still pawing at the water and all of a sudden it seems to sense me watching it, because it looks right at me. Now I don't know whether it really was Grandpa's curse caused it, but cows and McCrums are natural enemies – just like cats and mice – and as long as I live

I'll never like them. The way that cow looks at me I'm sure it knows, because before I can do anything it lowers its head, gives the water a final kick and charges straight at me, bellowing like it thinks the end of the world has come.

I look around, too scared to think straight. All I can see is amazed faces and all I can hear is a whole lot of splashing as people try to get clear of the beast. Then I see the Reverend, lurching toward me through the water, picking up his fat knees like it's real hard, a look of panic on his face. His chins are moving every which way, like he's a turkey running from the axe, and he's coming for me like his life depends on it. As he's between me and the cow, he's gotten a head start, and as he scrambles up the bank, his face as red as a beet, I can see a vein standing out on his neck like a rope.

At the last minute I make myself move, push Ida May's coffin over and throw myself on top of it. Then the light is blotted out by the bulk of the Reverend Cornelius Smith, flinging himself in his turn on top of me, and knocking all the breath from my body.

LEONARD RUNS AWAY

When I came around I was lying on a wooden floor and looking up at a yellowed ceiling. Just about every part of me was hurting, and when I raised my head I almost expected to see my body was quite flat, like poor Grandpa's after the stampede. I patted myself all over, groaning a bit, but found everything in the same place, and no bones broken.

It was only when I'd done prodding and poking myself that I realized I wasn't alone – there was a woman sobbing somewhere in the room. I looked up and saw Adeline and Leonard, sat on either side of the Reverend, who was laid out on the bed, his huge belly rising up from it like the moon over a cloud.

I got myself up off the floor, holding on to my back, and Adeline noticed me.

'Oh, Isaac, I was afraid you were dead, too! How are you feeling? Come and sit down.' And she tried to give me her own chair. I waved it away – apart from it being unmannerly to take a lady's seat, I was afraid if I sat down I'd never be able to haul myself upright again.

'What happened?' I asked her, my voice coming out in a feeble croak.

'Don't you remember? Father was a hero – and so were you. A cow got loose and stampeded across the river and you both flung yourselves on top of the mummy, to protect it. Although Father may have been trying to protect you, I suppose.' Leonard snorted at this, and Adeline gave him a perplexed look. 'I'm so glad you're alive, Isaac. But why did you do it – risk your life for someone who was already dead?'

'He's an idiot, that's why.' Leonard spared me from having to answer her. 'More to the point, why did Father do it? I know she's good for business and so is he,' he nodded in my direction, 'but he could have found another mummy. It wasn't worth dying for.'

'I guess it was just chivalry.' Adeline started crying again. 'It was his natural instinct to protect other creatures.'

I saw the look on Leonard's face: he didn't believe that for a moment. He was right, of course – what the Reverend was protecting was his reputation. If the cow had broken up Ida May's coffin then the whole congregation of pious folks would have seen his photographs of naked ladies – and seen that he kept them underneath the body of a dead woman. It wasn't a pretty picture, and it wasn't likely to have helped his ministry none. Then I realized I couldn't see Ida May anywhere. I looked all round the room, but there was no sign of her. 'Where is she?'

Adeline knew who I meant. 'It's all right, Isaac, she's safe. You managed to shield her, otherwise Father might have crushed her. The cow that was the cause of it all didn't do any actual damage. It jumped clean over you and charged off into the woods, with the boy who should have been taking care of it running after, cursing in the most profane manner.'

'So how did . . . ?'

'The doctor thought it was his heart. The years of appearances take their toll, even on one so strong.'

Leonard snorted again, and this time Adeline didn't let it pass.

'Pray tell me you mean by that, Leonard.'

'Come on, Addie, you must know as well as I do that it wasn't so much the appearances were to blame as all the food he ate, and the liquor he took, and the cigars he smoked.'

We buried the Reverend the next day, though it wasn't easy. It took two men to dig the hole, as it had to be twice the size of a regular grave. Then there was carrying the coffin. Six men would be enough, in the general way of things, but Leonard reckoned on ten, of which two was to be me and him. Course he had to pay the others, and the easiest place to find a bunch of fellas with nothing better to do is the saloon. Consequently, the other eight weren't as sober as they might of been, and I ain't too sure Leonard didn't have a couple of glasses to oil his wheels, neither.

So we weren't the most impressive funeral procession you ever saw. We got the Reverend off the bed and into the casket by way of a couple of ropes we passed underneath him and used to roll him over, then we pushed and pulled it out the room and down the stairs, bruising a few shins on the way. Lifting the thing was another matter. Trouble was, although he was uncommon fat, the Reverend wasn't uncommon tall, so the coffin was no longer than most, just wider and deeper, and there wasn't enough space for the ten of us needed to carry it. There was a fair amount of jostling and pushing going on, along with some cussing.

In the end we got the box up onto our shoulders, but of course Leonard hadn't been able to pick and choose who would do the job for him – he just took the ones that were willing, so they were all different heights. The darn coffin was rolling like a rowboat in a storm as we staggered toward the graveyard, and I was feeling like any minute we were all going to fall down under the weight of the Reverend, so's he'd get to squash me proper this time. I could hear a humming in my ears, and was wondering whether Leonard remembered that my fits were for real, and had thought what would happen iffen I had one now, when I realized the noise was coming from the rough-looking fella in front of me trying out a hymn.

Then I heard a splintering sound. I ducked my head to look under the coffin and saw a sharp piece of wood sticking down – and what looked like breeches material. The coffin bottom was giving way.

I tried to attract Leonard's attention, but he was right out in front and he couldn't hear me over the noise of the fella who was humming.

'Leonard,' I hissed, 'Leonard!' And then when that didn't work I muttered to the fella in front, 'Why don't you quieten down for a minute?'

He gave me a dirty look over his shoulder and carried on. 'I mean it! Quit that noise!'

'I can't,' he said out the side of his mouth. 'He's paying me to do it.'

'Paying you?'

'Yep. Said he wanted me to sing a hymn, but I ain't never had much of a memory for words, so I was just doing the tune.'

'Well, I need you to pass the message up to him that we gotta start moving quicker. The coffin ain't gonna hold – it's coming apart.'

Well, this time he did quit the humming, and he must've managed to get word to Leonard, because we began to shuffle faster. There was another crack from the coffin, and we broke into a trot. I was sweating like a hog, and it was running down into my eyes so's I could hardly see. Iffen one of us were to stumble I reckon we'd've had it, and the Reverend would've ended up in the dirt midst a pile of splinters.

Then all of a sudden we stopped, although of course the ones in front stopped first, and the rest of us banged into them. We might every one of us have ended up in the grave, but as it was we kind of shot the coffin into it. There was some awful cracking sounds, but it just about held, so poor Addie had something to throw some flowers onto.

Course, there was a good deal of moaning and complaining going on from the fellas who'd carried the coffin, and Leonard had to give them all a little extra for their trouble. Then we three went back with our landlady to her house, with a few of the people whom the Reverend had just baptized following us.

I couldn't help but mark that Adeline didn't look as upset as I'd expected her to be: her cheeks were much pinker than usual, and her eyes were sparkling. Maybe it was the running to the grave did it, but she seemed quite refreshed by the experience.

The following day I'm laying in bed, dreaming like I oftentimes do that Ida May is still alive, when I'm woken by a fearful shrieking.

'He's gone! He's gone!'

The next thing, Adeline comes running into my room in her night gown, her hair tied up in curling rags, waving a piece of paper in the air.

Now I wouldn't generally let a lady see me in my nightclothes, but the state she's in I reckon Adeline won't notice, so I get out of bed and I'm quickly pulling on my pants when the landlady appears, carrying a warming pan and giving me a stare that tells me she thinks I'm responsible for all this ruckus.

I own it must look bad, what with Adeline and me both being not properly dressed and her screaming fit to raise the roof and all, and I put my hands up over my head ready for the blow. Lucky for me Addie's holding up that paper so's you can't hardly miss it, because the landlady sees pretty quick that it, not me, is the root of the trouble and tries to get it off her. When I realize the danger has passed, I join in, and we're both jumping about after her like she's a dog that's stole some meat, until the old lady grabs hold of it and reads out what it says.

> *'Dearest Sister,*
>
> *I know you will be unhappy with my decision, but I am leaving without you. We have both spent our whole lives in the service of our father, who led us to believe that his life was dedicated to serving the Lord. Although you may not believe me, I think we were misled, Addie. His death has freed us, and we should make the most of this opportunity. I have taken the mummy, as I may be able to make use of it, and half the money in his strongbox, and left the rest for you. He has a good deal more in a bank in Tucson. I think you will be surprised by what you find there. I suggest you seek out our cousin O'Neill back in Tucson and bide with him and his family for a while.*
>
> *I beg you not to judge me too harshly.*
> *Your loving Brother,*
> *Leonard F. Smith.'*

When the landlady finishes reading, she lowers the letter and looks at Adeline.

'I am sorry, my dear. Whatever will you do now?'

At this Adeline commences to wailing again, and sags down onto my bed. I ain't sure what I'm supposed to do. Whenever Ida May was feeling bad about something she'd be sure and start throwing things. She did that a fair deal anyhow, but being upset seemed to sharpen her aim, so I used to try my best to keep out of her way. I don't recall ever seeing Ma cry, even when Pa and Neighbour Gustafson died.

It's fortunate the landlady is a motherly sort, and she sets down the warming pan and puts an arm around Addie's shoulders.

'There, there. At least he hasn't left you penniless. And there's a good deal a young woman of fortune can do in this world.'

I HEAR MORE ABOUT MY
CAREER AS AN OUTLAW

———◦◦◦———

*T*hat was the time in my life when I had the biggest decision to make: should I try to follow Leonard and somehow get Ida May away from him, or should I stay and look after Addie? Ever since I'd died – or not died, I suppose – my mission had been to get Ida May back and give her a decent burial, and I wasn't about to abandon her altogether – but then Addie had lost her Pa and been deserted by her brother.

Maybe I made the wrong choice, to get the living woman safely to her cousin's house and then go looking for the dead one, but iffen I'd've done it different I'm pretty sure I'd never have ended up here, surrounded by all these books, a respected citizen.

The first thing I did was pack our bags and settle with the landlady. She didn't look none too pleased to be sending poor Adeline off with just me for company, but I think she was relieved we were going. The Reverend Smith and his family had created altogether too much fuss in her town.

On the train Addie just sat looking out the window, sniffing from time to time. I kept watching her, on account of being nervous she might burst out with the weeping and wailing again, but after a while she fell asleep. Just as I was giving in to sleep too I heard shouting and the train came to a stop, shuddering, like she was protesting. There was more noise from up front and I heard a pistol being discharged. I didn't hear a body fall, though, so I reckoned it was a warning shot.

Adeline had woken up when the train stopped moving, and now she was looking around her, sleepy still.

'What? Why have we stopped? Are we at a station?'

'Not sure. It's most likely cows on the line,' I said, trying to sound like I knew what was happening.

A whiskery old gent sitting opposite to us was having none of it.

'Now, I don't want to scare you, miss, but I reckon it's a robbery. Happen all the time round these parts.' And he sat back and folded his arms as if he'd just told us he thought it might rain soon enough.

Adeline clutched my arm and looked at me with wide eyes.

'Don't you worry,' I said to her, 'they may not try to rob the passengers.' Now I don't think I was imagining it, but it seemed to me that Adeline was disappointed. I do believe she may have been looking forward to meeting some real outlaws.

After a while of waiting, the train jerked forward again and we moved slowly off. Everyone had been real quiet, but now talking burst out all around. The whiskery gent leaned forward and said to Adeline and me, 'I've been robbed four times, you know. Twice by that ruffian, Wilbur McCrum.'

I was hoping my face didn't betray me as I looked at Adeline, who was frowning and saying, as if to herself, 'Wilbur McCrum – don't I know that name from somewhere?'

'No doubt you've read about him in the newspapers, miss. He's notorious throughout the West. He's robbed trains, banks, even the fancier hotels – although I believe he started out with stages.'

'My! How does he manage to keep escaping, do you suppose?'

'Well, that's just it, miss. The posse *did* catch up with him one time – it was in the little town of Vacanegra, and they shot him dead.'

Adeline gasped and put her hand to her throat.

'And that's not all – they *drowned* the fella, too. He fell into the well, they fished him out and took him to the undertaker's and . . .' He paused for effect. 'He *disappeared*!'

'Disappeared? But how could that be? Dead men don't walk.'

'That's the question everyone in Vacanegra was asking themselves, especially the poor undertaker. I heard it drove him mad, trying to figure it out.'

I'd been sitting lower and lower in my seat, afraid he was going to mention Ida May, and that Adeline would make the connection with the mummy her father had been carrying around with him for so long. When I heard about poor George, though, I couldn't help but sit up and take notice.

'The undertaker went mad, you say?'

'So I heard. Poor fella just couldn't explain it. In all his years in the business he'd never once lost a body. Guess he felt he'd failed.'

'But surely some of his friends might just have come and stolen the body away, so they could bury him theirselves?'

'Well, that might seem the rational explanation,' and he dropped his voice, making Adeline lean forward in her seat, 'except there was no sign of a break-in, and most important of all, McCrum was *seen* slipping through the back of the lots, under cover of darkness. That fella rose from the dead, and you have to ask yourself – what kind of a person can do that?'

Adeline couldn't speak at first, but after a moment or two she whispered, 'Do you mean he was *a spirit from the underworld?*'

'Well, I couldn't take it upon myself to say, and I don't know any more than the next man about religion, but how else would he have escaped like that, and been able to go back to robbing, if he was just an ordinary man? And another thing – every time he pops up he looks different. One time I saw him, when he held up a train on this very line, and he was a tall, swarthy fella, another time he was fair, yet others will tell you he's short and fat, has ginger whiskers or a wooden leg. Some even say he's part Injun. There's only so much you can do with a disguise. Maybe he can really change his appearance.' And he sat back and folded his arms, looking well satisfied.

Adeline was a good audience for him, and I reckon she'd forgotten her disappointment at not being robbed herself. For the rest of the journey she prattled on about how dangerous the West was, and how she'd never realized while her dear Pa was sheltering her from all the villainy around her.

I let her talk. Truth to tell, I was glad of the chance to sit back and think some. I didn't like hearing stories about Wilbur McCrum, the outlaw, and I couldn't figure quite how they came about. I could see a body disappearing from an undertaker's would be likely to cause a stir, but why'd they think *I* was the one robbing all those banks and trains? Seemed to me there was a whole army of fellas out there taking other folks' money and not getting caught because people were willing to believe I'd risen from the dead.

Looked at another way, though, it might be a good thing. Isaac Boot wasn't robbing no one; he'd been working in a saloon, for a freak show and a preacher. A whole bunch of people got to see him and most of them would agree he wasn't capable of a robbery, even iffen he was to try. The only thing I didn't like was that Junior might get to hear about it. I didn't know what Lady M would've told him about his Pa, but iffen he knew my real name I didn't want him to grow up believing I was a bad man.

I GO ON MY WAY

*A*nyhow, after I'd accompanied Adeline to her cousin's, I had no real reason to stay. So, soon as I could, I put my bag over my shoulder and said my farewells. Addie cried, of course. She'd dried up before our journey to Tucson, but me going started her off again. I thought it best to leave her to Cousin O'Neill's wife and trust that she'd stop the howling once I was gone.

But where was I going *to*? I wanted to find Leonard and Ida May, but where should I start? I'd guessed that he'd taken Ida May with him because he wanted to sell her to a freak show, but what if he decided to keep her? He'd said he didn't have his Pa's calling, but once he'd seen how much money his Pa had saved up he must've realized that the kind of calling his Pa had was nothing but a sham. Perhaps he'd try his hand at preaching after all. Either way, finding him would be nigh on impossible.

First thing, I supposed, was to get me a job and some money. I was lucky to have spent that time with Mr Jenkins, as it meant I knew a fair bit about the black-smith's trade. Every town needs a smithy, and they don't just shoe horses – they can make railings, birdcages, pretty much anything out of metal. Ida May had reckoned a smithy was as close as you can get to Hell on earth, but I liked it. The heat and the noise suited me just fine on account of it stopped me from thinking about anything but the job I was doing, and there were times in those years when I'd've been quite content to settle down and spend the rest of my days blowing the bellows on hot coals or plunging glowing horseshoes into cold water.

Then I had to remind myself that I'd got responsibilities. It wasn't just me I had to think about, it was Ida May and Junior, too, and iffen I ever told myself it was too late for Ida May, that she was gone, I turned my thoughts to Junior. He wouldn't remember his Ma, but he had a right to know where she was buried, to have somewhere he could go and think about her, lay flowers if he wanted. So I made a vow: any time I found myself growing too contented in a place I'd pack my bags and move on, make myself uncomfortable so's I'd remember what I had to do.

That meant I spent a lot of time travelling, sleeping where I could, rolled up in a blanket under the stars when the weather was warm enough. I managed to find me a job in all manner of places, big and small. In Prescott I was even in charge for a while when the blacksmith came down with a case of the shakes, which is a real bad thing in that line of work.

I found that as I got older I got fewer fits, and that was a great help to me, for the fits frightened people and lost me a few jobs. Part of it was maybe being less afraid of them myself. When I was a boy I was always scared I'd have a fit and the other children in school would laugh at me, and Jonny Rose would torment me, and the more scared I was, the more likely I'd get one. As I'd gotten used to them, seen them as part of me, they grew further and further apart, till they scarcely bothered me at all.

THE CHURCH OF THE RISEN
AND FALLING CHRIST

Of course, partly on account of needing to find Ida May and partly on account of my vow never to get too comfortable anywhere, life wasn't exactly easy, and I had my down days like anybody else; liquor didn't make me feel better, but it did make me care less about what happened to me. On one of the days I was feeling real low I staggered out the saloon where I'd spent all the evening – and a fair bit of my week's wages – and couldn't remember the way back to my lodgings.

I walked about, paying no heed at all to where I was headed, twice knocking into passers-by, nearly getting into a fight with one of them over it. In the end I got so tired I just keeled over, as if I'd been buffaloed. I don't know whether I drifted into sleep or had a fit, but the next thing I remember is hearing singing, and when I opened my eyes I could see beautiful colours, shining on me like they were coming from the sky. I can picture it now.

Well, I've said before that I'm not one for religion, and my time with the Reverend Cornelius Smith has done nothing to change that, but for a moment there I do wonder whether I've died and gone to Heaven. Of course, when my head clears some I realize the colours are spilling out from a window in the building I'm laying beside. The singing is coming from there too, so I guess it must be a church or a chapel of some sort.

I haul myself to my feet and go to have a look. The double doors are heavy, but they open when I push, and inside I can see rows of wooden chairs on each side of the room, with a gap in the middle to walk down. There's a space at the front where I guess the preacher stands, but there's no one there now. It ain't a big place, and I reckon there's no more than about twenty people in there. I'd duck out again, but a woman sitting at the back turns around and smiles at me, and beckons me to sit beside her. Not wanting to be unmannerly, I slip in and do as I'm bid.

I don't recognize the hymn they're singing, and they seem to know it by heart, so there's no hymn sheet for me to read from. I don't mind; I've never had much of a voice, and I'm content just to listen to them. It's warm in here, from all the bodies, and I'm nearly lulled to sleep again. Then they stop, and a fella gets to his feet and walks to the front. At first I figure he must be the preacher, but he's dressed no different from the other fellas – an ordinary shirt and pants, working man's clothes – and I decide I'm wrong; he's just a member of the congregation. He stands there for a moment with his arms out in front of him, palms up, and his eyes raised, like he's looking to the Lord for inspiration, then he begins to speak.

'Last night I fell down, and as I lay on the ground I had a vision.'

A man over to my right calls out, 'And what did you see, brother?'

'I saw a world where peace reigned, where men and women went about their daily business with love in their hearts, where strife and conflict were unknown. And I awoke from my trance with this vision in my mind and I felt a great contentment – until I recalled what this world is truly like, how man pits himself against his brother, how covetousness and lust and anger rule our hearts. I ask you now, need it be so? If we live our lives as the people did in my vision, can we not persuade others to do the same? Let us pray now, for the strength to live that righteous life, that others may learn by our example.'

Now, I may not have seen the inside of a church too often, but I do know that the usual way to pray is to kneel down, or just bow your head. What these folk do is altogether different: they shuffle about, some of them go to the front, and then they fall on the ground. Every last one of them, man and woman, goes down and begins to writhe around, some of them muttering, some crying. Eyes roll back in their heads, hands are raised to the ceiling. Iffen I'd just walked in then and not seen what happened before I might've thought they'd all eaten something bad, and been poisoned by it.

Well, you can guess the effect all this rolling around on the floor has on me: before I know it I've joined them. When I wake up I can see boots. Everyone else is back in their seats, and the woman who invited me in is smiling down on me like she's a proud mother and I'm her boy who's just done something real clever. Hands reach from all around to help me to my feet again. I feel awkward about having a fit in front of a bunch of strangers, but when I look about me I can see that *everyone* seems to be smiling, like they're pleased with me. The fella who told us about his dream is still standing at the front, and he speaks.

'Brother, it seems you are one of us. You were drawn to our little community because you belong here. Please, join me.' He beckons me to come stand by him.

'Our numbers are small, but I believe that as time goes on, more people will come, and our message will be heeded by all the Christian world.'

The liquor I've drunk and the effects of the fit are making it hard for me to think straight. I narrow my eyes as I look at him, as if that will help. 'What message would that be, sir?'

He don't seem riled by my question. 'The Bible speaks of the Second Coming, and it is our belief that our Saviour has already returned. We believe he was reborn right here, in our own country, but sadly, just as before, we sinners failed to recognize him. Just as before, he fought the moneylenders and the Pharisees, but, this world being different than the one he was born into the first time, he had to fight them differently.'

A grey-haired woman in the front row carries on the story. 'He did it by robbing banks. He was born into a humble family, and he wanted to help the poor people who didn't have enough food to get them through the winter.'

A girl with long braids says, 'And he gave them all potatoes. Instead of loaves and fishes.'

I begin to feel a prickling under my skin.

'But people didn't understand,' says a young fella. 'They treated him like a criminal.'

The woman who called me in finishes off the story. 'This time, they didn't crucify him, they killed him the way they do it here: they shot him. But, just as before, he rose again. Because Our Lord wanted to show his sympathy for his suffering people, he made His son afflicted with fits, so we worship him in our own special way, here, in *the Church of the Risen and Falling Christ*.' She turns to look up at the window behind her and my eyes follow her gaze. What I see is a picture, in coloured glass, of a man – a small man, his arms outstretched and each hand holding a potato. The hair is an unreal kind of golden colour, but they've gotten the squint off real good.

I stare up at that window and my knees give out, making me sink to the ground. Of course, when I do that the whole congregation follows. Then I fall sideways in another fit, and the last thing I see is a whole bunch of legs, kicking and bucking like trussed-up steers.

I'm so tuckered out when I wake again that I just want to lie down and sleep – anywhere would do me – but the church folks don't want to let me go. They're getting a mite too excited by my fits for my liking. The fella who talked about his dream says, 'Few people who enter our church are moved by the spirit as immediately as you were. I truly believe you have been sent here, brother. Will you join us?'

There's a part of me wants to do just that. It's a long time since I've felt like I belong anywhere, and it would be kind of comforting to join them. But my head's spinning like I've been hit with a log. 'I'm real tired,' I say, 'I need to go and lay me down for a while.'

'The church has its own house, not far from here. You are most welcome to come and break bread with us and then rest.'

The thought of having the same roof over my head every day, a warm bed to sleep in and food on the table! I know I can't do it, though.

I have to get out of there before one of them takes a real good look at me and wonders iffen they've seen me somewhere before. I sure am glad I've let my whiskers grow, as they cover so much of my face. I can't hide my eyes, though, so I do my best to look at the floor the whole time, worried someone might notice my squint, add it to my fits and the general look of me, and realize who I am.

Iffen that happens it seems to me one of two things will follow: these good people will see that their whole religion is based on a lie and they'll lose their reason for living; or they'll think I truly am their risen Lord and follow me around, expecting miracles and the like, and being disappointed when I can't provide them.

And either way, how long would it be before word got out that the stories about Wilbur McCrum being still alive ain't just stories? The posse would be after me a second time and the members of the Church of the Risen and Falling Christ would see their Saviour shot or hauled off to jail to be hung. I decide to leave them with their belief that one day there'll be a better world where Christ could be born again and not get killed this time.

I have to think quick. 'That's mighty kind of you,' I

say, 'but my landlady will be expecting me tonight. She's fretful, and I wouldn't want to worry her. I'll go collect my things and I'll be back here tomorrow.'

I think maybe one of them will say they'll come with me, but I guess they're the trusting sort, because they let me go easily enough, smiling and patting me on the back, then walking me to the door and waving me off. I feel bad leaving them like that, but I know I have to do it.

TWELVE TREES

⟞⟝⟞⟝⟞

I'd sobered up by then and remembered where I was staying, so I went back there and packed my things. I took some bread and cheese from the kitchen, left some money on the table and walked out of town in the dark.

I wasn't afraid of the dark no more. Oftentimes it brought Sophia to mind, how her Ma let her come out to play at night. I didn't think of wolves or wild cats, neither. After that wolf left me alone when I ran away from the Reillys' I decided I'd nothing to fear from them. I still kept clear of cows as much as I could, but I'd come to realize it was other men who were most likely to do me harm.

I walked for five days and nights, sleeping in the woods, and once in an abandoned cabin whose roof had fallen in, to keep out the way of any road agents who might be about. I ate what I'd taken from my landlady's kitchen and drank from streams and puddles. I stopped off in two small towns just long enough to buy a little food, then went on my way again.

On the sixth day I was beginning to tire. It had been a dry spring and every breath of wind was stirring up the dust until it coated my clothes and got in my hair, beard – even my mouth. I'd had enough and I was ready to rest up, when I saw a settlement ahead. Maybe it was on account of the way I was feeling, but as I drew nearer it struck me as one of the prettiest little towns I'd ever seen. There was a pond with a few geese swimming on it and trees all around, and beside the pond was a wooden sign saying *Welcome to Twelve Trees, pop. 193.* Beyond that I could see a street of houses and stores with a boardwalk running down either side. There were people and a couple of tethered horses, but I couldn't see no cows. I decided right then that they'd need to change that sign to read *pop. 194,* leastways till my vow forced me to move on.

As I walk past the pond and into the town a young boy of seven or eight runs by me, chasing a small brown and white dog. I call out to him, but he waits until he's caught up with the dog and scooped it into his arms before coming back to me.

'I'm looking for somewhere to stay in town. Would you happen to know of anybody who's taking in paying guests?' I reckon a hotel would be too expensive for me; I have to save as much money as I can, until I find myself some work.

'Sure do. My Ma's got rooms she hires out. If you come with me and Wilbur I'll take you to see her.'

'Wilbur' must be the dog that's now squirming in his arms; it gives me a shock to hear my real name again.

I follow the boy along the street until he turns left. The town is bigger than I'd thought. He says his name is Arthur – Art for short – and as we walk he tells me, 'It's called Twelve Trees, but there's a lot more than twelve trees here. I reckon whoever named the town couldn't count no further than twelve, so that's when he stopped. I've tried counting them all, but something else more interesting to do usually comes along, so I quit. Ain't never reached the end yet, and I suppose they're planting new ones now and again, so I don't reckon I'll ever get to the end of 'em . . .'

There's more of this, but as he walks fast and he's ahead of me the whole time, and Wilbur the dog is whining and yapping, I don't hear it all. Before long we arrive at a two-storey house with flowers growing outside. A woman appears and takes the dog from Arthur. Then she notices me. 'Why, Arthur, who's this?' She's small and brown-haired. I don't know whether you'd call her pretty – I'm not much of a judge of these things – but she sure has a pretty smile, with dimples in both cheeks.

'Dunno,' Arthur says, 'but he's just arrived in town and he needs a place to stay, so I said you'd fix him up.'

'If that's convenient, ma'am. My name's Boot, Isaac Boot. I've been on the road for some time now and I figure I might stay here awhile.'

'Well, I'm Mrs Graham, Arthur's mother, and you're welcome to look at the room, Mr Boot. Our last guest had to go back east when his father died, and that was nearly a month past. We've missed the company. I believe it's good for Arthur to have a man to talk to.' Then she lowers her voice. 'His father passed on two years ago and since then he's rather run wild, I'm afraid,' and she gives me another of her pretty smiles. I have to say, iffen I was the sort of man who could change his affections the way you might change horses, then I might be tempted to court Arthur's mother. But my heart belongs to Ida May.

The room is big – although when you've slept in places as small as a manger and as big as the open prairie, you don't generally mind such things. There's glass in the windows and a quilt on the bed, and the floor looks swept and clean. Even living with a dog called Wilbur could be a good thing, as I'll get to hear my own name all the time and grow accustomed to ignoring it.

Later, over a dinner of pork and beans, we fall to talking about what work I might find around these parts.

'If you don't mind me saying, Mr Boot, you don't look like labouring work would suit you.'

'You're right, I ain't so big, but I have worked for blacksmiths before now, and I know a fair bit about shoeing and general iron work.'

'Our smith's got an apprentice – he ain't looking for another,' Arthur cuts in.

'That's true, I'm afraid, but there are several stores in town, and you might find something there, if you're good at reckoning up.'

'What about old George? How's your reading, Mr Boot?'

'Arthur! I'll trouble you not to be so impertinent! Please don't mind him, sir. As I told you, he lacks a firm hand.'

'Well, I *do* like to read, ma'am, as a matter of fact. I like it very well, but I don't have much opportunity to read books, mostly just newspapers. Why did you ask me that, son?'

'Because old George is stone blind and has a whole bunch of books in his house that he can't read no more, on account of his affliction. He's been asking around iffen anyone would come up and read them to him. He'd pay, and I reckon he's rich, else how would he have been able to buy all them books?'

'That's true,' says his mother, smiling. 'The poor man kept on reading with the aid of a magnifying glass for as long as he could – that may have made his eyes fade all the sooner – but since he lost his sight altogether he's been trying to find someone who'll be his eyes for him.'

'And there's no one round here will do it?'

'Half the men in this town can't read much more than their own names, and those that can don't consider reading a proper occupation. There may be ladies able to do it, but of course, it wouldn't be decent for a lady to spend her days alone with a man.'

'Well, I always liked to read. My Ma said it kept me quiet, stopped me having fits.' I hadn't meant to mention my fits, but I suppose it's better for them to know, in case I should get one in front of them.

'You have fits?' Arthur's eyes are bright as he looks at me.

'Arthur!'

I feel uncomfortable now. 'Sometimes I do. Though not as often as I did when I was your age. It generally happens when I get excited or upset. But there's no need to be frightened by them; if you leave me be I'll come out of it soon enough.'

I look at Mrs Graham, but she don't seem too troubled by the idea.

'Iffen you don't object, ma'am, maybe Arthur could take me to see the gentleman tomorrow?'

I MEET AN OLD FRIEND

‒‒‒‒ ⚬ ‒‒‒‒

The next morning Arthur was keen to introduce me to
the blind man, so we started out early. The house we
were looking for was at the end of its street, set back a
bit with a picket fence around it. It was clapboard that
had been whitewashed, but clearly not for some time, and
the grey wood showed through all over. The grass had
seen better days, too: it was overgrown and full of weeds.
As we walked up the steps to the door one of them gave
a groan like a man in pain.

Art rapped on the door with his knuckles, but I reckon
the creaking step was all that was needed to warn whoever lived there he had company. Art didn't wait around,
just opened the latch and went straight in. It was dark
inside; it being the house of a blind man, he had no need
of lamps.

I could see a figure moving in what I guessed must be
the front parlour, but there wasn't enough light to make
him out clearly – until he walked toward us, raising his
face up a little, the way blind people often do, and using
a cane held out in front of him, to tap against the
furniture, and be certain he could steer a clear path. His

hair was white, and stood out from his head like wisps of cloud on a July day; his eyes were milky and blank. I knew him straight away, however much he'd changed since he took the pennies off of my own eyes and they snapped open and saw him for the first time: George Beauchamp, the Vacanegra undertaker.

Well, I was so startled by the sight of him I felt a fit coming on, so I turned right round and walked outside again, sitting down on the front porch with my head between my knees. Now of course that brought Art out too, hollering after me, 'What's the matter, Mr Boot? You changed your mind 'bout the job?'

I couldn't answer him for a while, I was so busy trying not to give in to the darkness.

When I felt able I turned round to see Art standing in the doorway with George right behind, his hand on the boy's shoulder, looking bewildered.

'I just felt a little nauseous there, for a moment, but it seems to have passed. I'm sorry to act this way, sir, the first time we meet.'

'Think nothing of it, son,' George said, turning his head toward the sound of my voice.

'I hope it weren't Ma's cooking done that to you. She's pretty good as a rule. Never known her poison nobody yet.'

'Oh, no. It's nothing like that. I suffer from a nervous stomach, is all.' My voice was still shaky from the shock of seeing George again, but I hoped they'd just think it was on account of feeling sick.

'Let me get you a glass of water,' says George, making his way back into the house.

I get up, and Art and me follow him. George returns with the water, then leads us into the room where we'd first seen him.

'I dare say it's a bit gloomy. This place always used to need some extra light. There should be an oil lamp on the table and some lucifers in a box on the mantelpiece.'

Art goes and gets the brass box and sets about trying to get the lamp alight. Maybe the wick's damp, but it smoulders some and makes him cough. Still, it lights up the room, and then I can hardly believe what I see. From floor to ceiling along three of the walls there are book-shelves. On the other wall there are smaller shelves between the windows. And every one of those shelves is full of books. In some places they're even lying on their sides on top of the others. In my whole life I've never seen that many, let alone all in one place.

'Quite something, aren't they?' George is smiling fit to bust his face, as if he can see them still. 'Since my wife died, my books have been my only consolation. I had a good number before, but out of deference to her I tried my best not to take over the whole house. Since then I'm afraid I've let my passion run away with me. I order directly from booksellers in New York, Chicago – even London.'

London! I take down a fat volume and open it. Inside the cover, the paper is as fancy as any I've ever seen, patterned like feathers in dark red, with lines of white, yellow and blue.

'We were never blessed with children, you see. *These* are my children. I've had a good life, on the whole, but the greatest cruelty I've suffered, apart from the loss of my Josephine, has been the loss of my sight, and with it the ability to escape into all these different worlds,' and he waves his arm around the room.

Art sees his chance. 'Well, that's just what we've come about, Mr B. This gentleman I've brought to see you is Mr Isaac Boot. He's Ma's latest lodger, and he's a man of letters. He's looking for work, you're looking for someone to read to you – seemed only right to get you two together.'

I hardly fit the description of 'man of letters', but I don't want to call Art a liar, so I just say, 'I like reading, but I ain't seen many books since I was at school. Iffen you'll give me a try I'd like to work for you, sir.'

'Excellent! I don't mind telling you I've been going a little mad these past few months. Aside from the occasional visit from friends like young Art here, my only company is Mrs Temperley, my housekeeper, and although she's a good woman, she doesn't hold with reading any book but the Bible – which is fine, in its way, but a little restricting for me. I've spent most evenings this past winter listening to Mrs Temperley doing her best to save my immortal soul! Now, why don't you read something to me, and we'll see how we get on.' And George feels his way to an old brocade armchair and sits down like he's expecting to be entertained.

I perch on a bentwood chair and turn some more pages, past some pictures, a list of contents, some notes, to a page where it says *The Adventures of Oliver Twist* and the story begins.

'*"Among other public buildings in a certain town, which for many reasons it will be prudent to refrain from mentioning, and to which I will assign a fictitious name, there is one anciently common to most towns, great or small: to wit, a workhouse . . ."*'

I haven't even gotten to the end of the first sentence and I've already stumbled over 'fictitious' and 'anciently'. It feels like it ain't going too well, but George don't ask me to stop, so I carry on till the end of the chapter, which I'm glad to see ain't very long. When I get there I look up, and see George is still smiling, both hands holding on to his cane, leaning forward as if to hear all the better. Then I glance at Art, who's squirming on his chair.

'Will that do, Mr B? Only Ma said I was to go to school directly I'd brought Mr Boot to see you.'

'It'll do just fine, son.'

'But there were so many words I didn't understand . . .'

'Nobody's perfect. If I haven't learned that lesson in my unnecessarily long life then I've surely wasted my time on earth. If you're willing to acquire some new vocabulary, then I'll be only too happy to teach you, in return for your services – along with your remuneration, of course. When can you start?'

ISAAC BOOT, READER

⬥

$\mathcal{I}$t ain't until Art and me have gone down the front steps of George's house that the peculiar nature of what's just happened begins to sink in. I feel my legs give, and I sit down again right there and then in the dirt. Art raises his eyes Heavenward; I've a feeling he's getting to be a might sorry our paths ever crossed.

'You still feeling sick, Mr Boot? Will I go and see iffen I can borrow a cart to get you home in?'

'I'll be fine, son. I think my journey here's taken its toll of me, is all. A night or two of rest should see me right.' Art gets a hold of me under my arm and helps haul me to my feet and we go on our way, me a bit unsteady and leaning on him some for support.

I'm finding it hard to catch up with myself. Meeting with George again has given me a shock the like of which would've sent me into a fit for sure when I was a young man. George ain't by any means an uncommon name, so I'd no reason to suspicion that this George might be the same one I'd known back in Vacanegra. Iffen he hadn't gone blind since, where would I be now? Residing in the jailhouse, I guess. Or maybe he wouldn't have recognized me: I'm a good deal older, and I must look different walking about and talking to how I did when I was laying still in a casket.

It rained a little during the night, and as I walked to George's house the next morning the ground was still damp and the air smelt fresh. I was feeling good about going to work for George. It should've felt stranger than it did, being as how the last time he'd seen me I was laid in a casket and he was the one laid me out, but that was then and this was now. George had stopped being some-one in my past and I was getting acquainted with the new George, while he got acquainted with Isaac Boot, a living man who was going to read to him every day, and who had nothing to do with a dead outlaw called Wilbur McCrum.

Not that I was too sure about that any more. Was I Wilbur McCrum or Isaac Boot? I didn't live like Wilbur anymore: I hadn't robbed a stage or a bank for years, nor hidden out in a hut or a cave. Nowadays I ate and dressed at regular times and I had the kind of job a man might have who'd been to college and was real smart. Didn't look like Wilbur, neither, with my grey hair and my whiskers hiding my chin. The only thing the same was my eyes, and even they looked different now I was older: my squint was less obvious, maybe on account of the lines, and the way my lids drooped more.

After we stopped reading, George asked me to stay for supper. I couldn't very well say no to him, but I began to feel a little antsy. What iffen he was to start questioning me about my past? He had a right to know something about me, given I was going to be sitting in his house every day, looking around at what he'd got, with only his housekeeper to stop me stealing from him.

I said I'd have to go back to my lodgings first, just to tell Mrs Graham I wouldn't be eating there, and that gave me a little time to get things straight in my head. I reckoned I could tell the truth about my early years, as George wouldn't know anything about Wilbur when he was a child; I could even say I'd worked in the circus, just as a barker or a roustabout, instead of a freak. As long as I kept quiet about the lawbreaking and said nothing about fits I should be all right. The West was full of people who'd come from other parts of the country – other parts of the world, and done other things before. I wasn't the only one wanted to keep his past in the past.

By the time I came back in the evening I felt better prepared to face George and any questions he might put to me. I had to remember, as well, that I wasn't supposed to know anything about him, apart from that his wife had died and that he hadn't always been blind. I'd need to do some asking, too.

Evidently Mrs Temperley wasn't pleased to see me – she banged a dish of potatoes down so hard on the table I was surprised it didn't crack, giving me a hard stare while she did it. As soon as she left the room George said, 'You mustn't mind Mrs T. She's been a little protective of me since Josephine died. They were good friends, and she seems to have taken it upon herself to look after my interests as well as my person. She means well, but apparently believes that I lost my wits along with my sight. To her, every acquaintance I make is a potential thief or conman. Please don't take it personally.

'Now,' he said, finding the potatoes without my help, 'what brought you to Twelve Trees, and where did you live before this?'

I answered him as best I could, then asked him, 'What about you, Mr Beauchamp? Have you always lived here?'

'Call me George, please. I, too, have lived in various places. I was an undertaker by trade, my wife and I moved here after I sold up the business. Her sister lived in the town and we came to be near her. Sadly, both ladies have now passed on. It fell to someone else to bury them, and I'm glad of it, for I wouldn't have been able to bear it myself.'

He was quiet for a time, and I let him be, thinking of Ida May. It came as a shock to realize I'd hardly done that since I'd arrived in Twelve Trees.

After a while, George spoke again. 'It isn't pleasant for a woman to know that the man who comes home to her in the evening has been laying out corpses all day. My wife never said as much, but I knew she wanted me to give it up. And there was another reason.'

'What was that?' I asked the question because it was expected of me, not because I wanted to hear the answer.

'Something strange happened – something very strange that almost drove me insane.'

I held my breath and waited for what was to come.

'I lost a body.'

'Lost it? You mean you left it somewhere?'

'Oh no, I had it safe, right there in a casket, for all the world to see. Then one night it disappeared.'

'Did somebody steal it?'

'That would seem the most likely explanation, but I don't know who, nor why. It wouldn't make sense for bodysnatchers to take him: he was an outlaw, there was a reward on his head, but no one tried to claim it – except the fellow who shot him, but he was only given half the promised amount, due to the absence of a body. And there was something else – a strange coffin was left at the scene, one with a flap at the end, as if to allow for escape. I fretted and fretted over what it all meant, but the only thing I could come up with was that some friends of the deceased came to substitute the trick coffin for the real one, so that he could dig himself out with their help after he was buried and everyone would believe he was dead.'

'So you reckon he *wasn't* dead? How come?'

'Well, there you've got me. He looked dead, and he didn't appear to be breathing. Although another odd thing was that when I removed the coins from his eyes they opened, and I did fancy they were looking at me.'

'But iffen he wasn't dead – on account of he could hold his breath for a real long time, or something – why did they take him, and leave a mystery, instead of carrying on with the plan to switch the coffins?'

'Ah, there again, I don't know! Perhaps they quarrelled, perhaps they were interrupted and all decided to flee. Whatever the truth of it, it has certainly caused a good deal of speculation over the years. I don't mind telling you, Mr Boot, it put a dent in my belief that I was good at my job. If the man wasn't really dead, why didn't I notice?

'There's been all manner of stories about him since:

he's said to have committed crimes all over this part of the country – and who knows, maybe back east, too. You may have heard his name – Wilbur McCrum.'

I took a few deep breaths before I answered him, glad that he couldn't see my expression. 'I guess I have. Maybe I read about him in a newspaper.'

George nodded sadly. 'I used to take pride in being a rational man, but since the night that body disappeared I've never been sure about anything.'

I looked at poor old George and I wanted more than anything to tell the truth, make him sure about things again, but I knew I couldn't. He might go and call for somebody to fetch the marshal. And iffen he didn't do that, he might throw me out of his house and I'd have to pack up and move on. Even iffen he didn't do *that*, it wouldn't be fair to expect an old man to keep a secret, especially such a big one. After all, he'd be hiding an outlaw. I figured I'd gotten George into enough trouble already, he didn't need no more.

So I kept quiet.

I MEET MY NEMESIS

———◆———

I settled down real well in Twelve Trees. I liked the
place and I liked the people – leastways, the ones I spoke
to. Mostly I kept myself to myself, eating and sleeping
at my lodgings and visiting George every day to read
to him. Sometimes I felt bad, taking money for doing
something I enjoyed as much as he did, but iffen he
didn't pay me I'd have to go and find work somewhere
else, and then he wouldn't have anyone to read to him,
'cept Mrs T, with her Bible. I'd made a vow to move on
iffen I should ever feel too settled in a place, but this was
different – just like when I'd had to choose between
following Ida May and delivering Adeline safely to her
cousin, I was torn between staying with George and
trying to make up for the suffering I'd caused him, and
continuing my quest to find my girl. Once again, I chose
to stay with the living.

Time passed, measured by the chapters of books and the
growing of Art, who soon reached my shoulder, then my
ear, and before I knew it was looking down at me, instead
of the other way around. Iffen there'd ever been a time

when I should have courted his Ma it passed, and then it was too late: an attorney called Bill Wallace came to lodge with us, and before long he asked her to marry him. Of course, it wouldn't have been right for me to carry on living in the house after that, so George suggested I take a room in his place.

Mrs Temperley was none too pleased at first. 'It's very hard for a blind person to live with someone else, and it's very hard for a sighted person to think like someone who's blind. George knows exactly where everything is in his house, so he can find things when I'm not here. You'll move a chair to get better light, or make a fire and leave the fire irons in the wrong place, and he'll stumble over them and take a fall. And he's an old man, so goodness knows what that would do to him.'

'I'm sure you're right, Mrs T, but I've spent a lot of time in George's company, and I know his ways. I'll learn, just like you have.'

She didn't look too sure, but I knew she'd been worrying for a while about George being alone at night, after she went back to her own home. He'd looked pretty old to me when I first laid eyes on him, so he must be real old now, and I'd noticed he walked slower, not only on account of being blind, but because he needed to catch his breath.

So I moved my few things into a little attic room Mrs Temperley prepared for me. There were two other bed-rooms on the same landing as George's, but I reckon she put me up there to show me I was more like a servant than a guest, and I oughtn't to get ideas above my station.

I liked it, though. George's house was bigger than most all the other buildings, so I could see a fair way.

And that's how I saw him.

In *Oliver Twist* the bad man, Bill Sykes, dies because his dog leads the posse to him. George said that dog was Sykes's *nemesis*, and through my little attic window I saw mine.

What I see to begin with is just a fella staggering down the street. Now, in those days a man was most likely to be staggering for one of three reasons: he'd fallen off his horse; someone had just shot him; or he was powerful drunk. I watch for a minute or two, trying to decide which it is. The man don't look too clean, but that ain't unusual. It's when he starts to sing, or at least make grunting noises I reckon are supposed to be singing, that I make up my mind: he's just drunk. I keep on watching because you never know what might happen when a man's roaring drunk in the middle of the day; guns might well be drawn. Then he turns in my direction and raises his chin. I know he can't see me up here, but it's almost as if he can smell me, and that's when I recognize him: it's Jonny Rose.

I slide back against the wall, peering sideways over my shoulder to try to get a look at him, just as if he *had* drawn on me. He's moving on, slow and unsteady, calling out to someone I can't see, someone who maybe ain't there.

I sit in that spot for I don't know how long, fighting the darkness. At least I saw him before he saw me. That's always a good thing; it gives me the advantage over him, as he don't know I'm here. Or does he?

Why has Jonny Rose come to Twelve Trees? There are small towns springing up all over, why did he choose this one?

No, I can't believe he's come in search of me. Besides, he don't look like he's capable of tracking anyone down; it's just my bad luck that my worst enemy, my nemesis, has fetched up here.

But now he's here, what can I do? I can't just pack up and leave this time, not now I'm looking after George. I've run out on the old man once before; I ain't about to do it again.

Anyhow, it's possible Jonny Rose is just passing through. He might be gone by morning. Iffen he carries on like he's doing the sheriff might even run him out of town. Most likely all I have to do is lie low for a few days and then he'll be well away.

I stay inside the rest of the day, but the next morning I decide I have to venture out, just to lay my mind to rest. I go visit with Art and his Ma and her husband, I walk to the dry-goods store to buy some flour and eggs for Mrs T, then I brave a saloon – not because I want a drink, but just to prove to myself I have the courage to go looking for him.

I mean to go in, have one glass of whisky and leave, but I'm reading a newspaper when I hear a scuffle and look up to see a man holding another, smaller man by the collar. The big man is Jonny Rose and he's shouting, 'Why can't you watch where you're going?' and looking set to punch the other fella.

Other people sitting around the table try to calm Jonny down, but he begins to pull off his coat – which ain't easy, on account of he's swaying some. Then he calls out to the whole room, 'I'll fight any man jack of you! Anyone wanna take me on?' and he scowls round into all our faces.

Now maybe I should take my chance and try to sneak out of there, but I figure if I sit tight Jonny might not notice me, and even iffen he does, he might not recognize me after all this time. I'm wrong about that.

On account of all the liquor he's drunk, Jonny's movements are more exaggerated than usual, so he looks like an actor on the stage. His gaze passes over me, then swings back again. Iffen he was scowling before it's nothing to the black look on his face now, and as his bloodshot blue eyes meet mine I see that heavy jaw and thick grizzled hair as it used to be.

'Wilbur McCrum!' His voice is almost a whisper.

Folk have gone quiet, like they do when there's trouble brewing – everyone stops what they're about while they decide whether it's going to get serious, and iffen it is, whether they should get out the way or dive in – which means that most of the people in the saloon hear Jonny Rose say my name.

I feel my throat tighten, and the room starts to go grey. The last thing I need is to have a fit right here in front of everyone. I take deep breaths and try to look like I don't know what Jonny might be talking about, like I don't know who Jonny is.

Lucky for me, as soon as he says my name one of the other fellas at his table starts laughing. 'Wilbur McCrum? Wilbur McCrum, the outlaw? I don't see him around here no place.'

But Jonny don't take his eyes off of me; instead he raises his arm and points an unsteady finger. 'There. That's him, that's Wilbur McCrum. I'd know that bastard anywhere.'

The man who laughed stands up. 'I think your eyes must be playing tricks on you, mister. That man's Mr Boot, and we can all see he don't exactly look the type to rob banks or stages.'

There's laughter from all around, but it only makes Jonny madder. He takes on the stance of a man about to fight: head down, like an enraged bull. 'Why won't you believe me? It's him, I tell you, it's him. I should know if anyone does. That man's plagued my life. I ain't never gonna forget him!'

Then four men who are sitting by Jonny surround him, trying to quieten him down, and a fella at the next table to me says, 'I'd get out quick, if I was you. That fella's only been here a coupla days but I've already seen he's got a nasty temper when he's liquored up, and he likes to fight!'

Well, I don't wait around to be told a second time. I slip out while I have the chance, but as I pass his table Jonny stretches his neck to look over the heads of the other men and calls after me, 'It *is* him, I'd know him anywhere. That's Wilbur McCrum!'

Once I was outside I didn't know what to do. I was afraid of getting a fit, and afraid of Jonny following me, so I walked right to the other end of town and sat by the pond for a bit, trying to clear my head.

I reckoned I had to tell George the truth now, but I wasn't sure how to break it to him. However I said it, I'd deceived him and taken advantage of him being blind and there was no way I could see of making that look anything but bad.

After an hour or so had passed and I felt calmer, I headed home. I went inside the house and hung up my hat on the stand by the door. Then I heard his voice, thickened by all the alcohol and tobacco he'd taken over the years. I can hear it now, plain as the clock ticking on the wall.

'Oh yes,' he's saying, 'we go back a long way. I've known him since we were at school. You don't forget those days, do you? Even iffen you can't remember where you were last night.' And he laughs a horrible laugh from somewhere deep inside his throat.

I stand there with my arm still raised and my hand resting on my hat. Then my knees give way and I fall to the floor, pulling the coat stand on top of me.

'Isaac? Is that you, Isaac? You have a visitor – come see who it is.'

The thing I want most in the world is to be able to get out of there, to walk away and put as much distance between Jonny Rose and me as possible, but I know I can't leave George. Jonny Rose always did have a mean streak, and it don't look like the years have improved his temper none – he's an even meaner drunk. George is the smarter man, but he's old, and being blind means he can't judge a man's intentions the way he could when he could see. I just don't know what Jonny might do to him iffen I hightail it now.

I take some real deep breaths and get to my feet, then I go out back and fetch a large potato from a basket on the kitchen table. I put the potato in my pocket and keep a hold of it there while I walk very slowly into the parlour, thinking of Mr Jenkins and the warmth of his smithy. Mr Jenkins wouldn't have been scared of a mean drunk like Jonny Rose; he'd have laughed at him.

It ain't so easy to laugh when I see Jonny sitting on my reading chair opposite George. He looks at me like he hates me. Iffen George could see that look he'd know straight away this man ain't any friend of mine. As it is, he turns his milky blue eyes toward me and says, 'Now, isn't this a pleasant surprise, Isaac? Here's your old friend Mr Rose, come visiting.'

'How'd you find me?' I ask in a voice that's no more than a whisper.

'Lucky break. I didn't know you were here. I came looking for work – I just can't seem to hold on to a job nowadays – and I saw you in the saloon and asked around to find where you lived. Then I dropped by.'

'Why don't you stay to supper, Mr Rose? Today being Saturday, my housekeeper's not here, but she's left some cold meat and tomatoes. I'm sure Isaac can fix us a proper feast!'

Jonny smiles at me, but it ain't a real smile; he looks like a wolf who's cornered a deer.

'When did you change your name, Wilbur?' He speaks low, too, but there's nothing wrong with George's hearing. He frowns and turns his head in my direction again.

'What's he talking about, Isaac? I don't understand.'

'He's drunk, George. He's a drunk who once mistook me for someone else and won't let it go.'

'I may like my liquor, but you can't blame me for that – life's been hard for me, on account of you.'

'Life's hard for most folks – it's been hard for me, and look at George, his wife dead and his sight gone. You can't spend your whole life blaming me for one thing that happened when we were young.'

'What do you mean, Isaac? What happened?'

'Like I said, George, that ain't his real name. The name his Mama gave him was Wilbur – and his Pa gave him the name McCrum.'

It's strange, but even when a man's blind he opens his eyes wide when something shocks him. '*Wilbur McCrum?* What's he saying, Isaac? Is he saying that *you're Wilbur McCrum?*'

'I wanted to tell you, George, I really did. I just didn't know how, and I was scared.'

'Scared!' Jonny spits the word back at me. 'I used to believe that. I used to think you were scared of your own shadow, back when we was in school, but I don't believe that no more. What's a man who's died and come back from Hell have to be scared about?'

Poor George is turning his sightless eyes from one to the other of us, following our voices.

'I never went nowhere, Jonny. I just woke up, is all.'

'But they *killed* you. They shot you and you fell into that well. Iffen the bullet hadn't done for you, by the time they hauled you out you'd have drowned. What sort of man survives a shooting and a drowning at the same time? I should've realized when I found you digging up the money you robbed from the stage – you ain't what

279

you seem to be, Wilbur McCrum, and I do believe you're the very Devil!'

All the time Jonny's talking I'm trying to figure out what to do. He's really raging. I can see he's worked himself into believing I'm to blame for his life turning bad, and he wants revenge on me. I wouldn't mind so much, iffen only poor George hadn't gotten pulled into it.

'What's happening?' George asks. 'Who are you, really, and who is this man?'

'It's like he says, George, I'm Wilbur McCrum, pretending to be someone else so I don't get caught, and this man here, well, he's my nemesis.'

Maybe it's using a word he don't know upsets him, but it's then Jonny makes a move: he pulls his gun out of its holster and he levels it at me. George must feel the movement, because he swings his cane at Jonny, and that's bad, on account of at the selfsame moment I take the potato out of my pocket and throw it, aiming at Jonny's head. Now my aim never has been too good, so I don't rightly know whether I'd've got Jonny iffen he didn't move to avoid George's cane; the way it happens, though, the potato hits the oil lamp and knocks it onto the floor; Jonny loses his footing and goes down, too, and before I know it, his coat's on fire.

It's a terrible thing to confess to, but I have to admit that my first thought ain't that I should save Jonny, it's *Iffen I don't put out the fire, all George's books will burn*. I run over to George and pull him away, dragging him toward the door.

'There's a fire, George. You've got to fetch help while I try to put it out.'

Poor George stumbles down the steps and I hear him call for help as I turn to Jonny, who's on his knees now, struggling to pull off his coat. The only thing I can think of is to tug down the heavy drapes from the window and throw them over him. Then I roll him about on the floor until the flames are out.

I don't know if I have a fit or faint, but when I come to I'm on my back, with Jonny beside me, laying very still. His eyes are open, but they don't see me; Jonny Rose is dead. He ain't burnt bad enough for the fire to have killed him, so I figure maybe his heart gave out – the way he'd been drinking would've taken its toll of any man. I look at him laying there and think of how afraid I'd been of him just a moment ago, and how mean he was when we were at school. I remember his handsome face, laughing at me as I woke from a fit, looking down from his stage with fear in his eyes, and I'm still sorry – sorry he's dead, and sorry for what he'd come to before he died.

I crawl over to the door, haul myself to my feet and stagger outside. I find George lying on the ground, with a man I recognize as one of the neighbours kneeling beside him. George is having some kind of seizure – not like my fits, maybe it's his heart or something – I can see his leg twitching as the man tries to loosen his collar. He looks over his shoulder at me and says, 'What happened in there? Did the house catch fire?' But I'm coughing too bad to answer him and my world turns black.

GEORGE KNOWS THE TRUTH

⁓⧛⧚⁓

*I*t wasn't long before a whole bunch of people arrived. I was conscious by then and saw Mrs Temperley holding her skirt over her arm, running faster than I thought a woman of her age was capable, followed by the tall, spindly old doctor, more neighbours and the sheriff. Some of the neighbours came with buckets of water, but the first one to run in the house came out again directly with the bucket still full, hollering there was a dead man inside.

George was in no fit state to speak, so I told them what had happened, or a version of it, anyhow.

'I came home and heard George quarrelling with someone. I crept in as quiet as I could and saw a man I'd noticed about town, drunk and shouting. He was asking George for money, and George was saying he was welcome to some food, but he wasn't giving him money, because he knew the fella would spend it on intoxicating liquor.'

'I saw that man, too,' someone cut in. 'He came looking for work, said he'd turn his hand to anything, but no one would hire him because he was drunk all the time.'

'He was drunk all right. I was trying to make up my mind what to do – try and get him to leave or go out again and fetch the sheriff – when he made a grab for George's watch – the one he always wears on his waistcoat – and they started struggling. Course I had to step in then, but before I knew it, the lamp was knocked over and the fella was on fire. I put out the flames, but it was too late – he was dead.'

There were noises from the crowd, but not angry noises; just tutting and drawing in of breath. Someone put a blanket round my shoulders and patted me on the back.

'How's George?' I asked the doctor. His leg had stopped twitching, but he was still laying on the front porch, the doctor kneeling beside him, his bag to hand.

'Too early to tell. At his age a shock like this can carry a man off. But he's strong. If he makes it through the night I reckon there's a chance he'll be with us for a while yet.'

There was an argument then about where George should be cared for. Some folk said he couldn't possibly stay in a house where a man had just died; others said it was important for him to sleep in his own bed. In the end the doctor decided even iffen the fire was out, the smell of smoke wouldn't do a sick man no good at all, and George was carried to Mrs Temperley's house.

Mrs Temperley may not have been too friendly with me, but she was a good person to have around when things went wrong. She took charge straight away, seeing that George was made comfortable and making me drink plenty of water so's I wouldn't be coughing all night and keeping him awake. She still talked to me in a gruff kind of way, but it seemed more out of habit than because she meant it.

I have bad dreams that night. I keep seeing Jonny on fire; sometimes he's pointing at me, sometimes he's beckoning to me, like he wants to take me down to Hell with him. I keep on waking, so in the end I give up on trying to sleep and go sit by the window, waiting for sun-up, and thinking back over my life. It seems to me that most anyone I've lived with has ended up dead, and now poor George is set to die, too. Maybe I should just slope off again before anyone's awake, give George a fighting chance.

While I'm thinking this over, though, there's a knock on the door and Mrs Temperley comes in with a cup of tea.

'Thought I heard you moving around. Can't sleep, eh? Don't blame you. I'm the same way myself. It doesn't bear thinking about, what might have happened to poor George if you hadn't been there to save him.' She sets the tea down on the little table beside the bed.

'He's more than just an employer to me, you know. His wife was a good friend of mine. She helped me when I lost my daughter in childbed, so it was only right that I help George when Josephine passed on. This is rough country, I know that – but this town is about as peaceful as it gets, and a man like George deserves to die a peaceful death, in his own bed.'

'Do you think I should leave?'

'Heavens, no. If it weren't for you George would almost certainly have perished in that fire. He needs you to take care of him. I have to admit I wasn't sure about you at first, thought you might be out to rob him, but I don't think that now.' She sits studying me, as if she's trying to read me like one of George's books, then she says, 'Now, drink your tea and come down when you're ready.'

After I've had some breakfast I look in on George and find Mrs Temperley talking to him in a low voice. 'Let me sit with him a while,' I say. 'Why don't you go eat something? You need to keep your strength up, too.'

I sit by George's bed. He seems to have shrunk. When he smiles, one side of his mouth goes up, while the other stays down. When he speaks, his voice is so faint I have to lean forward to hear him.

'Why didn't you tell me?'

'I wanted to, George, truly, but I didn't know how. It seemed like iffen I was to tell you straight away, you wouldn't have given me the job, so I waited for the right time, and it just never came. I was too happy, just reading your books to you; I didn't want anything to spoil it.'

'What did you think I'd do – hand you over to the sheriff?'

'You might have done – you'd have the right to.'

'Now, you should know me better than that; my curiosity wouldn't allow me to, if nothing else. Are you going to tell me how, exactly, you rose from the dead?'

'I wasn't dead, is all. I just had the longest ever fit. Maybe the drowning made it worse – or the shooting.

Whatever it was, I woke up and could hear and see but couldn't move. Lucky for me it wore off before you put me in the ground!'

'Indeed. And that strange open-ended coffin?'

'Wasn't anything to do with me. That was your assistant. He'd figured out a way to make more money by reusing the casket. Him and the boy you had working there'd just brought it back when I woke up and they hightailed it, thinking they'd seen a ghost.'

'That Henry Fossey was a sharp one! No wonder they didn't mention having been there that night. I puzzled over that mysterious coffin for so long. Wait a minute, though – do you mean to say he was putting people in the ground in nothing but a shroud?'

'He was. Said it didn't make no difference, the worms would get them sooner or later. Said it was all about appearances, and it only mattered to the living.'

George goes quiet while he thinks about this. 'I left my business to that young man. I wonder how many people he's cheated since then.'

'Guess he's a rich man now.'

'I imagine he is. Well, I suppose that's the spirit this country was built on. If the white man hadn't been prepared to take from the red man, none of us would be here now.'

TWELVE TREES
GETS A LIBRARY

———⊶⫘⊷———

*C*onsidering all that had happened to him, George made a good recovery. He couldn't walk too far, and the left side of his face drooped some, but his mind was as lively as ever, and he could still talk like before. He decided that, as I'd led such a blameless life since I was shot, he was prepared to keep my secret for me, and we carried on as before. One day, when I was only a little way through a powerful long book named *Middlemarch* – I'd gone through just about everything by Charles Dickens, who was George's favourite, and I'd started on George Eliot, who turned out to be a woman with a man's name – George stopped me by raising his cane. 'There's something I want to discuss with you, Isaac.' (We'd decided it was best iffen he kept calling me that, just as Sophia had. It was easier than trying to remember to call me one thing when folks were about and another when we were alone.) I remember the conversation in exact detail, even though I'm nearly the age George was then – so this is going back a good many years.

'What is it, George?' I'm afraid he might want me to tell everyone who I really am, maybe give myself up to the sheriff, but I'm resolved to do whatever George wants.

'We need to consider the future, Isaac.' When I don't say nothing he carries on, 'We need to think about what's to happen to my collection – and to you – when I'm gone.' I still sit quiet. There's no use pretending George can live forever, so I hear him out.

'I want you to stay on here. As you know, I have no children of my own, and my books are the nearest thing to children I'll ever have, so I want them taken care of. At the same time, you'll need an income, so this is my proposal: you turn this place into a lending library. That way you can charge a small fee for every book you lend out and the books get to be read, rather than mouldering away on the shelves, unseen by anyone but you and the esteemed Mrs Temperley, when she has it in mind to dust.'

I think about this for a minute. I'd have to speak to a lot more people than I'm accustomed to, but then, why should that worry me? Now poor Jonny Rose is dead there's no one much remembers the real Wilbur McCrum, and I look so different to how I used to, and even more different from the legend, that there ain't really much danger. Anyhow, I reckon I owe it to George to do whatever he asks of me. Iffen that's what he wants, he's going to get it.

'I'll do it, George. I'll make a library here for you, and the whole town'll get to share your books.'

*

A couple of months later, as I was reading the last few pages of *Middlemarch*, I looked up and saw George sprawled on his chair, his eyes looking upward and his jaw hanging slack. I went over to him and gently shook his arm. 'George? Can you hear me, George?' I laid my hand on his waistcoat, where I thought his heart must be, but couldn't feel anything. I put my cheek to his open mouth, and there was no breath to feel. George was gone. I looked into his sightless eyes – they didn't tell me anything. Then I closed them for the last time. I took two pennies from my pocket and laid them on his lids; the opposite of what he did to me all those years before.

George had made a will, leaving his house and all the books to me, so long as I did what he'd asked and made it into a library for the townsfolk. Iffen I didn't take steps to fulfil his wishes within the first year after his death I was to lose any claim to his property and be turned out. Then a committee would take over and see to the setting up of the library.

The will had been drawn up by Mr Wallace, Art's Ma's husband, and when he'd finished reading it and then explaining it to me, he said they'd help. There was a fund for buying more books, and the booksellers who had supplied George would send me their catalogues, recommending those they thought our library should have.

That was one of the best times of my life, when I was making the George S. Beauchamp Memorial Library. A bunch of people took an interest, whether or not they'd liked George, or liked reading books. The general feeling was it would be good for our little community to be known for something like that, when most Western towns were famous for gunfights and lawlessness.

I missed old George, of course, but I was happy to be making his dream come true, and it meant I didn't have to fret about my future, neither. Not that I'd ever fretted much about it – the only plan I'd ever had, iffen you could call it that, was to find Ida May. Then, of course, meeting up with George again, I'd had to put even that aside, so's I could at least try to make it up to him. And I guess by this stage I was growing older myself, and quite liked being settled somewhere, so despite my vow, if setting up the library kept me in Twelve Trees a while longer, I have to own it didn't upset me much. It wasn't that I'd given up on Ida May – just that it didn't seem so urgent no more, not after all this time.

It was hard work, getting it all finally ready, and when the library opened for business there was a line of people waiting to come in. After two weeks or so, though, it slowed to a trickle, and I got to read quite a lot in between visitors.

The months went by real easy: I passed the time of day with my customers and read all the new books that were coming in. People were even starting to write stories about the settlement of the West, the cowboys in particular. The thought that anyone would want to read about the lives of those rough old boys made me laugh, but they were popular with the younger folk, the ones who didn't remember what those days were really like.

And that's how a man who'd once been the worst outlaw in the West became someone the townsfolk came to for information, and even advice. It surely is a strange world, where a man like Jonny Rose, who's handsome and popular, can end up a mean drunk, while a sorry creature like me ends up a pillar of the community.

I MEET THE NEW SHERIFF

꧁꧂

So there I am. I'm enjoying my new life: I'm doing what George asked of me; I haven't had a fit for so long I can hardly remember what they're like; I have a roof over my head, enough money to live on, and just enough company to keep me from having to talk to myself.

Then one morning a young woman comes in with a little girl. It's raining outside, and they've got caught in it without an umbrella.

'Hello, you must be Mr Boot,' the woman says, holding out her hand. Then she pulls it back and peels off her wet glove before offering it to me again. Her fingers are cold as a dead man's.

'Yes, I am, ma'am, and you're soaked through. Why don't you come warm yourselves by the fire?'

'Why, thank you.' She has a face that looks quite serious, but changes completely when she smiles. The little girl, who I guess is five or six, clings to her mother's skirts and peeps out at me with something like a scowl. She reminds me of someone, but I can't figure out who.

'I'm Mrs Grogan, and this is Grace. We've just arrived here. My husband is the new sheriff.'

Now that shakes me slightly. Even though I've been a law-abiding citizen for many years by now, I'm still as wary of lawmen as a bird is of cats: I try to keep away from them.

The old sheriff had grown fat and wheezy over the years and decided he wasn't up to dealing with criminals no more, so he's retired. Twelve Trees is generally such a quiet town, though, that there ain't much to do. Boys break a few windows when their ballgames get out of hand, once in a while a storekeeper might be accused of doctoring his scales and giving customers short measures, but we can go a long time without seeing a serious crime. Course, Jonny Rose stirred things up for months, and when something does happen it's generally someone from out of town like him is the cause of it.

Now all that might be good for Twelve Trees, but I wasn't so sure a young sheriff with time on his hands would be a good thing for me.

It's the very next day Mrs Grogan and her daughter come back, this time bringing two more people with them. The man is no more than a couple inches taller than me, and he keeps twisting his hat in his hands, as if he's awkward in company. He don't look much like my idea of a sheriff.

'Mr Boot, this is my husband, Jack Grogan. Jack, this is Mr Isaac Boot, the town librarian.'

I know it's a silly thing for a man of my age to feel proud when she says those words, but I do. I feel myself making a chest and have to remember to breathe out again.

'And this is Jack's mother, Mrs Annie Grogan.'

I have to say I never saw a mother and son so unalike as these two: where he is slight, she's tall and big-boned; where he's dark, she is fair; and where he seems shy, she stares at me like I'm an exhibit in a museum. She wears spectacles with real thick lenses that make her pale blue eyes look big and round, so I reckon the staring might be on account of not being able to see too well, but she sure gives me a good long look. She puts out her hand to shake mine, just like a man, but in a distracted kind of way, and she still don't take her eyes off of me. Her handshake is stronger than her son's – her hands are bigger, too. But I remember the Reverend Smith and his two skinny children, and I don't exactly favour my Ma *nor* my Pa, neither.

'I'm pleased to see this town has such a fine library,' the young fella says. 'It's the mark of a civilized place. Encouraging folk to read should help them learn about the world and stop them getting into mischief.'

Lawmen sure are different nowadays, I think to myself. Once upon a time the job used to be taken by fellas who liked nothing better than to buffalo a few drunks and sort out a brawl or two before bed. This one would rather read them a story. Still, that's a good thing for me, he won't be looking for trouble.

His Ma is bothering me, though: she's still peering at me through those spectacles and I can feel a sweat breaking out on my palms. I think I'd better make conversation with her, else I might fall at her feet in a fit and make a real bad impression.

'So do you like reading, ma'am?'

She looks at me like I've made a rude suggestion.

'Ach, I don't have time to sit around with a book on my lap!' She has some kind of an accent, Norwegian, maybe. I'm glad she won't be one of my regular customers, as she don't seem to have taken to me much.

'How about you, missy?' I crouch down to talk to little Grace, but she pokes her tongue out at me and runs to hide behind her mother.

The very next morning the younger Mrs Grogan comes back to see me again. Three times in as many days! She sets little Grace down in a corner of the library with some picture books to look at and then leans forward across the desk, speaking to me in a low voice.

'Mr Boot, I just wanted to say that I hope you won't be offended by my mother-in-law's manner. She's had a hard life in many ways, and as a result she can be very direct, as direct as any man, if not more so.'

I keep quiet; when a body has something to say to you, something they seem to have all prepared and ready, I reckon it's best to let them talk it through from beginning to end.

'Jack's father died when he was a baby. We don't know how, exactly. She may be forthright, but if there's something his mother doesn't wish to discuss, she clams up altogether, and she isn't someone you should rile by asking too many questions. She brought him up by herself, doing all the chores a man would do – chopping wood, hunting, trading furs. She's done everything for him; he's got her to thank for getting a college degree – he studied the law, you know.

'Anyway, I just wanted you to understand that if she

seems a little, well, rude, she doesn't really mean to be. It's nothing personal.' And she gives me a smile before turning to summon Grace. Her daughter is all ready for her – she's been glancing up at us every few moments, trying to figure out what we're talking about, I reckon – and now she jumps down from her chair and runs to her Ma.

'Can we go home now? I don't like this place, it smells funny.' She looks up at me and makes her eyes narrow and just in that moment I see the resemblance again, but I still can't figure out who she reminds me of.

I MEET UP WITH SOMEONE AGAIN

The Grogans settled in soon enough, and Mrs Grogan – Rose – became one of my regulars. Sometimes her mother-in-law would come in looking for her, and she'd often stare at me in the same way she did that first time we met. I never did get comfortable round her. Little Grace was another matter: she still stuck her tongue out at me by way of greeting, but then she'd smile, and it became a kind of joke between the two of us. I'd say hello to Jack Grogan when I saw him in the street, but he seemed like a quiet man, and as I'd never been one for small talk myself, we didn't have much to do with each other.

Then one winter's night there was a banging at my door after I'd gone to bed. I staggered down the stairs, tripping on one of the treads where the runner was worn and nearly tumbling down the last few steps. When I called out, 'Who's there?' and the answer came back, 'Jack Grogan, the sheriff,' I hesitated for a moment. Had he found out the truth about me; had justice caught up with me at last? Then I thought that whatever he'd come for, I had to face up to it sooner or later, so I pulled back the bolt and let him in.

'It's my mother, Mr Boot,' he said to me as soon as the door opened. 'She's very sick – pneumonia. She may not last till morning.'

'Your mother?' I couldn't understand why he'd come to me; I wasn't a doctor, what use could I be?

'She's asked to see you. I don't know what it's about, she won't tell me, but she says she can't rest until she's spoken with you.'

'But why me? I hardly know her.'

'I can't tell you that, sir. It may be that the fever's got to her brain and she's imagining you're someone else, but you'd be doing me a great kindness if you came home with me now.'

What could I say? I couldn't deny a dying woman her final wish, however odd it might be, so I pulled on some pants and a jacket over my nightshirt, took my hat off the coat stand and followed him.

It was a cold, clear night, and I could see hundreds of stars up in the sky, some bright, others so tiny and dim I wasn't sure if they were there at all. The cold air filled my lungs and made me catch my breath, almost taking my mind off the reason for this late-night walk.

In the warm hallway of the Grogan house, Rose took our hats and coats from us with hardly a word, and Jack led me silently up the stairs. Knocking gently on the first door he came to, he opened it without waiting for an answer, and showed me in.

The light in the room is dim: there's one electric lamp on a table by the bed, but it has a thin shawl draped over it. The old lady's propped up on several pillows. Her hair is in a loose plait that comes forward over one shoulder, her hands lie curled up on top of the covers. Her breathing is loud and slow, and the room smells bad; like stale vanilla and piss.

'At last,' she says, speaking with difficulty, 'I've been hanging on just to see you.'

Jack goes and sits on the bed and takes one of her hands, but she works it free.

'I need to speak to him alone; like we agreed.'

He glances over his shoulder at me, forehead creased with worry.

'If that's what the lady wants, it's fine by me.' I sound too jovial, but I don't know what I'm doing here, nor how to behave around a dying woman who's practically a stranger to me.

Jack goes out with a lingering look at his mother. 'Call me if you want me,' he says before he shuts the door behind him. I'm not sure who that's meant for.

I look at the woman in the bed and she looks back at me. Without the thick spectacles to magnify her eyes they look small and tired.

'Before we begin this, some water, please.' She raises a weary hand to indicate a tray on her dressing table, where a pitcher stands beside a glass and a small bottle of medicine.

I turn around, glad of something to do. I notice how my hand shakes as I pour the water in the glass. I'm about done when I hear a noise I haven't heard for some years: the sound of a pistol being cocked.

I freeze.

Then I hear something else I haven't heard for years: a voice saying, 'You always were a damned fool, Wilbur McCrum, and you still are.'

Very slowly, I set down the glass and turn to face her. She's pointing an old .45 at my head, holding it with both hands.

'You don't know me, do you?'

'No, ma'am, to the best of my knowledge we'd never met before you came to this town.'

She makes a noise deep in her throat that sets off a terrible coughing fit. I could take the gun off her now, but I don't move.

When she can speak again she says, 'Oh, we've met, all right. I wish we never had, but we have; we've met. I looked a little different then – more flesh on my bones – but it's hard to stay plump when you're working all the hours God sent you being the mother and father to someone else's child.'

Her accent seems to have got stronger and it seems familiar now. Suddenly I know, I know who she is. '*Helga?*'

'I recognized you straight away, in spite of your grey whiskers. Those eyes gave you away. I never thought I'd see you again, even though I read about you in the papers.'

'None of that was true. I stopped being an outlaw when I got shot.'

'I didn't believe those stories anyway: you didn't have what it took to do all those daring things. Ach, what's the point of this? I'm not going to shoot you.' And she lets the gun fall onto the quilt and lies back on her pillows.

Someone else's child. Suddenly I see little Grace, sticking her tongue out at me, and it's as if I've known all along who it is she reminds me of. My hand scrabbles at the bedpost as I try to grab hold of it for support.

'Jack?'

'Yes, Wilbur, he's your son.'

I hit the floor then, and the next thing I remember is someone banging on the door and Jack's voice calling, 'Mother? What's happening, Mother? Are you all right?'

'I'm fine. Mr Boot tripped over a chair leg, is all. He's not hurt. Now leave us alone, I still need more time to talk with him.'

I'm laying on my back and I can feel sweat trickling down my face and into my ears. I roll over and use the bedpost to pull myself up. I still feel woozy, unsure whether I'm dreaming.

'Welcome back,' Helga says. 'I think you should sit down before we continue our little talk.'

I pull up a chair and do as I'm bid. 'How come you ended up raising him? What happened to Lady M?'

'A year or so after it all happened and you left, a man came looking for her, said he was a private detective and he'd been hired by her son, back in Scotland. Turned out her husband had died and the son had inherited his house and all, and he wanted to find his mother and ask her to come home.

'She thought about it for a while. She liked running that joy house and we girls were like family to her, but in the end she decided she owed it to her son to go back, if that's what he wanted. She said Junior and me could go with her, but Scotland sounded too cold and wet for me, and anyhow, we agreed he should stay here because you were still alive, and while you might not be much of a father, you were the only one he had. It was her idea to call him Jack – that's what her own son was called – and he couldn't be Junior forever, could he?'

She's looking tired now. Her cheeks are sunken, her hands are twisted and appear old against the bright patchwork of the quilt. Even now I know it's her, I still can't see any sign of that big, buxom girl with all the false hair. I did this to her: I killed Ida May and I killed the old Helga, too, leaving her to wear herself out raising my boy.

'I'm sorry,' I say, moving closer. She pulls her hand back as I'm about to touch it.

'Too late for that. I made the choice. I didn't have to care for him, but I did. I'm not blaming anyone now.'

'Does he – have you told him about me?'

It looks as if she's making a real big effort to keep her eyes open.

'He believes his father is dead. What could I tell him – I'm not your real mother, she was a prostitute, just like me, and she was shot trying to help your outlaw father?'

'What do you want me to do?'

'I don't know, Wilbur, I don't know. I'm just so tired, I can't think anymore. I'm going to die soon, and I'm not figuring on making any deathbed confession. I want to pass on in peace with my family – still believing they *are* my family – by my side.

'Maybe I should have told him the truth, but the longer you live a lie, the harder it is to give it up. Perhaps I was wrong – guess I was – but can you blame me for it?'

'No,' I tell her, 'I don't blame you one bit.' And I pat her hand. This time, she don't have the strength to draw it away.

I GO BACK TO SEARCHING

Helga died the next day and was buried in the little cemetery by the church. The ground was frozen, but a whole bunch of townsfolk brought along their spades and helped dig the grave. Because she was the sheriff's mother everyone knew her, and most of the town seemed to be at the funeral. The sky was iron grey and flakes of snow stung our cheeks as we stood and watched the coffin being lowered into the ground.

She never liked me and never pretended she did, but I had plenty of reason to be there. If I hadn't made such a darn mess of my life her best friend wouldn't have died and left her with a baby to care for, and she might have led a very different life herself. I owed that woman a lot, and I couldn't blame her for keeping the truth from Jack – nor for wanting to kill me, neither. A lot of people have wanted to do that.

It made me think of Ida May, and how she should have a grave for him and me to stand and weep at. I decided I'd hidden away in Twelve Trees long enough; I had to go out there again and find my girl and bring her home. I did half think about telling Jack the truth first, and maybe asking for his help, but I couldn't be sure it was a good idea. What if the sheriff in him was stronger than the son, and he threw me in the jailhouse? Then I'd have lost my last chance to find Ida May again, and that didn't seem like it'd be fair on anyone, least of all Ida May.

I hadn't said anything to Jack about what Helga had told me. He and Rose had been taking turns to sit by her bedside, then they had the funeral to fix, and it wouldn't have been right to give him news like that at such a time – or so I told myself, anyhow. I *would* tell him, though, I was sure about that: if it had just been me he didn't know about, then maybe I could have kept quiet, let him believe his Pa was dead, but I owed it to Ida May to tell him about her. I'd just have to wait for the right moment to come along, was all.

Meantime, I started on a new search.

ON THE ROAD

———◆———

*O*nce my mind was made up, I had to figure out *how* I was going to do it. And just as I was trying to work that one out, an answer came along in the form of Art.

Art was a smart young man by then: he wore a brown suit a lot of the time, with the faintest cream stripe down it, and he slicked back his hair with a pomade that smelt of some kind of flower I couldn't quite fix on. He'd got himself a job travelling around selling cleaning products; folk had started getting electricity in their homes and they began to see into corners that had been in shadow before, and to notice there was more dirt around than they'd realized.

Art said it was good to see a bit of the world. He meant to see it all one day, but for now, he said, just the western states of the US would do him. To make it easier to get around he went and bought an automobile. He wasn't the first person in Twelve Trees to get one: that was Mr Hyram Smoker, who owned the *Twelve Trees Enquirer*, and who'd bought a Model-T Ford a while back. He wanted everyone to know about it, too, and he drove that thing up and down Main Street until he figured they'd all seen it, then he drove it up and down some more, just to be certain. Of course, like with every new invention, there were some who thought it was a wonderful thing, and some who thought it the work of the Devil, but just about everyone was curious.

Art's was a handsome thing all right, dark red – the first one I'd seen that wasn't black – with a soft roof you could pull back if you wanted and a polished silver-coloured grille at the front.

'It's a Dodge Brothers. Ain't she beautiful? Bill helped me buy her – but don't tell Ma that. He'd've liked to get one himself, but she says there's no need.'

I got in it straight away, while Mrs T stood by, arms folded across her chest, watching. Art cupped a hand round her elbow and tried to pull her to the door, but she resisted.

'What's wrong with horses, that's what I want to know?'

'Horses are fine creatures, but they are *creatures*: they need feeding and watering, else they die, and they get tired and can't go no further. An automobile can go for miles on a tank of gas, then all you need do is fill it up again and it can go miles more right away. It won't shy when it sees a rattler, neither, nor bolt and throw you in the dust if it hears a loud noise. This is progress, Mrs Temperley, progress.' And he went and slapped the gleaming metal, for all the world as if it *was* a horse.

'You young people think you've got the answer for everything, don't you? There's a reason folk have been using horses to get around since they first clapped eyes on them.'

307

'Yes, there was: Henry Ford hadn't been born!'

I could see Mrs T was weakening; she was tempted to get in that machine, and in the end she did. She sat up very stiff in her seat at first, but before long she was asking Art if he couldn't go any faster.

It felt fine, bowling along on the road out of town with the wind in your hair – although I have to own that with the roof down you got a bunch of grit in your eyes too, which spoiled the experience some, and by the time we stopped to go back I was coughing. Mrs T'd had the good sense to hold her pocket handkerchief over her mouth and clamp her hat to her head with her other hand, and her eyes were fair shining when Art handed her down.

'Well,' was all she could say, 'well, I never.'

I knew as soon as I saw that automobile that it was my best hope of getting out of Twelve Trees and finding Ida May. The railroad is fine, but you have to buy a ticket to somewhere, so you need to know where you're going; you can't just decide you like the look of that little track and go off down it the way you can when you're driving. I *had* to persuade Art to take me on the road with him. I could have told him about my quest, of course, but he might decide I was crazy and get me put in a hospital; my best chance was to appeal to his sense of adventure.

I asked him to take me on a longer drive, so we wouldn't be interrupted, and I said to him, 'How would you like to have a travelling companion, Art? It must get lonely on the road.'

'How d'you mean, Uncle Isaac?'

'Well, it's like this: I wandered a fair amount when I

was a young man, but mostly I was looking for work; I didn't get to appreciate the places I saw. Now I'm growing older I'd like to travel some, while I still can – before it's too late. You understand me, don't you, boy?'

'Sure, but it ain't glamorous, the kind of travelling I do. I go to the small towns and the lonely homesteads, not the big places with lots of stores; I'd never sell there. Half the time when people listen to me it's not because they want to buy anything, they just want to hear someone talk.' He shot me a glance, trying to judge whether he'd managed to put me off the idea. He must have decided he hadn't, because he carried on, 'And I have to bed down for the night wherever I can: it ain't unusual for me to have to sleep under a hedge.'

'But you've got the automobile now. With this you can cover much more ground than you could before, and you can sleep in it, too. Your own travelling hotel!'

I could see Art was doubtful about having an old man along on his journeys. I suddenly realized he was grown now, no longer a boy, and he might have more to offer lonely farmers' wives than just talk. Still, I needed him to take me along, and if I got in his way he'd have to put up with it; it was only until I found Ida May.

'I'll pay for all our lodgings, how about that, as my contribution to the trip?'

Mrs Temperley didn't approve of the idea one bit, but then I hadn't expected her to, and I wasn't about to listen to her protests. Art's Ma was clearly pleased, though, and offered to keep the library open while I was gone. I guess she reckoned that with me along Art wouldn't get into too much mischief. I believe the same thought had occurred to Art, too, as he wasn't his usual cheery self when we set off on our first trip.

Art allowed his Ma to throw her arms around his neck and plant a kiss on his cheek, and I allowed Mrs Temperley to drape a blanket carefully over my knees as if I was an old invalid off to take a rest cure. As soon as we were out of sight Art rubbed at his cheek, and I folded up the blanket and stowed it on the back seat.

I'd gone and bought some special driving goggles, for when we had the top of the Dodge down, and I tied an old plaid scarf over my mouth, so I didn't mind so much about the dust. I had a curious mixture of feelings as we sped along on that first day: it felt good to be on the open road – free, in a way – but all the same I wasn't free, I had a mission, a purpose, to fulfil. I might not need a blanket over my knees yet, but I was getting older, and I had to finish what was started all those years ago in Vacanegra. If I died before I found Ida May, she'd never be put to rest, and if that happened I reckoned I deserved to go to Hell.

AT LAST

When we reached our first stop I tried to help Art, unpacking all his samples and loading up his cloths with whatever wonderful cleaning product he needed to demonstrate, but it soon became clear I was in the way. The lady of the house was young and pretty, and she wasn't making big eyes at Art because she was interested in being a better housewife. I went and sat in the automobile until he was done.

We stopped in a few small towns and I paid for our lodgings, like I'd said I would. Mostly Art went to work by himself and I walked around, seeing what I could see, and enquiring about circuses. I didn't find any on our first trip, but I came across one on the second. The only freak in it, though, was a dwarf who was one of the clowns, and I didn't know him.

Six times I went out on the road with Art, and we found three circuses, but the only familiar face I saw was in the ticket booth of the third one: Baby Sue – although she was Grandma Sue now. But for her hair being white, she hadn't changed much, and she was real pleased to see me. She said Joshua had sold the freak show after I'd left

– to the freaks themselves, organized by Sophia – and she'd stayed on for a while, but then she'd met a man who wanted to marry her and he didn't want his wife to be a freak, so she'd quit.

Baby Sue couldn't give me any more information, though. I didn't meet with anyone else who might've had an idea where Ida May had gone. I realized I'd made a mistake not trying to go after Leonard when I had at least some chance of catching up with him. I was very close to despair – probably the closest I'd been since those days right after Ida May died.

Art could see something was wrong, but, being a man, he didn't ask me what it was. Instead he tried to cheer me up by suggesting we go to see a moving picture.

I'd read all about the movies, of course, but as Twelve Trees didn't have its own theatre I'd never seen one. I was a little worried in case all that movement and light should bring on a fit, but I didn't want to let Art down, so I agreed to go.

The town we're in is called Prisley, and it seems a lively place, with plenty of people walking up and down the streets in the evening – women, too, and none of them saloon girls. Most of the stores are built around a main square, with the movie theatre in the middle of one side of it. Over the doors it says in big letters '*The Bride in the Haunted Castle*'.

Inside there are long rows of seats, and we sit near the front. 'I'd like to see things from here for a change,' Art says, 'usually I'm in the back row.' There's a piano near us and a fella in a tuxedo starts banging on it real loud.

When the picture begins I nearly jump out my seat.

I've tried to imagine moving pictures before, but I ain't prepared for seeing people so big up there. At first I'm sat right back in the chair like a cat pressing itself against a wall when it sees a neighbourhood dog, but after a while I relax some, although I can't say I find the story much to my liking: it's about a young girl who's married a mysterious older man and is taken to his huge empty castle, where she soon decides something is wrong.

It's warm in there, and what with it being dark, and me not being too taken with the picture itself, I reckon I might have fallen asleep, if it wasn't for the piano starting up a sinister tune every time the villain appears. And then, near the end, I see something that makes me start in my seat like I've been shot.

The heroine of the story has found the key to a room her husband keeps locked and she's crept into it to find out what his secret is. They don't have electricity in that castle of his, so she's carrying a candle, and as she turns, the flame lights up first a stuffed owl, then a human skull, then the dried-up body of a woman. Straight away the girl drops her candle, but there's no mistaking that face, with its open mouth and gaps between the teeth: it's her – it's Ida May!

I do have a fit then, but I stay in my seat and the darkness hides what's happening from Art. I wake up to see the words *The End* and they begin to show the names of the people who've been in the movie and the ones who've made it. I try hard to remember one name in particular: *Director, Walter Kravitz*.

I guess I must look pale when I come out of the theatre, because Art claps me on the back and says, 'You were scared back there, weren't you, Uncle Isaac? I felt you jump when the girl saw that mummy. They do make it seem real, though, don't they?' Then he buys me a glass of beer to steady my nerves.

IDA MAY LONGDEN,
MOVIE STAR

⟶⟍⟋⟍⟋⟵

*F*inally my course was clear: somehow Ida May had ended up in a movie, and I had the name of the man who'd made that movie. If I could find him, he should be able to tell me where she was. How I'd get her back was another matter, but I'd think about that later.

If Art was surprised when I said I wasn't going with him on his next trip, he didn't show it. I guess he thought it had all been an old man's whim, and that I'd done wandering. When I told him I needed to visit someone in California, though, he couldn't help but look surprised.

'Uncle Isaac, you've not moved from Twelve Trees in all the years I've known you, and all of a sudden you've turned into a travelling man! What's happened to make you change your ways?'

I just smiled at him and said there were things I had to do that I'd left undone too long. He frowned, trying to figure out what I might mean by that, but he didn't ask me no more.

Mrs Temperley was a different matter. She made it plain she thought it ridiculous that a man of my age should undertake a long train journey for no good reason, but when she saw I was set on going, whatever she might say to me, she helped me pack my bag – although she didn't stop shooting me disapproving glances while she was doing it.

All the time I was travelling I was preparing different stories for this Mr Kravitz. Sometimes I was the owner of a freak show who'd been robbed of his main attraction, had thought her lost, but then seen her in the movie and come to claim her back; sometimes I was a rich man with a liking for odd things and I wanted to buy the mummy for my collection; sometimes I was just a man wanting to claim the body of his sweetheart. Trouble was, that one seemed the least likely to be true.

By the time I arrived in Los Angeles I was so tired I couldn't think straight. I'd never lived in a city, and the sight of so many people, so many automobiles, so many buildings was too much for me. The noise and bustle of a city, too, is hard to take when you've lived all your life on homesteads and in small towns: horns honking, fellas selling newspapers calling out for customers, everywhere people jostling for space on the sidewalk; folk crossing roads and shouting and gesticulating . . .

I had to sit down on some steps and catch my breath, else I'd've had a fit for sure. I was going to stay with a cousin of Art's Ma, and I had a piece of paper with her address written on it, and I kept showing it to people until I found the place. It was late when I got there, and she only opened the door a crack at first.

'I'd all but given up on you, Mr Boot. Thought you'd changed your mind! Well, I suppose you'd better come along in.'

The buildings there were so big that folk only lived in part of them, with a whole bunch of people in the same block. It was very different from the old pioneering days, when men like Pa moved out west so he could have a piece a land all to himself, somewhere you might not hear or see another person for weeks on end. I kind of liked it, though, and I'm sure Ma would have liked to have neighbours you could visit without having to leave the house.

Even though I was so tired, the noise and the street lighting and the thinking about everything I'd seen kept me laying awake in my bed. Then I fell into a restless sleep where I was dreaming of walking through crowded streets and seeing faces in those crowds. I saw Ma, and Pa, Nattie Reilly, Sophia – and Ida May. I saw Ida May again and again that night. Sometimes she was laughing and happy, sometimes she looked ornery, but then I saw her with the bullet hole in her forehead and I woke up hollering.

That didn't please my landlady, who came bustling in and switched on the light.

'Goodness me, Mr Boot, I thought you were being murdered in your bed, the noise you were making! What on earth happened?'

I explained I'd had a dream and she went away, muttering to herself, and made me a cup of hot milk to calm my nerves. I didn't feel too rested the next day, and neither did she, I reckon.

I took a taxi cab to the film studio, which was a new experience for me – an automobile you could hire for one journey, with a driver, too! I was surprised how far out of town we seemed to be going, though, and I wondered whether he might not have mistaken me for a richer man, one he could rob. In the end, though, we stopped by a row of big buildings that looked more like the kind of places you'd store machinery and such than make movies in. I figured I didn't know anything about it, though; maybe they worked out of buildings that seemed to have seen better days on purpose, so that robbers would pass them by.

I paid the taxi-cab driver and went up to the building marked *Lot 21*. There was a door with chipped green paint, propped open with a large ledger. I didn't like to see a book being used in that way, but at least it meant that when no one answered my call I could walk right in.

I went down a corridor, keeping my hand on the wall, as if feeling my way in the dark. I passed a few doors, but I could hear voices further on, so I went toward them. At the end I came to a big room, and as I looked in I was almost blinded by a light shining in my face. I put my arm up to shield my eyes and stumbled inside, hoping no one would notice me.

So there I am, leaning against the wall, taking deep breaths and blinking, until I stop seeing that light every time I shut my eyes. I'm at the back of a room full of people who're watching a woman in a long black gown which is all in tatters at the hem. There's a man and another woman, too, this one all dressed in white, with ribbons in her hair like she's a little girl, and all around there are things that look like broken tombstones, and what seems to be smoke curling about them. Between me and them there's a bunch of people and what I know must be a movie camera. I've seen plenty of ordinary cameras – I've even bought one myself, although I can't manage to take a single picture that comes out clear – but never one so big that the man working it has to sit on a special seat that's fixed to it.

Lucky for me, him and everyone else there is looking at the woman in black, who's shouting, 'How do you expect me to work in these conditions? This costume is impossible to walk in, *she* won't stop coughing ...'

The girl in white mumbles, 'It's the smoke, I—'

But she's silenced by the glare the other woman gives her, as she carries on yelling. 'I'm a professional, you know, I expect better than this.' And she pushes a hand into the hair on either side of her face and it comes off. She seems like she's bald, but I can see bits of her own hair sticking out from under some kind of cap that's keeping it flat to her head.

Just then a big man of around my age comes forward and wraps a solid arm around her shoulders. 'Now, Cecilia, you know we need the smoke machine to hide as much of the set as we can, and Sadie can't help it if the smoke sticks in her throat.'

'But I can't concentrate, it breaks the spell.'

319

'Well, Cecilia, that's just because you're so sensitive. You're an artist. You've got more imagination than the rest of us ordinary folk.'

I see the woman's expression soften some, and she begins to play with the hair of the wig she's holding. 'Well, just as long as we get this scene finished as soon as possible. I've got a date tonight. But first, I need a drink – and preferably *not* virgin's blood.'

There's some laughter from around the room, and the big man says, 'OK everyone, we'll take a break there. Back in half an hour.'

Some people file out while others coil up wires or look through the camera lens or shift lights around. The big man is heading toward the door, so I take my chance and move in front of him. 'Mr Kravitz?'

He steps back straightaway, looking at me suspiciously. 'Who wants to know?' His voice is much rougher now it's me he's speaking to.

'My name's Boot – Isaac Boot – and I'd like to talk to you about something.'

'You a bailiff?'

'No, sir, I'm a librarian.'

'You sure about that?'

'Absolutely, sir. I wanted to talk to you about someone I saw in one of your films.'

Kravitz looks over his shoulder as if he's checking whether anyone's listening to us. Then he says, 'How about we continue this conversation in my office? We can get some privacy there, and it's quieter.' He takes me by the shoulder and marches me pretty smartly back down the corridor and through into a room on the left. A young woman who's sitting at a desk, going through some paperwork, looks up in surprise as we walk in.

'Daddy! I thought you were filming. Who's this?'

'This is Mr, er . . .'

'Boot, sir, Isaac Boot.'

'Mr Boot, who's apparently trying to locate one of our actors. This is my daughter, Noreen, Mr Boot. Now, honey, how about a cup of coffee for Mr Boot and me?'

I can see the girl ain't too happy about that. She has brown eyes behind big spectacles and dark hair in heavy bangs over her forehead. Her nose is a little long, and she seems to have too many teeth for her mouth, but she has a lively, interested look about her, and I can see she'd like to stay and listen to our conversation. As it is, she goes out slowly. She don't get to hear nothing, though, as her father waits until she's gone and shuts the door before carrying on.

'One of my actors owe you money? Only I know what they can be like: easy come, easy go. Live like there's no tomorrow, most of them. It's not that I don't pay them well, you understand; they just spend it all.'

I forget all the stories I'd been fixing to use on him; besides, if he suspicions me already I figure it's best not to give him any more reason to mistrust me.

'This ain't about money, Mr Kravitz, it's about my wife.'

'Uh huh. I see.' He seems relieved, and sits himself down behind his desk. 'You trying to find her so you can divorce her? I've known a few actresses leave husbands behind when they come here hoping to become a movie star.'

'My wife is dead.'

He looks alarmed now, shifting a little in his seat.

'Well, that can't have been anything to do with me, my safety record's excellent. Never killed an actor yet. Few may have got hurt along the way, but never killed.'

'It wasn't anything to do with you, Mr Kravitz. She's been dead a long time. It's hard to explain, but she died and I wasn't able to bury her. The undertaker mummified her and she ended up getting sold . . .'

I can see from the change in his expression that he understands me now. 'You don't mean Egyptian Jane? You really believe she's your wife? But how?'

'Like I said, it's hard to explain, but I saw her again, after – after she died. I know what she looks like. I knew it was her as soon as I saw her in your movie. I know this sounds crazy, but I followed her for a while after she was sold by the undertaker; I meant to give her a decent burial, but I lost her. I'd given up hope of ever seeing her again until I went to a movie theatre and saw your picture. Where is she, Mr Kravitz, can I see her?'

He hesitates, frowning slightly, as if weighing it up. 'Well, I don't suppose it can do any harm,' and he beckons me over to a door behind his desk. It's a cupboard, and when he opens it, there's my Ida May, in her coffin, propped up against the back wall. She's shrunk some more since I last saw her, and her skin is darker, but otherwise she's less changed than I am by the years. On either side of her are rows of shelves, and on them are all manner of strange objects: jars with what look like parts of bodies in them and one with what seems to be a two-headed baby. It's too much for me, too sudden. I reach out a hand as if to touch her, but then my legs give way.

Kravitz catches me before I hit the ground and helps me over to a chair. I sit with my head in my hands, breathing deep until the blackness passes. Someone else enters the room. I smell coffee and hear the girl's voice saying, 'What happened? Is he ill?'

'He's overcome, honey. He's had a bit of a shock. You'll never believe this, but Mr Boot thinks Egyptian Jane is his late wife.'

'Oh, Daddy, how awful! I never thought there might be people still alive who knew her!'

'Tell the truth, neither did I.'

I look up, rubbing my hands over my head as if it might help clear it. Kravitz has taken two fat cigars out of his desk drawer and is offering me one. I shake my head, and he puts one back, then takes out a cutter and slices the end off the other.

'How did you come by her?'

'Fella by the name of Billy Richards sold her to me.' He lights the cigar with a match and takes a puff. 'Took her in payment of someone's gambling debts, off a man who said she used to belong to his father, a preacher. She'd been wrapped up in an old carpet and left in a closet for years, but the fella had gambled away almost everything he'd owned, so he offered her to Billy, and Billy took her, as he thought I might have a use for her. He was right – there's not many mummies around anymore. I'm not even sure if it's legal to buy and sell them, the law being what it is. She's very useful in my line of work, though: no need to make a dummy, or use a lot of greasepaint on an extra; she never complains, or says she's going to join a union. When the day's shooting's finished I just put her back in the cupboard until the next time she's needed!'

'Daddy!' Noreen jerks her head in my direction, evidently trying to remind him to be more sensitive to my feelings. 'Would you like some coffee, Mr Boot?'

I take a cup gratefully. I need it to make me feel more human again. As I drink it I have a chance to look around Kravitz's office. I wish I hadn't: there are more shelves around the walls, and they have the strangest things on them. At first glance they seem to be rows of heads and hands, cut off at the necks and wrists, but some of them are leaning over, others lying flat, and I can see they're masks. Horrible masks, too, with bulging eyes and big crooked teeth and fake blood. I go to put my coffee cup down and start at the sight of a dried-up 'gator baring its sharp little teeth at me.

I see Kravitz is looking at me and rubbing his chin, like he's figuring something out. 'I'd like to help you, Mr Boot, I really would. The thing is, do you have any proof of title to the item in question?'

'She's not an *item*!' I say, sitting forward on my chair, angry now. 'She's my wife!'

'Now, see, here's the thing: if she was your wife I find it hard to believe that you wouldn't have given her a good Christian burial at the time she died. And if you're the kind of man who wouldn't do that, then are you the kind of man I want to do business with?

'It's not that I don't want to believe you, Mr Boot – I

do, I really do. It's just that without *proof* I don't feel obliged to hand a valuable asset over to the first man to come along and claim it. Possession *is* nine-tenths of the law, after all.'

I stare at Kravitz's broad, shiny face, not knowing what to say: I haven't let myself think about what would happen if he refused to hand Ida May over to me.

Seeing my confusion, he carries on, 'But I'm not an unreasonable man, just a businessman. Movies are expensive to make and there's always a cash-flow problem: the cash used to make them flows out quicker than the cash you get for showing them flows in. I paid a fair amount for Egyptian Jane, and she's been useful to me, but I might be prepared to sell her for an appropriate sum.'

'How much were you thinking?'

'One thousand dollars.'

'A thousand dollars!' I don't know how I can get that much money, but I ain't going to tell him that. 'I'll have to see what I can do,' I say.

'You do that, Mr Boot,' and he hands me a little card with his name and address on it. Then he stands up to shake hands, propelling me toward the door, still holding on to me, as if he wants to be sure I don't double back and make a grab for Ida May.

As I walk down the corridor in a daze I'm startled by a strange figure ahead of me – a woman, all in black, in a long-sleeved gown that comes down to her ankles, and a hat with a veil over her face. You don't often see women got up like that anymore. As we pass each other we have to flatten out against the wall, meaning we're face to face – or face to veil. It could be anybody in there, but there's something familiar about her. I decide she's probably an actress trying to hide her face from the public, and maybe I've seen her picture somewhere.

I haven't gone far when I hear someone calling, 'Mr Boot! Wait, please, Mr Boot!' and I turn around to see Noreen running after me. As she catches me up she says in a low voice, 'I'm really sorry about what Daddy just said to you. He's not a mean man underneath, it's just that he's put a lot of money into his business and Mother never wanted him to. He feels he's got to make a success of it, and it's hard for someone like him to compete with the big studios. He's just trying to keep the wolf from the door.

'Why don't you give me the address of where you're staying? I'll talk to him, and if I can change his mind, I'll contact you.'

I MEET ANOTHER OLD FRIEND

⟞⟝

I went away from there quite low in spirits. I'd found Ida May again after so many years, yet it looked like I wouldn't be able to bury her after all. It seemed too cruel to bear. I wondered whether I should have told Jack everything and asked him to come along with me – Kravitz might have treated him differently. But I knew I couldn't have let him see his real Ma like this: kept in a cupboard with a whole bunch of curiosities. I'd tell him when the time was right, once I'd done what I had to do.

I'd got to think of some way to raise that money; I couldn't rely on Noreen to persuade her Pa to do the right thing. My mind was buzzing with all these thoughts and I was afraid I'd start having fits in the street and be taken to a hospital. I'd been a long time without one, but seeing Ida May like that had stirred things up good and proper.

I moped around for days trying to think up a plan. I considered borrowing money from the library, but $1,000 was a mighty sum, and it would mean going back to Twelve Trees, when I didn't want to leave Ida May. I couldn't rob a train or a bank no more, and I didn't have

327

nothing worth selling. Art wouldn't have it, nor would Mrs Temperley, even if I could've asked them. I was going crazy with the frustration of having finally found her but not being able to get her back, so I decided to go to the movies again, try to cheer myself up.

I chose one called *The Kid* this time, with a fella named Charlie Chaplin. Before we got to the main picture there was a newsreel. I wasn't paying much attention at first, but then I saw the second person in a week who looked familiar. He was a man of about my age, but much taller, and real thin. He was wearing a suit and a good overcoat, and a fancy black hat, and shaking hands with an important-looking man who carried his belly in front of him like a prize he'd won at the fair.

The fat man didn't want to let go of the thin one's hand. He was smiling and looking at the camera the whole time. The thin one, though, kept darting his eyes toward it and away again, like it made him uneasy. As it came in for a close-up he stared right into it, the way small children do when they're curious about something. I'd have known those pale green eyes even if I hadn't read the words on the screen that told me Mr Caleb Austin was being granted the freedom of the City of Los Angeles for his services to architecture.

I didn't stay around for the main picture. My heart was pounding when I got out onto the street again. Cal had been standing on the steps of a big building that said *Austin Towers* in big letters on the front; I knew I had to find that place.

The first cab driver I asked about it laughed at me, 'Do I know Austin Towers? Of course I know Austin

Towers – everyone knows it, you can't miss it.' When he'd done laughing at me I got him to take me there, although as it turned out to be only three blocks away it would've been quicker to walk.

I stood looking up at the biggest building I'd ever seen and realized I was shaking – with excitement, or maybe with nerves. All I knew for sure was I had to see Cal and I had to persuade him to lend me the $1,000 I needed to get Ida May back. Once I'd brought my eyes down to pavement level, though, I saw there might be a problem. There was a fella in a fancy green coat with brocade at the shoulders and a tall black hat on his head standing outside the grand doors of the building. It looked like I'd have to get past him if I wanted to go in.

I straightened my jacket, raised myself up as tall and as proud as I could, and walked over to him. He looked at me steadily, but said nothing.

'I wonder if you can help me,' I said, as nicely as I knew how, 'I'd like to speak with Mr Caleb Austin.'

'Oh, you would, would you? You and a hundred others, buddy. Mr Austin's not at home to people who want to show him their latest inventions, or ask for a job, or a handout, so please, move along.'

'You don't understand. I'm not here for any of those reasons: I'm an old friend of Mr Austin's, and I'd like to speak with him concerning a very important matter.'

'Sure you are. Sure you would,' and he inspected me from top to toe. The way he curled his lip showed how much he thought of what he saw.

'You may not believe me, but it's true. If you'd just

send this message to Mr Austin you'll see.' I felt around in my pockets for something to write on, but all I could find was Walter Kravitz's business card. I had a pencil stub, and I licked it, wrote *turn over* on the front of the card, and *It's me, Wilbur* on the back.

The doorman, who was wearing clean white gloves, held the card between his thumb and pointing finger. He studied the card at arm's length, puffed out his cheeks in a sigh, then looked at me again.

'Go on,' I said. 'What have you got to lose? If he don't want to see me, he'll say so, but if you don't let him know I'm here and then he finds out later, he might be so mad he fires you. Do you really want to take that risk?'

He frowned, but after a moment's consideration he pulled off a glove, put two fingers in his mouth and gave a piercing whistle. A young boy came running down the steps of the building, looking flustered. He was dressed in a green uniform, too, but with even more gold braid on it, shiny buttons down the front and a brimless hat that was held on by a strap under his chin. He looked like a drummer boy from some long-ago war.

'Raymond,' the doorman said to him, 'take this card up to Mr Austin and bring down his reply.' He didn't even look at the boy as he held the card out to him, and as soon as Raymond scuttled back inside he resumed his position, just standing there again, for all the world as if I wasn't there.

It seemed like a long time, but it was probably only a few minutes before the boy was back, running down the steps again so fast he had to hold on to his silly little hat.

'He says to send the gentleman right up, Mr Hawkins. I'm to bring him!'

The doorman looked thunderstruck, but he couldn't disobey an order, so he let me follow the boy inside.

We went through the doors into a big, empty hallway, all done in some kind of shiny stone. In front of us were more doors, in dark wood, with a row of buttons on either side. Raymond went over and pressed one and then stood waiting. I didn't know what we were waiting there for, but I'd managed to get this far, and I wasn't about to spoil it by asking stupid questions. I noticed something like half a clock face above the doors, but there was only one hand, and it was going backwards, each number it pointed to lighting up. Suddenly there was a *ping* like a ricocheting bullet, and Raymond pulled the doors back. They folded like an accordion, and inside was a kind of metal grille, which he folded back too. Beyond that was a small room. The boy walked into it and turned round. The way he was looking at me I could tell he meant me to go in there with him.

Now I'm not stupid, and by this stage I'd realized what this was. I'd read about elevators, but I'd never been in one and I was none too sure I wanted to; still, I had to see Cal, and if that was what it took . . . I stepped into that little room, trying to act as if it was the most natural thing in the world, and I did it all the time. The boy pushed another button and settled himself down on a little three-legged stool. Then my stomach seemed to travel up through my gullet into my mouth. I put my hand out to steady myself against the wall and tried to breathe deep so as not to fall into a fit in front of poor Raymond. I didn't look at him, but I knew he was looking at me, and I was most likely worrying him.

Luckily it wasn't long before we came to a halt and the boy opened first the cage, then the doors again. I staggered out, glad to be on a solid floor.

We were in a room as big as a saloon, but a lot brighter. The light was coming from three of the biggest windows I'd ever seen, straight ahead of me. I couldn't begin to imagine how it was possible to make a sheet of glass that big, let alone get it all the way up there. Between me and the windows was a tall thin figure, and as soon as he saw me he walked forward, not to shake my hand nor embrace me, but to put one hand on either of my shoulders as if to hold me still. Then he bent down to look into my face.

'I do believe it *is* you.' They were the first words he spoke to me after all those years.

'And I can see it's you, too.' No one looked at you the way Cal did: like you were a specimen he was examining, not a person at all. You could never see any feeling behind those eyes. Of course he looked older: there were deep lines running from his nose to his mouth and his hair was a mixture of grey and brown, but he hadn't altered as much as I had. Still, those eyes could see the truth of who I was, all right.

'Wilbur,' he said, shaking his head, like he couldn't believe it, 'Wilbur McCrum. You look old.' He still had me gripped by the shoulders, and I was aware of the boy, Raymond, watching us from the elevator doors. I nodded in his direction and Cal came out of his trance and told him he could go.

Still holding on to me, Cal led me over to a giant couch that looked like it was made of shiny black hide. 'All those years, Wilbur. What have you been doing for all that time? I heard you'd been killed, then I heard you were alive and still robbing banks. I didn't know what to believe.'

'It's a long story, Cal, and I'll tell it to you, but I've come here because I need your help.'

'Anything – just ask.'

'I need to borrow a thousand dollars to pay for my wife's funeral.' That was a huge sum of money, but I figured Cal must be so rich now he wouldn't realize how much it cost to bury an ordinary person.

'Your wife died! Poor Wilbur. My Mary died, too. Did you have any children?'

'Just one – a son.' I thought it best not to try to explain my situation just then, even if I *could* explain it. I'd come back and see him again once I'd paid Kravitz and Ida May was safe.

'We had seven children, Mary and me – five of them still living. I'm not sure how many grandchildren I have, it keeps changing.' At last he dropped his gaze from my face and I relaxed some.

'You know, if I hadn't got shot that time, and Dan hadn't taken me to cousin Samuel to get me patched up, I'd never have met Mary, never have settled down, never have gone back to school. I owe it all to you, Wilbur.' As he spoke he swept his arm around the room. 'I designed all this – can you believe it? Remember how when we were young buildings were never bigger than two storeys? Now they go right up into the sky; now I *live* in the sky!'

I took a good look out the window when he said this, and he was right: sky was all I could see. I started to feel peculiar again at the thought of the ground being so far beneath me.

'But I'm forgetting myself – you need some money,' Cal said abruptly, and he got to his feet and walked over to a desk in front of the window. Like everything else in the room, it was bigger than any other I'd seen. There was nothing on top of it but a pen, a bottle of ink and a blotter, but he took something out of a drawer and picked up the pen to write.

'I hope a cheque will do. If not, I'll send someone down to my bank.' He was waving a piece of paper about, to dry the ink, and when he thought it was ready he passed it to me. It said to pay the bearer $1,000. I stared at it, wondering if it was real, but I knew Cal never lied; I don't think he was able. What I wanted to do was take that cheque straight to Kravitz, but it was too late in the day to do that; I'd have to wait until morning. I told myself that after so many years another night wouldn't hurt.

'Wilbur!' Cal said suddenly. 'I should offer you a drink. I've got whisky.'

'How did you manage that?'

'When you're rich Prohibition doesn't seem to apply. Money can bend any law out of shape.'

It had been a long time since I tasted liquor, and it burned its way through my chest, adding to the lightheadedness I was already feeling on account of finding Cal again, and knowing I'd soon have Ida May back – not to mention the elevator.

'Do you and your son get along, Wilbur?' Cal asked me, leaning forward in his seat so that his knees were up to his elbows.

'Thing is, he don't even know he's my son.'

Cal thought about that for a moment, looking into his glass. 'Maybe that isn't such a bad thing. Let me tell you something: I don't really get along with any of my children, except Louisa, maybe, and she's as crazy as I am. My eldest, Frank, has got her in an institution now, and he'd like to do the same for me, too. He's scared, Wilbur. He knows I never much cared for money, and he's scared I'll do something with it that he thinks is stupid.

'Everything I've done – designing buildings – it was never about making money; it was about seeing what humans could do. I don't believe there's a limit, Wilbur. Man can fly now. People can go from one country to another in a few hours. There are new inventions every week. New ideas and ways of doing things that make life easier, giving people more time for leisure. And what do they do with it? Well, my son's either playing golf or checking his investments.

'I've never felt as connected to my own flesh and blood as I do to these buildings. The children were my wife's creations; the buildings are mine. I loved Mary, but now she's gone I visit with my sons and daughters and I don't know what to say to them. I look at them sometimes and wonder what on earth they're supposed to have to do

335

with me. When they were small they were little miracles, but now – well now, they just plain bore me, Wilbur.'

He sat in silence, thinking for a while, then he said, 'You know when I was happiest, Wilbur? It was the time when you and me and Dan were all together, living in the wilds, trying our best to be outlaws. We may not have been any good at it, but we were young, and we had our futures ahead of us – well, you and I did.' He was quiet for a while, then he carried on, 'I had so many ideas then. The awful thing about getting what you want in life is realizing that the best part was the wanting it. I loved dreaming about the buildings I was going to design, but once they were up, and that first thrill of thinking *I did that!* was over, all I could see were the flaws, the things I could improve on, and I wanted to start again, and do it better this time.' He grabbed me by the arm and pulled me to my feet, then led me over to one of those huge windows. I have to admit I was scared to go too near, so I stood with my back to the wall and peered through the glass by turning my head sideways.

I just couldn't believe what I saw. It was as if we were on the top of a mountain, and when I made myself look down I could see tiny, doll-like people and their toy automobiles. I raised my eyes again, quickly, and felt my way back to the couch.

Seeing my discomfort, Cal asked, 'Don't you like heights, Wilbur? I guess you wouldn't much like aeroplanes, then. I wanted to learn to fly myself, but Frank put a stop to it. He's an influential man, my son, and that worries me. He'd never have dared try to put me in an institution while his mother was alive, but now ... He's

336

watching my every move, Wilbur. If I do anything out of line he'll have me pronounced mentally unfit, and then I'll end my days in a little room with bars on the window.'

'Surely he wouldn't do that to his own father?'

'You don't know him. You may not believe it's possible for a son to hate his father, but I can tell you it is.'

The whisky and the view were making me feel sick. I stood up and had to sit back down again before I fell.

'I'll get my driver to take you back to your hotel. Unless you'd rather stay here?'

No matter how tired I was, I didn't think I'd be able to sleep in Austin Towers, not knowing how much air there was between me and the sidewalk. 'Thank you, but I'd rather go. I'll come back and see you again, if you don't mind.'

'Mind? You can't imagine how glad I am to see you! It's brought back memories that had lain buried for so long. I'd been lost to the world since Mary died; you've brought me out of myself again.'

As we stepped into the elevator I said, 'I'll pay the money back as soon as I can, Cal, I promise.'

'You will not! I'll never forget that you buried my brother, Wilbur. No amount of money can repay that act of kindness. Helping you bury your wife is the least I can do. And like I said before, if it weren't for you and that bolting horse of yours I'd probably have been killed or jailed years ago. I wouldn't be living like this, for sure.'

When we got outside Cal showed me to the longest, most shiny automobile I'd ever seen. He was about to open the door for me when the man in the white gloves hurried over and beat him to it. I got in and wound down the window to thank Cal again, but he silenced me by squeezing my shoulder and saying in a voice that sounded almost emotional, 'Goodbye, Wilbur. Goodbye, old friend.'

THE LADY IN THE VEIL

⊰⊱

I slept late the next morning, and light was streaming in through the window when I woke. I couldn't wait around to have breakfast as Cal had said I could use his limousine again, and his driver was calling for me at nine.

When I arrived at Kravitz's studio I found the door still propped open and walked in, like before. I went directly to the room in back, and as I got closer I heard a voice. I saw Noreen with another, older, woman beside her, and a whole bunch of people standing in silence, listening.

'So we won't be able to finish the picture. As you know, Daddy's backers had their doubts about making a movie about vampires – they didn't think women would come to see it. They're not prepared to put up more money now he's not around to finish it. I guess we'll never find who was right, but I promise I'll keep you all informed of what's happening.'

She turned away and pressed a handkerchief to her nose. The other woman put an arm round her shoulders and led her out, past me. As I turned and followed them down the corridor, murmurings broke out behind us. It was clear something bad had happened.

The old woman was just about to shut the door to Kravitz's office, but I put out a hand to stop her and went in.

'Who are you?' She looked pretty angry, and pretty fierce, too. Noreen noticed me then. 'Mr Boot! Oh, Heavens, what a time to be here!'

'I'm sorry,' I said, without knowing what I was supposed to be sorry for.

'I didn't mean it like that. It's not your fault, what's happened.'

'What *has* happened, Miss Kravitz?'

'It's Daddy!' and she looked as if she was going to cry. The older woman came over and took her arm again, looking at me like I was to blame. 'Mr Kravitz met with an accident.'

'An accident?'

Noreen found her voice. 'It was the stupidest thing. He always said to me, "Play to your strengths, Noreen, play to your strengths," but then lately he'd come up with a new catchphrase, "Diversify or die!" He'd got this idea that movies about cowboys would be the next big thing, and he was going to make one, so he got this machine made that was supposed to look like a bucking steer at a rodeo. It was like a bull on top, but underneath it was all metal and springs, but you wouldn't see that part – anyway, he just had to test it himself. Why would a man of sixty-five with a heart condition do something like that?'

'Because he's stupid and stubborn, is why.'

'Lillian!'

'You know it's true. There was no need for him to get

up on that bull, no need at all. The actor he was showing it to was half his age, and half as fat – and he didn't have a bad heart. What was he trying to prove? But why am I even asking? He's a man, and we all know they lose any sense they might have the first time they pull on a pair of pants.'

'But what if he doesn't get better, Lillian?'

'We'll carry on with our lives, same as always. You'd need to sell what's left of the business. Most of the money will go to the creditors, but at least he had the sense to take out insurance. You and your mother will be all right.'

I was sorry to hear about Kravitz, even though I hadn't much liked him. What I really wanted to know about was Ida May, but how could I ask Noreen while she was so upset about her Pa? Luckily I didn't have to.

'You've come about Jane – I mean, *your wife.*'

'I got the money your father asked for. Will you let me have her?'

Noreen's chin began to quiver again, and the old lady stroked her hair. 'Poor Mr Boot! Of course you can have her. We had no right to her in the first place.'

'So the deal still stands?'

'I won't take any money off you, Mr Boot. That would be wrong of me.'

'But your father—'

'I love my father dearly, but I don't always agree with him, and while he's in the hospital, I'm in charge here.'

'So, do you really mean for me to take her?'

'Please do. There may not be any more movies made here, and I certainly couldn't use your wife again now. And please accept my apologies for what we did, Mr Boot.'

Although I could hardly bear to leave, even for a short while, without Ida May, I'd have to go ask the driver to bring the limo as close as he could. Even then, quite *how* I'd manage was another matter. I couldn't carry her casket alone, nor roll her up in a blanket and put her over my shoulder, and I didn't think Cal's driver would take too kindly to moving her, either: it would be bad enough when he found out I was planning on treating his car as a funeral carriage. Anyhow, with all of this going through my mind I was finding it hard to think clearly and seeing stars in front of my eyes.

That's how come it took me ages to notice the automobile stopped directly in front of me and longer still to realize someone was winding down the window. Someone wearing a black veil that covered her whole face.

The veil moved in and out, blown by her breath as she spoke. 'I was hoping to see you again. I was taken by surprise the other day, not sure it was you. But I believe we're both here for the same reason – to take her home.'

I stooped down and peered from real close, but the veil was too thick for me to make out anything but a blur of features.

'Excuse me, ma'am, but do I know you?'

'You used to, Isaac,' and she pulled off one of her black gloves and held out a hand to me. A hand glittering with rings. A hand covered in coarse grey hair. 'Why don't you get in? Then we can talk properly.'

I looked over at Cal's limo. The driver was leaning on the bonnet, reading a newspaper. 'I'll be five minutes more,' I called to him, and I got in beside the veiled lady.

'How did you find this place?'

342

'Same way you did, Isaac: I went to the movies and saw her. When I spoke to the unfortunate Mr Kravitz he told me it really *was* you I'd passed in the corridor. I think he was a bit suspicious of me, but he said you'd be back with the money. I thought if I waited here every day then I'd see you again, sooner or later. If you didn't manage to raise enough I was going to offer to appear in his next movie, in exchange for her.

'Now, would you mind if I took this off? My nose is really itching me and I'm dying to scratch it.'

I shook my head, and she lifted the veil and threw it back, then turned to face me. The wiry hair was mostly white now, but she still looked like a mule – a clever, kindly mule.

'Just as well we were neither of us handsome when we were young, don't you think, Isaac? We had no looks to lose but plenty of wisdom to gain.'

'Where are you living now, Sophia?'

'Coney Island. Most of us decided to carry on together after Josh gave up the business, but over time people quit – touring gets harder the older you get – so those of us who were left settled there. Mary-Lou and Lionel are still with me. We've done well, Isaac. And you're looking quite dapper yourself.'

'You'll never believe it, Sophia, but I run a public library now.'

She threw back her head and laughed. 'So how did you come by the limo and the driver?'

'He works for a friend – the same friend who lent me the money to get Ida May back.'

'Like I said, I would have helped you with that.'

I didn't know what to say to her; I was overwhelmed by the generosity of my two old friends. A few days earlier I'd believed there was no prospect of getting Ida May back, but now my dream was coming true.

HOMECOMING

⟞⟞⟞ ⟨ ⟩ ⟞⟞⟞

$\mathscr{S}$ophia agreed to help me get Ida May home and even offered me the use of her automobile if I didn't want to alarm Cal's driver too much. It was a bit of a squeeze in there, with Sophia, Ida May and me, so I told Sophia that as I had to see Cal again anyhow, I might as well ride in the limo to Austin Towers, with her and Ida May following.

As we got close, though, there were a couple of police wagons blocking the street. The driver asked an officer what was happening and he leaned his head in the window and said, 'A jumper. Some rich guy threw himself out a window of his own apartment block. Road's closed off till they clear up. You'd think someone like that could find a way to do it that wouldn't stop the traffic. Not that I'd wanna kill myself if I had his money.'

The driver turned a shocked face toward me, then got out the limousine, leaving the door open. I didn't need to wait for him to come back and tell me who it was, though; I already knew. I felt some sadness, of course I did: I'd only just found Cal again after all those years, but knowing what his life had become I felt a kinda pride in him, too. He wasn't going to let his son lock him away; he even got to fly in the end.

I got out and squeezed in beside Ida May in Sophia's automobile. I turned to her, and for a moment I didn't see what was there; I saw her as she was when we first met – a young girl with an ill-fitting dress and a fierce expression. 'I'm taking you home, honey. At last, I'm taking you home.'

Through all that long journey, miles passed when we didn't speak. Evidently as she'd gotten older Sophia had calmed down. We did tell each other some of the things that had happened since we'd last met, but it's hard, when you've lived so much life, to make a story of it. She said one thing that surprised me, though: she had a daughter. I didn't want to ask the question that was buzzing round my mind, but she knew what I was thinking.

'No, Isaac, she's not hairy, and she doesn't look like a mule. Her daddy was a smooth-skinned man, and it's him she favours.'

She was quiet for a time, then she went on, 'In part it's because of her I wear the veil. She's a young woman now, and she doesn't need people seeing she's got a freak for a mother. She'll be wanting to marry and have children herself someday soon, and what chance does she have of finding a husband who won't run away as soon as he sees my face?' She looked sad at this, just for a moment, but then seemed to brighten again.

'Anyway, how about you? Did you go back for your son?'

'I didn't, but I met up with him by chance when he

was a grown man. As a matter of fact, you'll be meeting him when we get to Twelve Trees. He's the sheriff there.'

'The sheriff! Well, who'd've thought the son of a notorious outlaw would grow up to be a lawman! This is quite a country, Isaac, ain't it, though? What does he think of all this: you going off to find his Ma and bring her back?'

'Well, that's just it, Sophia: he don't exactly know about it.'

'You haven't told him?'

'That's not all I haven't told him. He don't even know I'm his father.'

She thought about that for a while. 'I see. Are you *going* to tell him?'

'I've always figured I would, one day. I've just never found the right day, is all.'

We sat in silence for a while after. It was companionable silence, but when I wasn't talking I was thinking about how I'd be received when I arrived home, driven by a mysterious veiled lady, with a coffin in the back of her automobile.

When we get to Twelve Trees it's a day like any other: although it's early, people are walking the streets, going about their business; the storekeepers are opening their shutters and setting their wares out on the pavements – and there's Mrs Temperley on the sidewalk with a basket over her arm. Her face, when we draw alongside, is a picture. She looks from me to Sophia and back again, quite unable to hide her curiosity.

'We thought we'd lost you, Isaac! Some of us wondered

whether we'd ever see you again. And who is this you've brought with you?'

'An old friend, Miss Sophia – what *is* your last name, Sophia?'

'Hopwood. Sophia Hopwood.'

Mrs Temperley's giving us both a fixed smile, but then her eyes stray to the back seat. 'Gracious me!'

'About that, Mrs Temperley – that's my late wife.'

'Your wife! You never mentioned a wife before this!'

'We hadn't seen each other for many years, but at last I'm able to do the right thing. I plan to give her a good Christian burial here in my home town, and one day I'll lay by her side again.'

Mrs Temperley can't think of a reply to that, but I know now I've told her of my intentions it will be all around town in no time.

THE FUNERAL

$\text{---}\!\!\!\text{III}\!\!\!\text{ }\!\!\!\text{(}\!\!\!\text{ }\!\!\!\text{)}\!\!\!\text{III}\!\!\!\text{---}$

The preacher was a little taken aback when I asked him to bury Ida May. He wasn't accustomed to conducting funerals for people from out of town. In the end I felt I had to show her to him, just so he believed there truly was a body in the casket, and not some stolen loot. I told him how she'd been dead a long time, and been ill-used along the way, and how it was my fault, and I needed to make amends. When he saw the bullet hole in her forehead he looked at me, wide-eyed, but he acted like a true man of God, and didn't ask me what had happened. I figured having Sophia along helped my case, although I have to own I lied to him about the way she dressed: I said she'd been burned in a fire, and didn't want to be seen on account of the scars.

I used Cal's money to pay for everything: he was gone and didn't need it any more, and his children would be wealthy enough not to miss $1,000.

Sophia threw herself into organizing it all. I'd never gotten used to the telephone – it didn't feel natural to be speaking to someone I couldn't see – but she was happy to use it, and arranged flowers, a horse-drawn carriage and a new fancy casket in place of the old one. I do believe Mrs Temperley's nose was put out of joint some, having another woman take over like that, but Sophia knew how to handle her: any time Mrs T approached her looking like she'd worked up a full head of steam, she'd throw back her veil and give one of her brightest smiles, showing all her teeth, and that would be sure and knock the wind out of Mrs T's sails.

It's a beautiful day, the day of the funeral. The sky's a bright clear blue, with a few fat white cotton-ball clouds on the horizon. We put her in the black carriage that's lined with ruched black silk and drawn by six black horses with great black plumes on their heads and black blinders. Mrs Temperley and Sophia walk along behind with me, Mrs T quite swelled up with the drama of the occasion and staring fiercely at the crowd of well-wishers, in case there are any wagging tongues need silencing.

I do believe every single inhabitant of Twelve Trees is in that graveyard, all curious to see the old librarian who's suddenly produced a wife, and a dead one, at that. Folk love spectacle, and they love intrigue, and after living such a quiet life here for years, I'm the unlikely person who's giving them both. No one is about to miss it.

It's a strange thing for me, to be standing at last by Ida May's grave. Now I'm here, at the centre of the thing I've wanted most for all these years, I remember what Cal said about the wanting being better than the getting. I've spent so long hoping for this moment, and now it's here I hardly feel joyful. Not that you'd expect me to be, at a funeral. I look over at the Grogans and see they're all sombre but dry-eyed. Of course they are – they have no idea the woman we're burying has any connection to them at all. As we walk away and the church bell tolls, I feel flat, finished.

MY SWANSONG

---

*T*hat wasn't the end of my story, neither. I'd vowed to bury Ida May and I'd done that, but I still had to tell Jack the truth. Once the excitement was over I planned to go to the sheriff's office and turn myself in.

I didn't know whether I'd end up in the bosom of my family or in jail, but I knew it was the right thing to do. All my life I'd been the kind of man who came around the corner just as the parade disappeared over the hill; finally it was time to take charge, be the man at the head of the parade for once.

When I told Sophia of my intention she wanted to come with me, but I said I'd rather go alone; this was between father and son. So I went to the kitchen and slipped a potato into my pocket, keeping my hand on it for reassurance as I walked across the street.

Jack was sitting at his desk when I arrived, writing something. He looked surprised to see me – I'd never had cause to come to his place of work before.

'Mr Boot! What can I do for you?'

But I just stand there, trying to remember the fine

352

sentences I've composed in my head whenever I've thought about this moment, but nothing will come to me.

'Would you care to sit down, Mr Boot? You look rather pale – are you ill? The funeral must have exhausted you.'

I sit, as he suggests, but still the words won't come. I have half a mind to turn around and go back home again, but then I think about Ida May all alone in the churchyard.

'Mr Grogan – Jack – I'm not who you think I am.'

He frowns, and when he does that I can see his Ma in him. Then he settles himself back in his chair, fingertips together, listening.

'I used to be known by another name.' I pause, feeling the sweat starting on my brow. 'You may have heard the name before. My real name is Wilbur – Wilbur McCrum.'

He laughs. He can't help himself. I guess it does seem ridiculous.

'Mr Boot, Wilbur McCrum was a notorious outlaw, and he's been dead for years!'

'Well, yes – and no. I was shot and taken for dead, but I was in a fit. I escaped from the undertaker's, took a new name and eventually fetched up here.'

'And became the town librarian?'

It's plain to see he don't believe me.

'I know it sounds peculiar, but it's true, honest. And that's not all I have to tell you.'

He's leaning forward now, elbows on the desk.

'I'm your father, Jack.'

This time he don't laugh, just stares at me.

'My father's dead, Mr Boot. He died in 1893, before I was old enough to form any memory of him.'

353

'That was the year Wilbur McCrum was supposed to have died.'

'My father's name was Clarence Grogan. He was a farmer.'

'She made him up, Jack, to spare you the truth.'

'My mother wouldn't lie to me.'

'Jack.' I lay my hand over his. 'She wasn't your mother. She brought you up after your real mother died, and I'll always be grateful for it. Your real mother was my wife.'

I watch as all the colour drains from his face, then he pulls his hand away and jumps to his feet.

'That woman we buried yesterday, my mother? It's not possible!'

'I know it's hard to take in, son, but it's true. Nobody wanted to lie to you, but it was the only way, believe me.'

'No! I don't believe you, I won't!'

He turns away from me, biting at his thumbnail as he does so, and I can't hold it together any longer: I slide off the chair and into a fit.

I wake to find Jack leaning over me. He looks more concerned than angry now.

'Should I fetch the doctor?'

'No, no,' I struggle to sit up, 'I'll be all right in just a minute. Been having these fits my whole life, they pass soon enough.'

When I say that, Jack frowns again and sits back on his heels.

'What is it?'

'Just a memory; something I'd forgotten until now: being cradled by my mother in her lap, by the stove in our little cabin. I was prone to fevers that would often lead to fits. They stopped as I grew older.' He seems lost in his thoughts for a moment, but then he looks at me. 'I'm sorry, Mr Boot, but you have to leave now. I have genuine criminals to look out for.'

He's helping me to my feet when the door flies open and Sophia runs into the room so fast she nearly knocks me to the floor again.

'You have to believe him, it's true!'

Poor Jack looks thunderstruck at this new intrusion. Sophia's panting, like she's run all the way, and she leans on his desk to catch her breath. 'Mirror?' she gasps.

Jack points to a door and she grabs us both by an arm and pulls us into the small washroom. The mirror ain't very big, but she stands us shoulder to shoulder, gently takes off my spectacles and makes us look at ourselves. I've not noticed it before, but there's no mistaking it: Jack has a slight squint.

'That happens sometimes when I get upset,' he says quietly, as if reading my mind.

'Can't you see the resemblance?' Sophia turns his head to face the mirror again.

At first he seems to be humouring her, but after a moment or two his expression changes. He drops his gaze and goes back into his office.

When we follow him he's toying with the papers on his desk. I can't guess what he's about to say and his silence is almost unbearable. Have I done wrong, telling him the truth – have I shattered his notions of who he is? Maybe I should just go back to the library, hand the keys to Art's Ma and leave this place for ever.

Finally, Jack looks at me. 'If I truly believed you were

Wilbur McCrum I'd be bound by my duty as an officer of the law to arrest you and see you stand trial for your crimes. As a lawman, though, I can't bring myself to believe your story.'

Sophia gasps, but he holds up a hand to silence her and goes on, 'But my wife is not an officer of the law, and you know better than anyone how fond she is of a good story. If you were to come to supper with us tonight I'm sure she'd be eager to hear what you've told me, and she might take a different view. And as she is not an officer of the law, her interpretation of your story would, of course, be a different matter.' And he looks me in the eyes and we hold each other's gaze for a long moment.

Of course I could carry on – I could tell you how I turned and left, how Sophia followed me, and how excited she was, and I could tell you about dinner that night and how nervous *I* was – but I reckon you've got the idea of it by now. Yes, that's the story of Wilbur McCrum, and it's drawing close to the end for real now, for I've caught a chill and my old bones are too tired to recover. I can't complain, seeing as how I've had so many extra years since I died the first time, and good years, too. Wilbur McCrum, the outlaw, may not have made much of his life, but Isaac Boot, librarian, was a good enough citizen. Between them they had a son who's grown into a decent man – even if the credit for that lies elsewhere.

Jack and Rose are the only ones who know my real identity – they thought it best not to tell Grace, and she calls me uncle. I don't believe she's too clear whether I'm kin or not, and I'm leaving it up to Jack to decide what to put on my grave. Meantime, Grace reads to me most evenings, just as I used to read to George. She's good at it, too, and she helps her Ma run the library. Mrs Temperley comes to sit with me, and even though she must be older than me she's still getting about, seeing to other people's business.

Other people's business! I saw plenty of that all right – I saw many things and met a lot of people on my travels through this life. Some were good and some were bad, but they all brought me to where I am now, and where I am now is where I was meant to be, I'm sure of it. I wasn't much good in the outside world, but in George's library I could go wherever I wanted, be whoever I wanted and leave behind that little man with a squint who was so afraid of cows.

There's a story that a swan sings before it dies, and you could say this has been my last song, but there's one more thing remains to be done, now that I've come to the end of it, and I've sent for Grace to help me. I'll be able to tell it's her on the stairs from the way she stamps when she walks. She's not a demure young lady, that's for sure, but she knows her own mind, and it's how I know I can trust her to help me. What I want her to do is take this book from me, once the ink is dry, and find a place for it somewhere on the shelves of the library. Perhaps she'll be curious enough to read it first, but I suspect an old man's memoirs will seem a dull prospect to her. She'll most likely slip it in, unnoticed, among the rest of the books. One day, perhaps, someone will take down this volume, blow the dust from its cover and read the truth about the strange life and many adventures of the man born Wilbur

McCrum who died Isaac Boot. Outlaw. Librarian. Widower. Father.

Before that can happen, though – well, I've come to the end of my journal and the end of my journey, and this time, when I die, I'll stay dead; my eyes will stay closed, there'll be no waking. I'm ready for my final sleep, and perhaps I'll see my Ida May again.

Hush, I can hear Grace's tread now on the stairs – or maybe it's Ida May, come for me already. Stamp, stamp, stamp . . .

Acknowledgements

The list of acknowledgements could go on for several pages, as a lot of people have helped me along the long road to publication. I apologize to anyone I may have omitted. In roughly chronological ordger, thanks to: Anna McGrail for being both mentor and inspiration to me; Maura Dooley, Pamela Johnson and Romesh Gunasekara, my tutors at Goldsmiths College; Maria MacDonald for her infinite patience with my ability to master information technology and my general incompetence; David Cross at the Arts Council for helping me apply for the grant that enabled me to finish the novel; my agent, Ben Mason, for seeing something glinting in the dust and picking it up; to my friends from Goldsmiths, Ashley Dartnell, Sara Grant, Kellie Jackson, Emily Jeremiah, Vinita Joseph, Elizabeth Mercereau and Sandra White, who helped me keep the faith; and finally Sam Humphreys, who combines excellent editorial instincts with great tact.